This en
had bee

Never had he been forced to study so much. And never had studying been more difficult for him.

Studying at Pam's kitchen table caused his mind to wander out of finance and into other places, including the double bed in the room at the end of the hall. He had spent one night there and every night since reliving it.

But after they made love, Pam had backed away from him, informing him that she cared too much for him ever to allow him back in her bed.

Women! Were they all as confused as Pam? But then he didn't care about the state of other female minds. It was Pam and Pam only he was obsessed with. And part of the obsession was his overwhelming need to move in with her, to *live* with her, to shave in her bathroom, wake up in the morning in her bed . . .

ABOUT THE AUTHOR

As the daughter of an army officer, Indiana-born Anne Henry moved frequently during her childhood. Now she makes her home in Oklahoma, where she edits alumni publications for the University of Oklahoma. Anne is a mother of three grown children.

Books by Anne Henry

HARLEQUIN AMERICAN ROMANCE

 76–CHEROKEE SUMMER
 90–THE GLORY RUN
114–THE STORM WITHIN
135–A TOUGH ACT TO FOLLOW
171–I LOVE YOU, JONATHAN SKY
212–A MIXED MATCH
252–A COLONEL FOR JENNY

Robbing the Cradle

Anne Henry

Harlequin Books

TORONTO • NEW YORK • LONDON
AMSTERDAM • PARIS • SYDNEY • HAMBURG
STOCKHOLM • ATHENS • TOKYO • MILAN

Published April 1989

First printing February 1989

ISBN 0-373-16292-8

Chapter One

"Did you get a sitter for Friday night?" Brenda's voice asked over the phone.

"Not yet," Pam admitted, grabbing the saltshaker from Tommy as he toddled by.

"Come on, sis. This man is a dreamboat, and he really wants to meet you. George and I have been telling him all about my beautiful, charming sister."

"What did the 'dreamboat' say about Scott and Tommy?" Pam asked, walking to the end of the telephone cord and peering around the corner into the living room. Scott was sitting in front of the television, watching a game show. Tommy was standing by the sofa, examining their saintly mongrel's ears, something he did a lot. Maybe he would be a vet—or an ear doctor.

"Ah, well, I can't remember," Brenda was saying, "but I'm sure Robert loves children. He and his first wife have twin daughters. He showed us their pictures. Darling little girls. He has them every other weekend, Wednesday evenings for dinner and two months in the summer."

"Brenda, everyone loves their *own* children. You didn't tell him I have two children?" she asked.

"*I* didn't, but I'm sure George did. Come on, sis. What do you say? All work and no play make Pam a dull girl. And Robert is terribly good-looking, incredibly successful, has a terrific sense of humor, a beautiful home. He's a specialist in international tax law, and George's firm is one of his clients. Believe me, sis, this man is the answer to a single girl's prayer."

"I'm not so sure any man would answer this single girl's prayer. I think I'd prefer winning the Publisher's Clearing House Sweepstakes. More nights of uninterrupted sleep would be nice, too."

Pam stared at her reflection in the hall mirror. She saw a woman in need of a haircut looking back at her. Her fingernails needed manicuring, her brows needed plucking. Pam turned her face from one side to the other. Not a bad-looking woman, considering the time she *didn't* spend on herself, but date bait she was not, and right now she didn't have the time or money to get herself into shape. And she left her boys with sitters far too much the way it was. At this point in her life, a date with Tom Selleck wouldn't seem worth the effort, especially after she finished with her current catering job. She knew that all she'd want to do come Friday night was curl up in bed with a good book. In fact, she already had it picked out. A new Carolyn Hart mystery.

"Promise me you'll go," Brenda said. "You need to have a little fun in your life. All you do is work and take care of children."

"I also spend time with my dear sister and her charming husband, enter contests and read. However, I admit work and children do take up most of my time, but the children are a joy as well as a responsibility. And if I don't work, said children don't eat," Pat reminded her sister, who was childless by choice and modeled at Neiman Marcus. Brenda's husband, George Harrington, had graduated from the University of Texas but was a British citizen, and they had spent the first year of their marriage in London so George could take a year of training at the home office of his new employer, a computer manufacturer. Now they were living in Dallas, where George worked as a well-paid junior executive for the company's U.S.A. subsidiary. Their lives were a continual social whirl and quest for physical fitness. They considered themselves a new breed of young adults, making their lives more intellectual, exciting and fulfilling by not having children. Brenda was a fashion plate. George was terribly British and orderly. At times, Pam envied the order but not the childlessness of their lives.

"I know you have to work hard, sis," Brenda was saying, "but all the more reason why you should have a little fun once in a while to reward yourself for the drudgery. Your life depresses me."

Pam started to explain that "drudgery" was hardly an appropriate word. She adored mothering her children and found that catering—when everything went well—could be surprisingly satisfying work. Starting a new business always meant hard work and stress, but it also offered excitement and optimism. Brenda meant well, however, and Pam knew her sister worried about her. It was nice to have someone who cared.

"I'll see if Cindy can come," Pam said, relenting, and then hung up the phone. Poor Cindy was plump and shy and never had dates. She seldom turned down Pam's request for a sitter. And who knows, Pam thought with a surge of wistfulness, maybe Robert would turn out to be a really swell guy. In spite of her protestations, Pam had to admit having the right swell guy in her life might be kind of nice. She wasn't sure where she'd work him into her busy schedule, but she did get lonely at times.

She was also a realist, however, and past experience had taught her that the Roberts of the world weren't looking for additional children in their lives, especially ones in diapers. Most women her age at least had school-age children. And Pam really didn't blame the men. She didn't want any more children in her life, either. The knowledge that Robert had twin girls made him seem less attractive to her before she ever laid eyes on the man. Children from previous marriages brought complications and jealousy to relationships. Already she knew her boys were sweeter than his girls. It might not be logical for her to feel that way, but it was normal. Too bad Robert wasn't a sterile childless widower who'd always yearned for children.

Pam made a face at herself in the mirror. "Dream on, woman," she said out loud. "While you're at it, let's make Robert an incredibly *sexy*, sterile childless widower who's always yearned for children—and doesn't consider diaper changing women's work."

She went to the living room and scooped up Tommy. "Come on, Scott," she said to her older son. "I want you guys to come out in the kitchen where Mommy can keep an eye on you."

"Mary won a washing machine," Scott said excitedly. At age two and a half, he took game shows very seriously.

"Good for Mary. Let's go to the kitchen, honey. You can have some apple juice and crackers."

Reluctantly, Scott allowed himself to be pulled up by the hand. Mary was stroking her new washing machine ecstatically. Did she want to risk it and try for a dryer? the host asked.

The audience screamed advice. Mary nodded. Yes, she would take the risk.

Pam waited with Scott to see what happened. The wheel went round and round then slowly inched its way toward a smiling devil. Mary lost.

"Poor Mary," Scott said.

Yes. Poor Mary. But she knew the risks. Just like Pam herself when she decided to risk her savings against a better future for herself and her sons.

And even if she lost, Pam decided, she wouldn't always be wondering if she could have gotten by the smiling devil.

PAM CHECKED HER LIST AGAIN to make sure she had everything. She was operating on too tight a schedule to have to load the kids back into the station wagon and make a return trip to the grocery.

Paprika. She'd forgotten paprika. Awkwardly, she turned her full shopping cart back toward the aisle with spices—2A. She spent so much time here, she knew the layout of the supermarket as well as any employee.

Tommy was starting to fuss in his seat in the cart. It was past his lunchtime. "Just a little longer, honey. Mommy will hurry." She looked around for Scott. "Now, where's that brother of yours?"

"Scott," Tommy said, and looked around for a minute until he caught sight of the box of Oreos in the basket.

"Cookie," he demanded.

"Not until after lunch," Pam said automatically. She retraced her steps with the cart, looking down each aisle as she passed it. Ah, the joys of grocery shopping with two toddlers. She did all right until the food portion of the shopping cart got too full and she had to put Scott out to walk. He was getting more adventurous with each shopping trip. Last week he'd wandered into the stockroom, and Pam was frantic until she found him.

"Where is that little varmint?" Pam said more to herself than Tommy, who was trying to get himself turned around enough in his seat to reach the Oreos.

"Sit down, Tommy. We'll have cookies at home."

"Cookie," Tommy whined in his starving-child voice.

The crash came from the back of the store. Pam felt a sinking feeling in her stomach and headed down the cereal aisle.

Tommy spotted Captain Crunch. "Crunch," he cried, holding out his arms as his mother sped by.

The display of canned chili had been spectacular. Pam had noticed it on her first tour of the store. As part of the store's Texas Days Sale, some enterprising young stock person had built a six-foot pyramid and topped it with the Texas state flat. Other displays in the store featured a chuck wagon full of bottles of barbecue sauce and the largest can of ranch-style beans in the world.

The cans of chili were rolling everywhere—except for the one Scott was holding. A look of amazement covered his face.

Pam had to take a minute to compose herself before swooping in on her child and the disaster he had caused.

A plump stock boy with braces retrieved the flag from the floor and called, "Hey, Joel, some little kid wrecked your pyramid."

A tall boy with curly auburn hair came trotting up.

"Hey, Tiger, what'd you do that for?" he asked, mussing Scott's hair. "You've wrecked the engineering triumph that was going to win me a sure berth in the stock boys' Hall of Fame."

Scott sheepishly held out the can of chili.

"I'm sorry. Let me help you pick them up," Pam said, bending over and retrieving two cans. "I can't manage both children in one cart. I guess I'm going to have to start using two. Oh, golly, what a mess! There must be a hundred cans."

"Two hundred and seventy-two, to be exact," Joel said.

"Scott, help pick them up. You were a bad boy."

Scott hunkered down on his plump legs and solemnly picked up another can to hand to Joel.

Joel laughed. "Thanks, Tiger. Aren't you the little guy who visited us in the back room last week?"

Pam collected an armload of cans and looked around for a place to put them. "Shall we rebuild the pyramid?"

"Don't worry about it, ma'am," Joel said. He had a dimple in his right cheek when he grinned. He looked like someone who grinned a lot. "We'll take care of this," he told Pam reassuringly.

"But I feel so responsible."

"Look, wrecked displays, spilled milk and the like are a way of life in a supermarket. Besides, I would have had to take it down this weekend anyway. The Hawaiian Holiday Sale starts next week. I'm going to build a volcano out of cans of pineapple."

The plump boy came down the aisle pushing three carts in front of him. He and Joel began putting the cans into the carts.

Pam picked up another armful, then looked around for Scott. He was toddling down the aisle toward a woman in a wheelchair. Pam raced after him, picked him up and started back toward the disaster scene in time to see Tommy retrieve the package of cookies from the back of the shopping cart.

And suddenly Oreo cookies were rolling out among the cans of chili.

Pam uttered an oath under her breath.

Joel and the other boy were looking around them in amazement. Joel began to laugh. "Lady, you've got a two-kid demolition team on your hands."

"Tell me about it," she said helplessly. She fished around in her purse for two five-dollar bills. "I think the best thing for me to do is get them out of here. I'm really sorry for all the extra work we've made," she said as she held out the money.

Joel waved her away. "It's not as bad as yesterday's broken jar of honey—large economy size. Don't give it a thought. Goes with the territory."

"On the other hand . . ." the younger boy said, eyeing the money.

Joel flashed him a look.

"You're awfully nice," Pam said, smiling. Joel was not only nice, he was very nice-looking and not a boy, really. A young man. Twenty or twenty-one.

He smiled back at her. Yes, a very nice-looking young man.

Pam wished she'd bothered with makeup. She wondered what her hair looked like.

"Cookie," Tommy wailed. "Cookie."

"He's hungry," she explained, holding tightly to Scott's hand.

Joel reached into the cart and handed him one of the loose cookies.

"Me, too," Scott said, holding out a plump little hand.

"You come here a lot, don't you?" Joel said, bending over to pick up some cans.

"Yes. I operate a small catering business and shop for a lot of groceries."

"Must be tough with these two guys. Does anyone help you?"

"No. No one helps me. Are you sure I can't give you something for your trouble?"

"Naw," he said. "Take the crew home and feed them. The little squirt looks like he needs his lunch and a nap."

The younger stock boy looked like he wouldn't have minded having something for his trouble.

Pam put the money back into her purse. "Well, good-bye. Again, I'm sorry. Tell them bye-bye, boys." Tommy had Oreo cookie all over his face and hands. Scott was carefully licking off the white stuff. He looked up long enough to say "Bye."

As Pam pushed the cart up the aisle, Tommy reached out his hands and pointed at the cookies being left behind on the floor. "Cookie!"

She heard Joel's laughter.

"Think you'll ever have kids?" the younger boy asked him.

"Sure. Cute little guys, weren't they?"

Pam smiled. Tommy and Scott were cute little guys.

JOEL WATCHED THE DEPARTING woman for a minute. "Nice lady," he said.

"Yeah," Paul said without enthusiasm. "I guess."

"Pretty, too."

"Yeah, I guess. But you're engaged, remember, and that woman's too old for you anyway. Get to work so I can go on break. I haven't had my morning Pepsi, and I'm suffering from withdrawal."

As Joel picked up cans, he continued to think of the pretty woman and her two cute kids. He'd noticed her before. He'd admired the nice way she had with her children. With all the groceries she bought, he wondered if she had six more at home or a husband with a voracious appetite.

She wasn't wearing a wedding ring. She said no one helped her, and something in the way she said it made him think she meant more than her catering business.

Catering. Joel himself had considered going into hotel-and-restaurant management for a college major but had opted for safe and sane accounting—and not out of any particular love of the field. But he could study accounting at a nearby city college that was not only less expensive than other colleges and universities but offered many of their classes in the evening, on weekends and even at seven o'clock in the morning to accommodate working students.

After three years of study he still wasn't too enamored with the field, but maybe that was because he was having a hard time visualizing himself spending the next fifteen or twenty years of his life working with columns of figures at the head office of Anderson's Food Marts, Inc. Stephanie Anderson and her father had it all worked out, however. Eventually, he'd be a vice president, probably even run the company someday—a golden opportunity for a young man who came from nothing. And he was damned lucky to be engaged to a girl like Stephanie, who could have had any guy she wanted. She was beautiful, rich, cultured, smart. And Mr. Anderson had taken a fatherly interest in him. He'd even offered to pay the expenses for Joel's last year in college if he would give up his job and transfer to Southern Methodist University, the prestigious Dallas school that Stephanie attended.

But Joel had declined Mr. Anderson's offer. It was difficult to make the Andersons understand why, but he wanted the satisfaction of finishing college under his own steam. He'd been raised on welfare money. Working his way through college was earning him self-respect. Stephanie had pouted a lot about his decision. Had she ever! She wanted to make him a part of her world and had even picked out a fraternity at SMU for him to join.

With all the cans of beans picked up, Paul went scurrying off for his break, and Joel pushed the full shopping carts to the stockroom. He glanced at his watch. An hour until lunch. Then he was scheduled to work until three. He could study a couple of hours before coming back for the evening shift. Stephanie complained a lot when he worked double shifts on weekends, but he was worried about paying his tuition next fall. Paying his summer-term tuition had cleaned him out. Sometimes he wondered if he wasn't an idiot not to take up Mr. Anderson's offer and become a full-time college student his senior year. But he was going to be owned by the Andersons soon enough the way it was. And working had its compensations, he decided, thinking of the episode with the catering lady and her two boys. He realized he was grinning. What a circus that had been! Cans and cookies everywhere. The lady had been so upset, the boys so funny.

"Cookie," Joel said out loud, imitating the toddler.

That cookie kid's mommy was nice. Mighty nice.

WITH HER EYE ON THE CLOCK, Pam fed the boys and got them ready for their naps. Guiltily, she wished they'd sleep all afternoon and give her time to get the Pattersons' dinner party organized.

Barney, the old yellow mongrel who had started living with them last fall, followed her down the hall as she carried Tommy to the boys' bedroom. Tommy was already nodding by the time she put him in his bed. He reached for Puppy, his favorite stuffed animal, and was instantly asleep. Pam took a minute to run a loving finger along the pure line of his cheek. Precious baby. He was growing up so fast—already fifteen months. She wished there was a way to slow time down so she could better relish each stage of her boys' lives.

Tommy's thumb went automatically into his mouth, an arm clutching Puppy close to his chest. Puppy was missing both eyes and much of his stuffing, but he was preferred over the other stuffed citizens of Tommy's crib.

Barney followed Pam back down the hall to the living room, where Scott was playing with his cars on the coffee table. The dog curled up at her feet, and Scott crawled into her lap for the reading of *The Little Engine That Could*, his current favorite. Last week it had been *The Cat in the Hat*. Scott nodded off before the little train got the toys for the good boys and girls over the mountain. Pam pulled the afghan over him and left him on the sofa. She didn't want him disturbing Tommy when he woke up.

As soon as she left the room, she heard the tags on Barney's collar jingle as he jumped up on the sofa beside Scott. The dog wasn't supposed to get on the furniture. Six months ago, when it became apparent no one was going to answer the lost-dog ad she placed in the classified section of the *Dallas Morning News*, Pam had held the big homely dog's head in her hands and explained, "Okay, dog, I guess we've been adopted, but I do have my rules. I absolutely will not tolerate an animal on the furniture. I will feed you, and in exchange, I would appreciate you scaring away would-be burglars."

Since that time, she and Barney had been playing this silly game. He waited until she left the room to jump onto the sofa or Scott's bed. If the dog heard her coming, he'd jump down. But Barney slept soundly enough to be unaware of all but the most severe thunderstorms, and a burglar could come and go safely with no threat from the big, homely dog. Pam caught Barney on the furniture almost daily. He'd jump down and slink into a corner, his big soulful eyes asking her to please love him anyway.

Dumb old dog, she thought, not bothering to go back to chase him off the sofa. He'd just climb up again the minute her back was turned. Barney was winning the war. But he was good for the boys, and she kind of liked the old mutt herself. And the sofa was already stained and worn. What were a few dog hairs?

Pam tied on her apron and looked about her cluttered kitchen. Thank goodness she'd prepared the chicken Kiev and almond tort yesterday. This afternoon she needed to finish the hors d'oeuvres, make the lobster bisque and get the vegetables and the salad ingredients ready for last-minute preparation. Then, when her baby-sitter arrived at five-thirty, she would take the food over to the Pattersons', where she would assemble everything and supervise the serving. The Pattersons were her best customers. Philip Patterson was senior partner in an old-line law firm, and his wife, Buffy, was a grand matron of Dallas society and famous for her dinner parties. Her picture was frequently found in the society section of the *Dallas Morning News*. The Pattersons' son was getting married next month, and Pam would be kept busy over the next weeks with prenuptial events, including a rehearsal dinner for forty, her biggest catering job to date. Just thinking about it made her nervous. She hoped the boys stayed healthy and Cindy, her baby-sitter, didn't find that job she was looking for. Cindy had been applying at fast-food restaurants and movie theaters for an evening job. Pam dreaded the thought of finding another sitter.

Catering, Pam now realized, was a demanding business at best, but trying to conduct it around the schedules of two small boys made it especially difficult at times.

But she could operate the business out of her home. With her boys being so young, that seemed like a very important consideration. And she was earning money doing what she did best.

When Pam had been faced with the prospect of supporting herself and her children, she knew that her best chance for earning money had something to do with food. During her teenage years, she had worked summers in her grandparents' restaurant in Santa Fe and later had gone to chef school during her four-year stint in the Army. During her last assignment at an Army base in Oklahoma, she'd run a mess hall that fed hundreds daily, so she definitely knew her way around a kitchen. But normal Army fare such as meat loaf, mashed potatoes and chocolate cake was not appropriate for catered affairs. The Army hadn't taught her gourmet cooking. That she was having to learn on her own.

At first, the food she attempted had been too exotic, and she experienced a few embarrassing failures. And she hadn't charged enough. Now she was less timid about pricing and less experimental about recipes, relying on garnishes and sauces to glamorize more standard fare. But she did try to have one out-of-the-ordinary dish with each meal. Tonight it was the bisque—served with dollops of caviar and sour cream.

She was learning with each job, and her business was growing, but she still didn't earn enough money to make ends meet. The problem was time—either too much or not enough. She would go for days or even a week with no work. Then she would have more than she could handle. At times, especially after a lean month, she wondered if she shouldn't just give up the whole idea and get a regular job. But that meant taking two babies to all-day child care—something she would rather avoid, if possible, especially while they were so young.

She had promised herself that she would try to make a go of the catering business until her savings ran out. Then, if it looked like a lost cause, she'd get a salaried position. After six months, she was close to the end of her savings. Jobs were starting to come more regularly, and she was earning more with each one, but it was still touch and go. If she could hold out long enough, she knew she would not only break into the black but make enough to support herself and her boys.

Pam refused to think about failure. She felt certain the work was out there. At almost every event she catered, one of the female guests would find her way to the kitchen with compliments and inquiries.

Pam finished making the hors d'oeuvres and preparing ingredients for a salad, storing each in a plastic bag until time for tossing with her own tarragon-vinegar dressing. Then it was time to make the delicate bisque that had so pleased the hostess at the anniversary celebration she'd catered last week.

Pam assembled the ingredients for the thick soup, only to realize the cream had gone bad and she'd gotten home without the paprika.

The two neighbors she knew well enough to ask to stay with her sleeping sons long enough for her to dash back to the grocery would be at work. If she woke up the boys from their naps, she'd never get everything finished.

She tried her sister's number. No answer.

Pam looked in the yellow pages for a store that delivered. Only one was even remotely in her part of town, and when she called, the man who answered informed her that the store delivered only for its regular customers.

Pam called the local Anderson's Food Mart and asked if they would deliver for their regular customers. The answer, of course, was no. Pam hung up, then with her hand still on the receiver she dialed the number again.

"Is Joel there?"

Shortly, Joel was on the line with a brisk hello.

"I'm the woman whose son destroyed the chili display."

"Tiger's mom," he said brightly. "What can I do for you?"

"Could I pay you or one of the other stockroom workers to deliver two pints of cream and a can of paprika?"

"You sound desperate."

"I am. The boys are asleep. I've got to have a complete dinner ready for delivery at five-thirty. If I wake the boys now, the rest of the afternoon will be a disaster."

"I get off at three. Is that soon enough?"

Pam gave him the address.

THE DOORBELL WOKE up Scott.

"Hi, Tiger," Joel said to the sleepy boy trailing an afghan across the entry hall, his thumb firmly in his mouth. "Looks like I woke you up."

Pam picked up her groggy son and accepted the small sack from Joel. "Come in," she said. "I'll get my purse."

"Here, let me have the kid," Joel said.

Before she could protest, the slender young man had taken Scott from her arms, afghan and all. She hesitated, then went off to find her purse.

The phone rang. Mrs. Patterson wanted to know a good dessert wine to serve with the torte.

Pam suggested a Madeira or champagne. She couldn't be more specific. Wines were still a mystery to her, but she would learn. That and a hundred other things. She was going to be the best damned caterer ever to hit the city of Dallas—she hoped.

When Pam returned with her purse, Scott and Joel were in the living room playing with the toy cars. *What a lovely young man,* Pam thought, as she paused to watch them. He seemed genuinely to like children. *Nice.*

But then he was little more than a boy himself.

Joel offered to stay a while and keep Scott entertained so Pam could get things under control in the kitchen. "Are you sure you don't mind?" she asked.

"Hey, a chance to play cars with a two-year-old doesn't come along very often," he said with a slightly lopsided grin.

Later Joel helped her load the station wagon, and she fixed him and the boys an early supper of waffles and sausage. Joel fed Tommy so Pam could check her lists one last time to make sure she hadn't forgotten anything.

She took a few minutes before Cindy arrived to sit down at the table and have a cup of coffee. What a nice little group they made. Two sturdy boy babies in their high chairs. A man—albeit a very youthful one—joking with them and feeding Tommy bites of waffle. And herself. The mother person. It all seemed so normal.

Such a nice young man. Joel's grin was endearing. His easy sense of humor a delight. And he liked little boys. She hoped her sons grew up to be as kind and charming.

Chapter Two

The dinner was hectic. Mrs. Patterson's maid was sick, and Pam had to serve. Mrs. Patterson started the meal late, and the guests lingered over each course. Pam kept a worried eye on the clock. She'd promised Cindy she would be home by midnight. Her mother maintained a rigid curfew, even in the summertime.

"Don't fix Kiev anymore," Mrs. Patterson snapped at Pam after she had said good-night to her last guest. One of the female guests hadn't been careful enough cutting into the chicken Kiev, and butter had splattered all over her dress. "And couldn't you have managed a more exotic topping for the torte than whipped cream?"

"Perhaps. Actually, I thought the meal went rather well. I had several lovely comments from your guests. And now, I'm really sorry, Mrs. Patterson, but I need to leave. My sitter's parents expect her home by midnight."

"Leave! Why, look at this kitchen!"

Usually the maid was in charge of cleaning up. Pam had managed to clean the dining room and load her station wagon with her own pans and utensils, but the kitchen was still a disaster. Dirty dishes were stacked on the counters. Used utensils filled the sink. Leftover food covered the kitchen table.

"If I'd known I needed to clean up, I'd have made arrangements to stay later," Pam explained. "I really need to go now."

"Mrs. Sullivan, if you want to continue working for me, I suggest you find some way to get this mess cleaned up before you leave here. And no, I don't want it left overnight. I want it done now."

Pam called Cindy's mother, who would agree to only one extra hour. Cindy had another baby-sitting job at eight in the morning, it seemed.

An hour wasn't enough. Pam called her sister.

"You're kidding," Brenda said. "You want me to go over to your house and spend the night because some woman won't clean up her own kitchen?"

"I'm really sorry, Brenda. You know I wouldn't ask if I wasn't really in a bind. I've got several hours of work ahead of me. I need the favor in the worst way. I can't afford to antagonize this woman or Cindy's mother. Mrs. Patterson is my best customer, and Cindy's my best sitter."

"Okay, honey. Call your sitter and tell her I'm on my way. George says he'll come, too. Do the boys ever wake up at night?"

"Well, yes, sometimes," Pam admitted. "Scott especially. Sometimes he wants his diaper changed or just a little cuddling. He'll usually go right back to sleep. Tommy may want a bottle or his pacifier. And his diaper changed, of course. Do I still have to go on this date tomorrow? We're all going to be tired after tonight."

"You certainly do, Pamela Sue Hunter Sullivan! You're going out with Robert John Fenwick III if I have to baby-sit those kids myself. I'm tired of feeling guilty over my good life when my big sis is having such a rocky time."

"And a man can make it all better, I suppose?" Pam asked sarcastically.

"Damned right, if he's a dear like my George. I wish George had a twin. You could use a wonderful man like him."

"George's twin would probably be just like George," Pam reminded her sister. "He wouldn't want kids, and he'd marry someone younger than he was."

George and Pam were the same age—thirty. Brenda was twenty-six.

"You're impossible," Brenda said. "Get to work. We'll bed down in the guest room."

"You'll have to move the pile of unfolded laundry from the bed. And put the ironing board in the closet. Leave the bedroom door open so you can hear the boys."

It was three o'clock in the morning before Pam pulled her station wagon into the driveway. Lights shone from most of the windows of her small house. She went racing up the walk, certain some disaster had befallen her household. Her brother-in-law and Scott were both asleep in the living-room rocker. Barney was asleep on the sofa. The television was flickering blankly.

The coffeepot was still on in the kitchen. Animal crackers were scattered about the table. The milk carton was open on the counter.

Brenda and Tommy were asleep in the guest room. All the stuffed animals had been transported to the guest-room bed.

Pam put her sons into their own beds. She sent George to his sleeping wife. Unloading the station wagon would have to wait until the morning. She brushed her teeth and fell into her own bed. *Please let the boys sleep past six.*

Past seven would be lovely.... Would eight o'clock be too much to ask?

PAM GOT A FULL REPORT in the morning over coffee. After Brenda and George arrived, both boys had awakened and been so excited to see their only aunt and uncle in attendance that nothing would do but a little post-midnight playtime.

"By the way, who's Mary?" George asked with a yawn. "Scott seemed worried about her washing machine. The little tyke really talks quite well now, you know. Like a person. I'm rather impressed."

"He *is* a person, George. Mary was a contestant on a game show. Game shows are his current passion. Mary lost, and Scott worries about losers. You two can't imagine how much I appreciate this. I'll make you a pie."

"Apple, please," George said, not taking his eyes off Tommy. He seemed fascinated by his younger nephew's attempts to feed himself oatmeal. "I say, is he always this messy?"

"Yes," Pam admitted. "Both of them are. I have to take the high chairs outside and hose them down every second or third day."

"But don't you get ants and bugs and such from food always being dropped on the floor?" George's British nose wrinkled as he looked at the crumbs.

"'Fraid so."

"And the infants must be cleaned and fed and watched after continuously?" he demanded.

"Something like that. But they're kind of cute, don't you think?"

George looked from one boy to the other, studying. "Yes, by golly, they are that. But does cuteness balance out all that bother?"

Pam laughed. "For me, yes. I wanted children in the worst way. And they have been more than worth all the bother."

Pam felt her sister's eyes on her face and knew what Brenda was thinking—that these two children had cost her a lot.

PAM STARED GRIMLY at the clothes hanging in her closet. "Drinks at the Crescent Bar followed by a small dinner party at the home of George's boss," her sister had said. "It's the queen's birthday. The men will wear suits."

Now, just what was she supposed to wear? Pam thought frantically. The Crescent Bar was posh—a yuppie watering hole for Dallas's young, successful and beautiful. And she was certain everyone attending the dinner party would be impeccably attired.

The few dressy garments she owned were out of style. Her taller, thinner, younger, more elegant sister would look like a fashion plate, while she herself would look dated and a bit frumpy. She should have thought to borrow something from Brenda. But she hadn't, and now it was too late. Her sister's clothes probably wouldn't fit anyway. Living her life in a kitchen had put extra pounds on Pam's hips, a trend she was trying to reverse.

She pulled out a black faille cocktail suit that she'd once thought was smart. Now it looked severe, maybe even matronly, but she steamed the wrinkles out of it, anyway. The suit would have to do. Maybe it would look better on.

The next problem was her hair. After washing and drying it, Pam tried to coax it into a style. It looked clean but limp. She not only needed a cut, her last perm had chosen this week to vanish. She tried more styling spray and fluffed a bit. Finally, she tried the curling iron, lots more hair spray and serious fluffing.

Then she took time to feed the boys and put on their pajamas. Cindy arrived and took over evening playtime.

The suit still fit but was definitely severe. Pam added a silk scarf in bright fuchsia that Brenda had given her two years ago for Christmas and had never been worn.

George and Brenda arrived promptly at six. Brenda was outstanding in a red outfit sporting a miniskirt worn with red stockings and matching high-heeled shoes. She took one look at her sister then marched Pam back to the bedroom to change her small pearl earrings for large rhinestone ones, to coax some height into her hair with ornamental combs, to retie the scarf and to roll the skirt at the waistband and hike it up a few inches. "Better," Brenda said. "I give you these scarfs and combs and earrings. How come you never wear them?"

"Wear them where?" Pam laughed. "To do laundry?"

She tolerated her sister's adding more blush to her cheeks and eyeliner under her eyes. Somehow their roles had gotten reversed. At one time, Pam had instructed Brenda in the mysteries of makeup, the drama of dress. Now she felt like the younger sister gratefully benefiting from the big sis's expertise.

But then, she lived in a world of children—a Humpty Dumpty world combining the opposing forces of imagination and practicality, a world of Big Bird and washable clothing, of Dr. Seuss and stripped-down decor. Mommies in makeup and pretty clothes seemed out of place. Mommies who wore chenille bathrobes and talked to teddy bears were right at home. Any sophistication she had once possessed got left in the maternity ward. But maybe not all of it. Fascinated, Pam watched in the mirror while her clever sister worked a minor miracle on a worn mother of two.

Brenda stepped back to assess, then added a bit more blush. "Voilà!" she said. "Stop hiding your light under a bushel, sister of mine. You're a knockout when you work at it."

"Knockout" was stretching it a bit, but Pam admired herself in the mirror and had to admit her sister's efforts were effective.

Pam smiled at her sister in the mirror. Brenda winked. It was fun to look pretty and to be going out. Pam felt her spirits soar. Maybe they'd have a terrific time. Maybe her date would be fantastic.

Robert John Fenwick III was waiting in the elegant lobby of the Crescent Hotel. Unlike the few previous dates Pam had had since arriving at her single state, Robert was actually tall, dark and handsome. His tummy was board flat, and his shoulders broad. His eyes were black, his eyebrows expressive. He reminded Pam of a young Tyrone Power, and she felt a flush of nervous warmth. He was out of her league.

Even this place was out of her league. Marble floors. Enormous crystal chandeliers hanging from high, ornate ceilings. Groupings of velvet-covered Victorian furniture. The lobby looked more like it belonged in a palace than a hotel.

The bar area was large and tastefully wood paneled. The four of them found seats at the bar. All about them attractive, fantastically attired people were laughing, talking, sipping their drinks. Pam ordered a frozen daiquiri. The other three ordered Scotch and water. When the drinks arrived, hers seemed frivolous and unsophisticated.

Robert was wearing an impeccably tailored, under-stated suit of a Western cut. On his feet were black eel-skin boots that must have cost hundreds of dollars. Her own black patent pumps came from Kinney's and cost $29.95.

Robert's job occasionally involved traveling, he ex-plained, and he had just returned from Tokyo. He told of attending Japan's traditional Kabuki theater, which he enjoyed immensely. "Do you travel much?" he asked Pam.

"No," she said. Her sister interrupted with a story about London theater before Pam could explain why.

"How long have you known George and Brenda?" she asked.

"Several years now. I met George in London when I was doing some work for Dover International. We've been seeing each other socially since he and Brenda moved to Dallas. When I discovered that the gorgeous Brenda had an unattached sister, I could hardly wait to meet her," Robert said smoothly, his hand touching Pam's arm and lingering.

He was charming, she had to admit. And the best-looking man in the room, even better-looking than George, who was also darkly attractive and looked mar-velous tonight in a gray linen suit worn with a pink silk dress shirt.

"And now that I have met her," Robert went on, his voice warm and soft and just for her, "I am wondering when I can have her all to myself."

Pam sipped her drink, not knowing how to respond. She was flattered but uncertain. It was lovely to have a handsome, successful man pay attention to her, to com-pliment her, but she felt like a participant in a charade. The woman perched on a bar stool in a hiked-up skirt, sipping her drink and looking reasonably chic was not her. Robert had no notion at all of the true Pam Sullivan, who usually wore stretched-out sweats or faded jeans, whose house was shabby at best, whose life was full of dirty diapers and spilled milk, whose feet ached from the unaccustomed high heels on her feet.

But the game was fun. And the mirror over the bar reflected back a pretty woman with a handsome date. The liquor in her unsophisticated drink made her feel a little light-headed and more carefree than she had felt in a long time.

She watched in the mirror while brother-in-law George whispered something in her sister's ear. They were holding hands; their shoulders were touching. Brenda smiled and kissed her husband's cheek then whispered something back. They still acted like young lovers. How nice. How very nice.

Over Pam's protests, Robert ordered her a second drink. He asked her if she liked rodeo.

"I've never gone," she admitted.

"Never gone! A Texan who's never been to a rodeo. That's practically criminal, and we're going to have to fix that situation right away. There's a big professional rodeo over in Fort Worth next weekend. We can go to the Cattlemen's Restaurant first for the best T-bone on the face of the earth."

"I have to cater a party Saturday night," Pam said, both sorry and relieved at the same time.

"Then we'll just have to take in the Sunday afternoon performance and have that steak afterward," Robert said, his hand once again on her arm. "Then we can go dancing."

Dancing. It had been years since she'd danced! She and Marty used to dance, before the babies were born. Ballroom. Western. Disco. Pam loved it all. Marty used to say they'd been born to dance together, and it did seem that way. At least on the dance floor, they had been good together. Maybe great. Sometimes other dancers would stop and watch while they performed like Fred Astaire and Ginger Rogers, swooping, dipping, twirling. Now Pam's dancing partners were Scott and Tommy, who thought it was great fun when their mother turned up the radio and twirled them around the living room.

"Do you like to dance?" Robert asked.

"Yes," Pam said softly. "Very much. It's been a long time, but I used to really love it."

"Then it's a date?" he asked.

Pam hesitated. How could she be gone all afternoon and evening on Sunday? She couldn't afford a sitter for that long, and she hated to leave the boys so much. She had three catering jobs next week the way it was. She sometimes wondered if, after expenses, Cindy didn't clear more than she did.

Brenda leaned over and whispered, "Having a good time?"

Pam smiled and nodded. Yes, she was. "What are you doing next Sunday?" she asked her sister.

"Playing in a tennis tournament with George. Why?"

"Oh, just wondering."

"Has he asked you out?" Brenda said, her eyes gleaming. "Go for it, sis. He's a catch."

Pam didn't like her sister's word choice. "A catch." As though she were a huntress on the prowl. If anything romantic was going to happen in her life, she wanted it to be spontaneous—eyes meeting across a crowded room, immediate recognition of a soul mate. No hunting. No game playing. But it probably only happened that way in the movies.

While they waited for the second round of drinks to arrive, Robert showed her the pictures of his two daughters. They were six, identical and darling. He seemed pleased at Pam's compliments. "Yeah, they're dolls," he agreed. "It's important for me to keep a good relationship with them, but it's hard. You ought to try entertaining six-year-olds. Do you like children?" he asked abruptly, putting his billfold back in his pocket.

Pam smiled. "Oh, my, yes," she said, reaching in her purse and pulling out pictures of her own.

Robert looked at the photographs and frowned. "Cute kids. Who are they?"

"My sons," Pam said with a dirty look at Brenda and George. They hadn't told him.

"Oh? I hadn't realized you had children," Robert said, his voice suddenly cooler. "When Brenda said she had an unmarried sister, I assumed she was younger and well, ah, unencumbered."

Sudden silence fell over the group. The pianist was playing nimble jazz, the perfect background music for relaxing yuppies. A couple next to George was discussing the latest Woody Allen movie. She liked it. He didn't.

Bits of another conversation about the Dallas Cowboys' upcoming football season floated from a nearby table. Mediocre at best, one man insisted. His companion disagreed.

"Well, I say, we'd better down these drinks and be on our way," George said too jovially. "It's time to pay tribute to the queen."

Brenda squeezed her sister's arm. "I'm sorry, sis."

"You should have told him," Pam said, not caring if Robert heard.

"I know," Brenda admitted. "I just thought if he could meet you first and see how sweet and darling you are that he'd be a little more accepting about Scott and Tommy.''

By this time, Robert had recovered. ''Listen. There's no problem here. I love my kids. Pam loves her kids. Let's have a good evening.''

For the rest of the evening, Robert was attentive, but it wasn't the same. The flirtatious edge had gone from their banter, and they were just making the best of things. Apparently Robert wasn't in the habit of going out with women who had young children. Like most men in his age group who had children by a previous marriage, Robert obviously didn't want additional children encumbering his life. Who could blame him? Pam felt the same way herself. And maybe at this point in her life, she also didn't need a man to complicate things. The only sort of man she would be interested in was one who liked her sons, who would welcome them into his life, and such a man might not exist. Most men this side of forty were either like Robert with children from a previous marriage or bachelors wanting to have children of their own. More and more, Pam wondered if a second marriage would have to wait until the boys were grown, even though she hated for them to grow up without a man's influence in their lives.

Ah, well, at least she didn't need to worry about getting a baby-sitter for next Sunday.

The party was held at the Turtle Creek home of George's boss, the president of Dover's Texas subsidiary, and was populated by an eclectic group composed of leading Dallas civic and cultural leaders and British citizens living in the city.

Pam overheard her brother-in-law telling his wife that she was the most smashing woman in the room. He was right. Brenda was incredible with her model's figure, gorgeous hair, perfect features. She exuded an aura of glamour that turned heads and made her husband proud. But Pam had no doubt George would still love Brenda when she was old and not so glamorous, and he would still be telling her she was the most smashing woman in the room. Being around those two left Pam with a bittersweet longing. People were happiest when they had someone to love, someone to share their lives with.

Pam had done a couple of catering jobs in the sprawling Turtle Creek mansions, and she decided she could have done a better job with the catering at this particular function. The buffet was unremarkable.

Robert was having a difficult time restraining himself from the pursuit of a fresh young British secretary who worked at the city's British trade consulate. Pam could tell he was fascinated with her accent, her bright blue eyes, her peaches-and-cream complexion. She had no doubt the girl would be receiving a call at work on Monday morning from a handsome Texan who wanted to pay her court.

"It's all right," she told Robert. "Go find out her telephone number."

He looked a bit sheepish. "You're really quite a lady," he said.

"Sure. That's what all my dates say when I give them permission to go check out the competition. Just make sure she doesn't have kids."

While Robert was on his mission, an aristocratic-looking man in a tuxedo approached her. Pam assumed he was one of the Brits and was surprised when he addressed her in a bit of a Texas drawl.

"He's crazy," the man said, nodding his head in Robert's direction. Robert's head was bending close to better hear the words from a pair of brightly painted British lips.

"Not really," Pam said. "We weren't suited at all."

"A blind date?"

Pam nodded.

"You go out often?"

Pam nodded no.

"Why not? A pretty young woman like you surely has lots of opportunity."

Pam regarded the man. Unless she missed her bet, the tux was tailor-made, not rented. His hair had not been cut but styled. His diamond tie pin was at least two carats, but at least he wasn't wearing one of those obnoxious diamond Rolex watches that so many rich Texans wore. Old money, she decided. The man was about forty. Either divorced or a philanderer. The look on his face was admiring.

"No. Actually, I don't have much opportunity to go out," Pam said peevishly. "Most men run the other way when they hear about my two small sons."

The man smiled. "Why? Do you take your sons on dates?"

Pam laughed. "No."

"Good. All I'm interested in is your company. I don't care if you have twelve children, as long as you leave them at home. How about having dinner with me tomorrow night?"

"Leaving children at home means hiring a sitter. And all *I'm* interested in is a man who wouldn't mind staying home with me and my kids once in a while."

"Too bad," the elegant man said with a sigh. "I cook for my ladies and buy them lovely gifts. I take them on fabulous trips and am most attentive to their physical needs. But I have nothing to do with their children."

The man took her hand and raised it to his lips. "Sure you won't reconsider?" he asked.

Pam shook her head no. He held her hand in both of his now. His skin was warm, his eyes compelling. Pam knew she was in the presence of a real pro when it came to seduction. But at least he was honest about it.

"I'm afraid not," she told him, "but thanks for the compliment. I've never had such a glamorous proposition. It will give me something to smile about when I'm stirring the oatmeal."

"Good luck," he said. His smile was as warm as his skin.

She watched him make his way to the buffet table, allowing herself to speculate about what it would be like to be with such a man. At one point in her life, she might have been insulted by his attention. But she supposed he was the sort of man put on this earth to make lots of women happy rather than one woman miserable. The happiness he promised was fleeting, however. Just an illusion really.

"Do you know who that man was?" Brenda demanded, handing Pam a glass of wine.

"Oh, just one of my many admirers," Pam said. "He wants me to go on a fabulous trip with him and be attentive to my 'physical needs.' But he wouldn't let me bring Scott and Tommy."

"He is J. Winston Marchland."

"Ah, I should have recognized him from the society pages. How remiss of me. Dallas's most eligible bachelor."

"Did he really want to take you out?" Brenda said in awe.

"So it seemed."

"Well, are you going?"

"Of course not," Pam said. "He's looking for good times. I'm looking for commitment."

"Are the two mutually exclusive? George and I are committed, and we have a good time."

"With Mr. Marchland they are. He prides himself on treating his *ladies* well."

"Pity. Just think, you might have gotten your picture on the society page."

"That's not very high on my list of life goals," Pam said.

Seeming quite pleased with himself, Robert returned from his reconnaissance mission to join them for the toast to the queen. Along with the other guests, many from Great Britain and other nations, they lifted their glasses and sang "God Save the Queen." George's baritone voice rang out above the rest.

"Does it make you homesick?" Pam asked her brother-in-law.

"A little," he admitted. "But I find myself becoming more American all the time. I like the sunshine and wide open spaces. I like hamburgers and adore apple pie. And I absolutely could not manage without *Monday Night Football*."

After the party George and Brenda dropped Robert off at his car in the Crescent parking lot. He shook hands with Pam. "It was great," he said. "You're a class act, Pam. Those two sons of yours are lucky little fellows."

Pam invited Brenda and George in for a cup of decaf to round off the evening. Cindy had dozed off on the sofa. Two candy-bar wrappers were wadded up on the coffee table alongside two Diet Coke cans. When the teenager woke up, she guiltily stuffed the wrappers into her pocket.

"Any problems?" Pam asked.

"Tommy's nose is running again, and he keeps waking up. And I wish Scott would move on to another book. I'm sure getting tired of that talking train," she said good-naturedly. "Mrs. Patterson called. She said you *must* do a lunch for ten on Tuesday. She apologized for the short notice but didn't sound sincere. You're to call her in the morning at eight-thirty sharp."

"That woman is both my savior and a cross to bear," Pam said with a sigh. "I'm beginning to feel owned."

George walked Cindy home while Pam perked some coffee. When he returned, the three of them tiptoed in to check on the boys.

Tommy was sleeping on his tummy with his diaper-clad bottom in the air, an arm clutching Puppy to his side. He sounded a bit stuffy but was sleeping soundly. Scott and Barney both had their heads on the same pillow.

"I say, is that sanitary?" George whispered.

"No," Pam answered. "Not much about kids and dogs is."

Needing physical contact with her sons, Pam patted two smooth little heads and touched two plump little hands. How she loved them. These two small human beings filled her heart and gave her life purpose—and made her afraid. It was hard to be alone with so much responsibility.

Seated at the round kitchen table, Brenda said, "The boys really are rather adorable, aren't they?" She ran her hand dreamily through her long, silky blond hair.

"Some of the time," Pam said. "Do I detect a note of wistfulness?"

"Oh, heavens no," Brenda said, sitting up straight and adding sugar to her coffee. "George and I agree wholeheartedly. No children. Can you imagine these hands tending children, cleaning up after children?" Brenda held up her beautiful hands with their long, red, perfectly manicured nails, then glanced around her at the cluttered kitchen with its twin high chairs, playpen, rows of clean and dirty baby bottles, the stained tile on the floor that never seemed quite clean.

"We discussed children at great length before we got married, and we're in complete accord," George said in agreement, taking his wife's elegant hand. "When Brenda feels like mothering, she can mother me. I'd be much too jealous for her to love another human being the way you love Scott and Tommy."

Brenda reached out and tickled her husband's chin. "Koochie, koochie, koo," she said. "Is it time for Mommy to put her babykins to bed?"

"No, stay a bit longer," Pam said. "How about some brandy? I'm not ready to face the ghosts of the night just yet."

Brenda reached over and touched her sister's arm. "What do they look like—the ghosts?" she asked gently.

"Their white sheets are generally covered with dollar signs. And instead of 'whooo,' they say 'pay me, pay me.'"

"Do any of them strum on a guitar?"

"Yes," Pam admitted, "but not as often now."

Quite irrationally, Pam felt the sting of tears in her eyes. Damn. She went to the cupboard to search for the brandy. The bottle needed dusting. She didn't have any brandy snifters but brought three wine glasses instead.

"Have you ever asked Mom and Dad for money?" Brenda asked, pouring the brandy.

"No. Their retirement income is limited, and they need it for their own expenses. I just wish they could afford to come to see us more often. We had such a good visit when they were here last month. They're good for the boys.''

"Listen, sis, if you get in too much of a bind, we can help..." Brenda began.

Pam held up a hand to silence her sister. "If I get in too much of a bind, I'll get a salaried job and put the boys in day care. Maybe I should have done it in the first place. It's just that I liked the idea of working at home and dreamed about building a successful business that would someday give me more than a mere sustenance income. I'd like to farm out some of the cooking to other home-bound women like myself. I'd like an assistant or two to help run things and make deliveries. But maybe the dream is a luxury I can't afford.''

"But you won't do anything stupid like getting evicted because you wouldn't ask us for help?" George asked.

"No. Thanks. And please stop being so sympathetic. I'll manage one way or the other.''

"What this little family of yours needs is a second income," George said brusquely.

"Yes, but unfortunately, Scott and Tommy are too young to get a job.''

"Was it a complete bust with Robert?" Brenda asked. "He seemed like such a nice guy.''

"Yeah, it was a bust, and yes, he was a nice guy. Listen, I know you guys mean well, but don't do that again. If a man doesn't want to date a woman with kids, let him say so up front.''

"But you'll never have another date in your life," Brenda wailed.

"So be it," Pam said with more conviction than she felt. "I have other things.''

JOEL WASN'T AT THE FOOD MART when Pam went shopping on Monday. She kept looking for him, intending to thank him again for helping her the week before.

Pam felt a sense of disappointment when she realized the young man wasn't in the store. Scott would have enjoyed seeing him again.

Pam started to ask the plump stock boy when Joel would come in, but decided that was unnecessary. She certainly wasn't coming back today if she could help it. Perhaps she'd see Joel another day.

Tommy was fussy. His runny nose was turning into a full-blown cold. Pam hurried about the store, shopping for the luncheon tomorrow. Mrs. Patterson was having out-of-town guests—relatives of her son-in-law-to-be. She had requested Pam's curried chicken salad made with walnuts and grapes.

Mrs. Patterson was the kind of woman who expected miracles on short notice, and she never said thank-you. But she paid well. And her guests often called Pam for their own parties. Buffy Patterson was the key to her success if there was to be any.

PAM HAD A SMALL wedding reception scheduled for Saturday afternoon with a small budget to match. Friday morning she was back at the grocery store shopping for sale-priced cheeses and the ingredients for meatless finger sandwiches.

Joel was nowhere to be seen.

"Doesn't Joel work here anymore?" Pam asked the plump kid—Paul, she heard one of the other boys call him.

"Sure," Paul said. "But during the week, he goes to class in the mornings. He doesn't come in until three."

Paul kept a wary eye on Scott, who was circling a display of tomato soup.

"Class?"

"Yeah. He's a student at Dallas City College. He's taking summer classes now."

A college student. He'd be surrounded by young coeds. His grin and his curly auburn hair would charm them. How could they not? Pam felt jealous. And old.

SHE HADN'T BOUGHT CHIVES. They weren't necessary, but Pam decided they would improve the taste of the egg salad. She'd run back to the store when the boys woke up from their naps.

Her hair was impossible, but lipstick and blush helped compensate. Not that it mattered. She was just going to run into the grocery. For chives. That nice young couple was having to make do with minimal reception fare, but she could at least provide them with tasty egg-salad finger sandwiches.

She took one last look in the mirror and promised herself a permanent after she got paid for the Pattersons' rehearsal dinner.

Joel was there, mopping the produce section.

"Hi, gang," Joel said with a wink for Pam. "Say, did I ever tell you two guys that you sure have a pretty mom?"

Scott put out his arms to be picked up. Joel parked his mop and obliged. "How ya doing, Tiger? Wrecked anything lately?"

He reached over and tickled Tommy's chin. "How about if we go see if we can talk those ladies in the bakery out of a cookie?"

"Cookie," Tommy said, his face lighting up.

Joel laughed.

The bakery ladies fussed over Scott and Tommy. And Joel. Pam had the feeling Joel had talked them out of cookies many times before. The ladies beamed at him like two proud aunts. Pam beamed with them, trying on the role of an older woman enjoying the company of a nice young man. The smile felt stiff on her face.

Chapter Three

Joel realized he didn't like Stephanie's father. He'd never allowed himself to think such a seditious thought before, but now, as he listened to the man drone on and on, retelling once again the story of how he'd built his business from his parents' neighborhood grocery store into the chain of sixteen central Texas stores that it was today, Joel realized he was not only tired of the story but of the man himself. Percy Anderson was pompous and boring. A "conversation" with him meant nodding occasionally and trying to look interested.

"I've kept my eye on the hands in the till and worked hard," Percy's monologue continued. "Let me tell you, no man ever died of hard work. You can't be afraid of hard work and succeed. And I've always hired hard workers. I don't believe in carrying deadwood on the payroll."

Joel wondered how many times he'd heard the man say it all before. Percy liked to hear himself talk and said the same things over and over.

Before, Joel had always been able to convince himself the man was amusing, a real American classic. Tonight he wasn't amused. *My future father-in-law,* he thought ruefully.

The meal had been ostentatious, as always. Mildred Anderson equated rich sauces with gourmet, and her cook sought to please. Joel wondered if Percy ever longed for the chicken-fried steak and gravy that he'd surely been raised on. Or fried catfish and slaw. But down-home cooking never made its way into the Andersons' twenty-room mansion.

"Joel, is something wrong with your crepes?" Mildred asked, putting a jeweled hand on his arm.

"Joel is tired," Stephanie spoke up, her voice carrying a sarcastic edge. "I thought he'd have a little free time when school let out, but oh, no. He's taking summer school in the mornings, studies in the afternoons and works evenings at the store. I'm surprised he found a way to sandwich us in tonight. Usually he schedules his social activities between ten and eleven at night."

"Now, honey, the boy's a hard worker," Percy said. "You can't fault him for that."

"It would have been nice to have him at my best friend's engagement party last night," she went on, ignoring her father's defense.

"I'm sorry about the party, Steph," Joel said. "But even if I could have gotten off, I couldn't afford to rent a tux."

"*I* could have gotten you off, and *I* would have rented you the tux," Stephanie insisted.

Joel didn't answer. They'd discussed it before.

After the dessert of Bananas Foster Flambé had been served, Percy invited Joel into his study for a brandy. Joel turned down an offered cigar, sipped at the expensive liqueur and steeled himself for what was coming.

"My little girl is mighty unhappy these days," Percy began. "She'd like her young man to squire her around a bit more, spend more time with her, escort her to parties. Have you thought any more about going to SMU your senior year, son, letting me help you out financially? I admire your pride, Joel, but, hell, what's the point? Stephanie's my only child. All this will belong to you kids someday," Percy said with a wave of his hand.

"I've gotten this far on my own, and I'd like to finish college under my own steam," Joel said. "And, yes, it is a matter of pride. I've paid for every cent of my education myself, and I'm proud of that fact."

Percy talked on a while longer, about taking advantage of opportunities when they come your way, striking while the iron was hot, not looking a gift horse in the mouth. Then he switched to a detailed description of the match that won him the state amateur tennis title for men over fifty. Joel listened politely until Stephanie came to reclaim him.

They went for a drive in her Firebird. They usually used her car. His battered van was roomier for necking, but she was afraid of being seen in it. Joel often wondered why she didn't give up on him and go find a rich boy to go out with, one who could afford a tux for parties and fit in better at sorority dances. But since she'd spotted him last summer working in one of her daddy's stores, Stephanie hadn't wavered from her course. She'd had a summer job of sorts working for her daddy and was picking up time cards from store managers. After that, she thought of other reasons to come back—almost daily, sometimes twice a day. She wasn't bashful, he'd give her that. And she was so damned gorgeous that he started daydreaming about her with great regularity. She was a stunning girl with a mane of thick blond hair and flashing brown eyes. Her long legs were smooth and muscular and brown, her bust round and firm. Studying became an ordeal for Joel, but mindless activities like

stocking shelves and sweeping floors were greatly en-
hanced by imagining what Stephanie Anderson would
look like in a bikini, what it would be like to kiss her, to
do other things.

He wondered if he'd ever have the courage to ask out
the daughter of the big boss man himself. But he realized now that when Stephanie decided she wanted something, she never left things to chance. When he got off
work one evening, she was waiting for him in her flashy
red car. "Let's go to dinner," she said brightly. Her white
sundress looked fantastic with her tan.

"I can't afford it," Joel admitted reluctantly.

Stephanie laughed and drove them to Friday's, where
she used her American Express Gold Card to pay for
their margaritas and fajitas.

She picked him up every night after that. Often he had
to study, and she would drop him by his apartment after
pouting her way through a quick meal. Other times they
would have a leisurely meal and go park in a secluded
lane by her house. It seemed that Stephanie had made up
her mind that Joel was another self-made man just like
her daddy, and that was the sort of man she thought she
should marry. And she liked his hair, his strong shoulders and arms, the way he kissed. He liked the way she
kissed back. They kissed as much as they talked. After
summer school ended, he pretty much gave the month of
August over to her, working the early shift at the store,
spending afternoons and evenings with her lounging by
the Andersons' pool, playing tennis on their court, skiing
at the lake behind their boat. Stephanie was as smashing
in a bikini live as she had been in his daydreams. And all
that wealth turned his head. On August eighteenth, Stephanie announced that she loved him. He saw no reason

not to love her back, or at least he had convinced himself it was love he felt.

Now, almost a year later, he wasn't so sure. They drove to their special place and necked a while, but his heart wasn't in it.

Finally Stephanie pushed him away, fixed her makeup and suggested they go get a Coke.

"I take it Daddy didn't convince you to transfer to SMU," Stephanie said from her side of the booth. She was pouting. Joel used to think it was cute when she pouted.

Joel took a sip of his Coke before responding. "I need to finish what I've started at DCC. And besides, I'm not SMU material. Those are rich kids out there, Steph. Future yuppies. I'm definitely more City College material."

"Well, if you're going to marry me, it's time for you to make the transition," she said. "There's nothing the matter with yuppies. Aren't you planning to be upwardly mobile? After all, you're a future executive with Anderson Food Marts."

"Sure, I want to be successful. But I've been doing a lot of thinking, and I don't want success just handed to me. Maybe we should make it on our own for a few years before I go to work for your dad. I'd like to earn his trust first."

"You mean take a job at Sears or something?"

"Yeah, or maybe at a hotel or restaurant. They need accountants, too. I wouldn't mind having a business of my own someday."

"Surely you don't expect me to marry an accountant who works at Sears," Stephanie said in her most withering tones.

"Why not? You and your dad claim you admire me 'cause I've pulled myself up by the boot straps. But now you want to cut them off. You can't have it both ways, Steph. I can't be both my own man and your daddy's boy."

"I don't believe I'm hearing this," she said, her brown eyes narrowing. "It was all decided, and now you're wanting to change everything."

"You and your dad decided everything, but you forgot to consult me."

"You never said a word before," Stephanie said, anger creeping into her voice. "You went along with everything."

"Yeah, I guess I did," Joel admitted. "I'm not too proud of that now. I was so impressed with you and your big house, and you're a hard person to say no to. When I start kissing you, I don't care much about anything else."

"Tonight the kissing wasn't so hot, was it? And now suddenly you have courage. What's going on with you, Joel?"

"I'm having second thoughts about marrying my way into the country-club set, I guess. I'm not sure I belong there."

"I knew you were raised common," Stephanie said with a toss of her wonderful hair, "but I didn't realize you *were* common."

"Yeah, I'm pretty common, just like your immigrant grandparents were down in their neighborhood grocery store. Sometimes I wish you'd remember them more when you start acting like Miss Dallas Debutante. I grew up in foster homes, and I don't intend to forget it. I think we could have a good life together, Stephanie, but I want us to do it on our own—at least for a few years. I know your dad's going to want to retire one of these days, but until then, why don't we go someplace else and get out of his shadow for a while—spread our own wings.''

Stephanie grabbed the car keys from the table and slid out of the booth. ''I can assure you I have no intention of ever leaving Dallas or my daddy's shadow!''

Joel didn't have money for a cab. It took him an hour to walk back to the Andersons' house. He glanced up at Stephanie's bedroom window. It was dark. He climbed into his van and coasted down the driveway before starting the motor.

His apartment had never looked seedier. The bed creaked as he fell across the sagging mattress.

''PAM, THIS IS ROBERT FENWICK,'' the voice said over the telephone. ''Remember, the jerk with twin daughters?''

Pam laughed. ''Don't be so hard on yourself. How was Miss British Secretary?'' Trailing the cord behind her, she walked to the stove and checked the pies in the oven.

''She hates jazz,'' Robert explained. ''I hate heavy metal or whatever that loud stuff was she likes. And she collects teddy bears. Her apartment is full of them. I hate to admit it, but she's too young for me. How are your sons?''

''Terrible. Wonderful.''

''I know what you mean. My terrible, wonderful twins will be with me this weekend. I wonder if you and your boys would like to join us on a picnic or some other G-rated excursion.''

''Why?'' Pam asked.

''Honestly?''

''Yes.''

"Well, I'm crazy about my daughters, but I dread these weekend visits. Wednesday evenings are fine. We go out to dinner and a movie or order a pizza and watch television, then I take them home. And this summer wasn't so bad when I had them all the time. With the girls actually living with me, we get into a routine that has a semblance of normality. I don't feel like I have to spend every moment with them or buy them presents all the time. But on these weekend visits, I feel like I have to do special things. You know, entertain them continuously, spoil them, make sure they know Daddy really loves them. It's gotten to be a real drag. And most of the girls...ah, most of the *young women* I've dated aren't interested in being part of my visitation weekends, or if they are, they soon get uninterested after a stimulating afternoon watching a movie about nauseatingly cute bears or jarring their dental work loose in bumper cars. I thought maybe it would help if us single parents joined forces."

"My boys are just babies—hardly compatible with six-year-olds," Pam said, picking up a sponge and cleaning flour from the counter. "And I don't have time for movies and bumper cars," she added.

"Please," Robert pleaded. "Just give it a try. I've thought about you a lot, wishing I'd behaved better when we went out. It was nothing personal, believe me. I thought you were quite lovely and enjoyed your company very much. I just didn't expect you to have children."

"So, this isn't a date per se?" she asked. "It's more two single parents joining forces to provide an excursion for their children."

"Yeah, I guess. Something like that. But I wouldn't ask if I didn't want to see you again. After going out with a succession of sweet young things who wouldn't know how to manage a kid even if they wanted to and think Neil Diamond is square, I've been wondering if maybe I ought to rethink my criteria for a datable woman. So maybe I'm inviting you for a combination family excursion and sort-of date. I'd like for us at least to be friends, Pam."

She considered. Robert Fenwick was a nice enough man with a quite legitimate concern about whether a woman he might become involved with had children or not.

But that didn't mean they couldn't be friends.

"Are you catering?" Pam asked.

"No, I think Colonel Sanders will get the contract."

"Okay. I'm game."

Pam thought about calling Brenda but decided against it. Her sister would make too much of the invitation.

While she washed the lunch dishes, she watched as a flirtatious cardinal paid court to a female in her backyard. Such a contrast—the male, vivid and bold, the female, gray and subdued. Pam wondered if cardinals mated for life or if the handsome male was just passing through.

The birds were nesting in her oak tree, which was a wonderful, stately tree that pleased her greatly. It was the oak that had made her decide to bid on this house instead of other repossessed houses the government sold at auction last fall. The oak and the deep backyard were the only things special about the otherwise nondescript dwelling. A tree like that would shade her sons, mark the seasons for her, be a home for birds and squirrels.

The house's shabbiness had made it affordable. A fixer-upper. Her father had cosigned the note for the mortgage, and her parents had stayed a month helping her move in and make the house habitable. Her father replaced rotten boards on the siding, patched the roof and replaced the broken windows in the utility porch. Her mother had helped Pam scrape and paint the inside.

The house was modest, but it was hers, and Pam dreamed about how nice the house could be if she added on a family room, recarpeted, papered the living room, put in a new kitchen floor and a hundred other things. She used daydreams about fixing up her house to help push other, deeper longings from her mind.

Her dad had promised to mend the fence in the backyard and build a sandbox during his next visit. She hoped her parents came soon. She'd like to be the daughter again for a time, to be fussed over as only a loving mother and father will do.

Her parents had retired to Santa Fe, where they had both grown up. They had kept her mother's family home with that plan in mind. Pam loved Santa Fe and had considered moving there herself. That's probably what she should have done. But last fall when she bought the house, she was still hoping. What if Marty came back? She wanted to be in the Dallas phone book so he could find her. He didn't know her parents had moved to Santa Fe and wouldn't think to look for her there.

Of course, if she'd been thinking straight, she would have acknowledged that Marty could have tracked her down if he'd wanted to, no matter where she lived. It wasn't like she wouldn't leave a trail. But she didn't want to leave anything to chance, and at the time, she had no pride when it came to Marty. She wanted him back.

From the first moment she had seen Marty singing in the Lone Star Bar, Pam had been smitten. His cowboy hat was pushed back on his head, and his guitar hung about his neck on a sequined strap. And he sang of loving. Good loving. Bad loving. Pam had never liked country-and-western music before, but that night it spoke to her.

The audience was predominantly female—women of all ages. Marty was a sexy young man with a sexy voice, and he knew all those women were admiring him, and that just made him tip his hat back still farther and his voice grow throatier.

His singing gave Pam goose bumps, made her lean forward in her chair, tense, tuned in. This was why she had gotten out of the Army and come back to Dallas, so she could come to this nightclub on this night and hear this man sing. It was destiny.

Dallas was where she had first met Marty and where she hoped he would someday come back to her.

Of course, there were other reasons why she stayed in the city after Marty walked out on her and the boys. These were the ones she told her parents—better work prospects, cheaper housing, Brenda's return to the city, more young people. But all of them were secondary. She still dreamed of opening the door one day and having Marty standing on the front porch, cocky grin in place, or of picking up the phone and hearing his voice.

For a long time, she woke up every morning hoping this would be the day that Marty came home. Sometimes, especially when her hair looked nice and she had on something pretty, she acted out little scenarios of how it would be. She would open the front door, gasp, fall into his arms, cry, listen to him begging forgiveness. He couldn't live without her. He loved her more than life itself. What a fool he had been. Could she ever forgive him? He'd never hurt her again. Never. He wanted the four of them to be a family.

But in recent months Pam wondered if she hadn't crossed some sort of magical line. The house had helped a lot. It held no memories of Marty. She didn't dream of Marty's homecoming anymore. She was stronger now and saw her former husband for the irresponsible man that he was. When Pam thought of Marty, her heart felt frozen and hard. He had melted it many times before, but finally she felt strong enough and responsible enough to banish him from her life. She had even acted out a different scenario for a while, telling him she didn't want him anymore. And now, finally, she no longer bothered with Marty scenarios. He wasn't ever coming back. It was just as well.

THE LOVELY JUNE WEATHER brought people to the park—joggers, cyclists, picnickers. Pam was glad she had come. How nice to be outside and surrounded by active, happy people.

The twins—Julie and Janet—were beautiful carbon copies of each other. Pam was fascinated that two human beings could be so exactly alike. "They're really something, aren't they?" Robert said proudly.

At first the girls were intrigued by the two little boys, but when they discovered Scott and Tommy weren't dolls and had minds of their own, the girls soon ran off to play on the swings and slides. Robert and Pam each pushed a boy in the baby swings. The girls kept calling, "Watch me, Daddy. Watch." And Robert would turn to wave and call out encouragement.

Pam couldn't tell the girls apart. When she spread out the lunch on a picnic table, one twin turned up her nose at the fried chicken. The other complained because there wasn't any Dr Pepper.

"What's our present this weekend?" the first girl asked her father.

"Do you want another doll?" Robert asked hopefully. "We can go to the mall later."

"I want a Care Bears Country Home," the twin who didn't like chicken announced.

"And I want a ball gown for my Barbie," the other said.

After lunch, they all walked over to the wading pool. While the twins played in the deeper end, Pam and Robert rolled up the legs of their jeans and waded around with Scott and Tommy. "I'd like to have a son of my own sometime," Robert said.

"Then most likely you will," Pam told him over the squealing voices of excited children.

"Right now, I need to figure out a way to be more of a father for those girls. Their mother is starting law school in California—and getting married again. She's offered to renegotiate custody. She wants the twins holidays and summers and for me to have them during the school year."

"How do you feel about that?" Pam asked.

"At first I was overjoyed, then I got real scared. How can I take care of two little girls? Shop for dresses and little girls' underwear. Visit their school. I wish I'd already remarried. I think I'm ready, but anyone I married would have to really want my daughters and be able to love them and mother them. I realize I haven't been going out with that sort of woman."

Pam looked around at the other children in the shallow pool. Her boys were the most wonderful, of course. She realized, however, that the other parents felt that way about their offspring. Robert even liked his bratty little girls.

Tommy was satisfied sitting in a few inches of water and splashing. Already Pam's and Robert's clothes were more wet than dry. Scott was braver than he had a right to be and kept having to be put back on his feet. He'd come up sputtering and set off again, undaunted.

"I have a woman coming in later to watch the girls this evening," Robert said. "She agreed to take on two more. Would you have dinner with me?"

"Oh, that's awfully nice of you, but the boys need baths and their own beds. I don't have enough diapers. They both wear them at night."

"I have a bathtub. We can buy diapers on the way."

"But I'm not dressed for dinner," she said, looking down at her wet jeans and cotton blouse.

"We'll go to the Cadillac Bar for Mexican food. Jeans are no problem there."

"Look, because I took a day out of the kitchen today, I'll have to get up at dawn tomorrow to catch up."

"Come on, Pam. You know what they say about all work and no play."

"You sound like my sister," Pam said.

"She and I are right."

Robert's hair was charmingly windblown. His teeth were white against his tanned skin. He was a very attractive man, but even though Pam found his attractiveness pleasing, Robert didn't make her heart race or her breath quicken. She wished her flesh would glow when he brushed against her, but it didn't.

"Play doesn't pay the bills," she observed.

"You've had it rough, haven't you?" The concern in his voice was sincere.

"I'm not complaining."

"What do you think of my daughters?"

"They're beautiful and completely spoiled. Why don't you just treat them like you did before you were divorced?" Pam asked, surprised at her own bluntness. "Tell them 'no' once in a while. They'll love you even if you don't buy them a gift each visit and make every minute they're with you fun-filled."

"I know," he said miserably. "I've fallen into every trap open to single fathers. I've got to change things, or pretty soon I won't be able to stand my own kids. And I really care about them."

"I can see that you do," Pam said. She felt sorry for him. Divorce was a bad deal for everyone concerned. Sometimes it was necessary, she supposed, or one had no choice in the matter, but it always seemed to make more problems than it solved.

There was a guard at the gate of the residential complex where Robert lived. The wooded grounds were beautifully landscaped. His paneled front door had an ornate brass knob.

The interior of his apartment was large and tastefully decorated with plush Persian carpets and artwork that did not come from a starving-artist sale. Pam ran ahead of the boys, pushing objets d'art out of their reach.

"I can't leave my boys in a place like this," she called over her shoulder to Robert. "They'll destroy a masterpiece."

At that point the doorbell rang and Robert admitted a Miss Duff from the agency. She was a severe-looking woman with her hair in a tight bun. She wore a navy suit and sensible shoes. Just as Tommy was about to open a coffee-table book on Asian art, Miss Duff said "No" in a voice that made Tommy turn and look openmouthed. "No," the woman repeated.

"What are the children to have for dinner?" she asked Robert.

"I thought I'd leave money for you to order pizza and soft drinks."

Miss Duff turned up her nose. "I'll fix them something nutritious. Come, children, we'll go wash our hands, then see what the kitchen has to offer."

The children stood staring.

"At once," Miss Duff snapped.

Scott and the girls went. Tommy toddled after them.

"Is she a moonlighting prison matron?" Pam asked in awe.

"She comes highly recommended."

"By whom? The KGB?"

"An agency. At least we won't have to worry about anything happening. I'll bet she could manage King Kong."

"Scott and Tommy will cry when I leave them. They're not used to her. They always have the same sitter, and they've never been here before."

"They'll survive," he insisted. "We won't be gone long."

Pam went to freshen up in a bathroom that was larger than her bedroom. Its mirrored walls reflected her faded jeans and wrinkled blouse. She smoothed the blouse as best she could and took pains fixing her makeup.

The boys cried. Miss Duff was surprisingly kind. "You haven't left them very much, have you?" she asked sympathetically. Pam realized the woman was actually quite lovely behind the severe hair and no-nonsense demeanor.

"Yes, I have," Pam said, taking Tommy from the baby-sitter's arms. "I work many evenings, but they are always left in their own house with the same sitter."

"They will cry for a time, but I'll keep telling them you'll be back soon," Miss Duff assured her. "Do they like to be read to?"

"Look, you're very kind," Pam said, "but I'm just not up to the trauma of leaving them."

Pam turned to Robert. "I'm sorry, but I don't want to do this. If they'd had some time to get used to things, I'd feel differently, but this isn't fair to them. They're afraid."

"Then let's take them to your house. Miss Duff and my girls can stay there."

Pam hesitated then walked over to the window for privacy. Robert followed. "After being here in your lovely apartment, I'm not sure I want you to see my house," she explained.

"I'm not a snob," Robert said.

"What do you want from me?" Pam asked, putting her cheek next to Tommy's smooth head. He was still whimpering, clinging to her blouse.

"I want a relationship with a woman who can mother my girls. I'm just trying to find out if you might be that woman."

"I'm not one of those women who can raise a houseful of kids, Robert. I've reached my limit with Scott and Tommy. Truly I have. I want to be the best mother in the world for them, and I think that's all the mothering I have in me. That said, however, I might be willing to attempt a relationship with you if I thought we had anything going. I want someone who's crazy about me. Such a man may not exist, but I need a man who will think about me first thing in the morning and last thing at night. Corny as it sounds, I want true love. My prince doesn't have to live in a palace, but he's got to love me as much as I love him. I settled for less than that once, and I won't make the same mistake again.''

"How do you know we won't end up with something special like that?" Robert asked.

"Do you think we will? Do I stir strong emotions in you? Come on. Be honest.''

Robert hesitated too long. "No," he admitted finally. "But that doesn't mean you won't someday. And I think we can be good friends. Partners.''

"Why don't you hire a housekeeper and not be in such a hurry to find a stepmother for those girls? See if Miss Duff or someone like her will take over your household. She'd straighten out your girls in no time. Then take your time finding wife number two. You're on the right track asking out a mature woman for a change, but this particular mature woman has all she can manage with her own two kids.''

"YOO-HOO, ANYBODY HOME?" Brenda's voice called.

"We're in the bedroom," Pam called back. She had just given the boys baths and had them on her bed for diapering and pajamas.

She pinned on Tommy's diaper and bent over to nuzzle his stomach and make him laugh. Clean baby skin was her favorite smell.

Tommy squealed delightedly, and Scott presented his own tummy for some of the same.

"Hi, sister and nephews," Brenda said, and sat down on the bed to receive a hug from her naked older nephew. "Careful, honey. Don't wrinkle my dress," she cautioned, holding Scott at arm's length. "Uncle George and I are going out.''

Brenda was wearing a yellow sundress that looked fantastic with her perfect tan. Her blond hair was swept to one side and adorned with a gardenia. She looked gorgeous as always, and as always made Pam feel drab and a bit envious.

"I turn somersaults," Scott told his aunt excitedly, and proceeded to put his head down in the middle of the bed to demonstrate. Brenda grabbed him to keep him from going over the end.

"Wow, that's terrific. Anybody win a washing machine today on television?" she asked.

"Sally won a swimming pool," he said, suddenly serious. "It was blue."

"You're funny, you know. And so are you, Pamela Sullivan," Brenda said. "George just told me that you'd turned down a date with Robert Fenwick. Are you crazy or something? The man is perfect."

"Perfect for what?" Pam asked, fastening Scott's diaper and pulling on his pajama bottoms. He'd been dry two nights in a row. Maybe he wouldn't need a night diaper much longer.

"You know damned well what he's perfect for. Courtship. Marriage. Happily ever after. Financial security. A college education for the boys. Some new clothes for you. Weekly beauty-shop appointments. Manicures. You wouldn't have to cook for that horrible Buffy Patterson anymore."

"He's not that rich," Pam said.

"No, but he probably will be. Come on, sis, what gives with you? I go out of my way to fix you up with a really nice guy, and you blow it."

"Come on out in the kitchen while the boys have bedtime snacks."

Pam picked up Tommy. Brenda and Scott followed her down the hall. Barney joined the parade from the living room.

"You haven't answered me," Brenda said.

"He doesn't make my heart go pitty-pat. Okay? And I don't make his so much as flutter," Pam said as she put Tommy in his high chair. "It's just not there, Brenda, so stop pushing on me. I'm not in the poorhouse yet, and when I get hooked up with a guy, his bank account will not be a consideration. Move, Barney," she said, pushing the dog with her foot. "Do you always have to get right in front of the refrigerator?"

"Forget his bank account then. Robert's a nice, good-looking guy who wants to date you. What's the matter with that?"

"He wants a stepmother for those two girls. He sees me as a ready-made mother person."

"Well, you are."

"Don't be so dense, Brenda. I can't take on two more kids, especially for a man I'm not in love with."

"Pam, you've already ruined your life. What's two more?"

Pam closed the refrigerator door and turned to face her sister. "Is that what you think?" she asked. "That I've ruined my life because I have children? Because I have *Scott and Tommy*?"

Brenda put Scott into his high chair and sat down herself. "I don't know. Yes and no. I look at this plain, little house and your difficult life and your unpermed hair, and I think I'd die if I had to live like this. Then I look at you kissing these babies and loving them, and I don't know what to think."

Pam slammed down an apple and a paring knife in front of her sister. "Peel this, please, unless you think it will ruin a nail. You know what, Brenda? I feel sorry for you and George because you've made this no-kids decision. You are missing a lot."

"Kids scare me to death. You lost Marty because you had children. George's parents hated each other but stayed together because of their children. George and I love each other so much, and it seems like people end up loving and worrying more over their kids than each other."

"What about Mom and Dad? They loved us and each other. And after all these years they still hold hands and cuddle."

"I don't know many couples like Mom and Dad," Brenda challenged. "George and I have a good marriage the way things are. I don't want to risk ruining it with children. I don't want to end up like you—alone and with two kids to raise all by myself."

JOEL'S HEART WAS POUNDING as he dialed the number. He wondered if he'd have the courage to let it ring, but he did. Four times.

"Hello."

"Mrs. Sullivan?" Why was he asking? He would have known her voice anywhere.

"Yes."

"This is Joel Bynum." Would she even know who that was? he wondered. She didn't know his last name. "From the Food Mart," he added.

She laughed. "Yes, I know. How are you, Joel?"

She was using the voice a grown-up lady would use talking to someone young. He didn't like that. She didn't sound like that when she came to the store the other evening. She was kind of girlish and breathless. She even blushed when he said she was pretty. And she was. Not drop-dead gorgeous like Stephanie, but in an approachable way, like the pretty ladies on television who advertise lemonade or station wagons.

"I'm fine," he answered. "Busy, of course, what with the job and summer school and studying. And you?"

He hoped he didn't sound as nervous as he felt. She must wonder why in the world he'd be calling her. And he wasn't all that sure himself. All day long he'd planned to call Stephanie and maybe apologize, although it wouldn't have been very sincere. But here he was calling Pam Sullivan instead.

"Good," she answered. "Busy, too. I have more catering work than I can handle. I still don't make enough money, but I certainly work a lot."

"And the boys?"

"Terrific. Scott wants to know where you are whenever we go to the store, but we almost always shop in the morning."

"Yeah, I know. I watch for you anyway. Every time I see a woman with two kids, I look to see if it's you." He cleared his throat before continuing. The time had come to state a reason for the call. "Say, I don't have to work tonight, and I was wondering if you and the boys would like to have a hamburger with me and maybe go walk around the West End. There's a jugglers' convention in town, and the jugglers will be doing street performances. I thought the boys would like that."

At first there was silence. Damn. She was probably offended. Angry. To her, he was just a kid.

"Why, that's awfully sweet of you," she said, her voice uncertain. "But why would a college boy want to spend Saturday night with an older woman and two kids?"

"Because the college boy likes the older woman. And her two kids. I think about you sometimes. Is it all right if I call you Pam?"

"Yes."

"I think about you, Pam. I'd like to see you again."

When Joel hung up, he was feeling rather proud of himself. He'd done that well. And it was true. He did think about Pam. But he still thought about Stephanie, too. A guy would have to be a fool to pass up a rich doll like Steph. A real fool.

But he felt his spirits brighten at the prospect of spending an evening with Pam and her two little boys. He took extra care shaving, and he sang his way through his shower. "Old MacDonald had a farm, E-I-E-I-O. And on that farm, he had some chicks, E-I-E-I-O...."

Chapter Four

"Hire me," Joel said, flashing that irresistible boyish grin. "I'm the answer to all your prayers. Hard-working, clever, terrific personality."

"You're not serious," Pam said, shocked by his offer. She had just been making conversation, explaining the problems she was encountering with her catering business, wishing out loud she had some help.

"Why not?" Joel said with a shrug.

"I can't afford to hire someone," she said. "I was only indulging in a little wishful thinking. And if I could hire an assistant, I'd need someone who had some experience."

"I've worked in restaurants and groceries since I was fourteen, so I do know a bit about food. Quite a bit, actually, when it comes to eating on next to nothing."

Joel was sitting on the sofa, holding Tommy. Barney was in front of them, tail wagging, his brown eyes begging for attention. The unoccupied portion of the sofa was rapidly filling up with toys as Scott brought them from his room one at a time to show Joel.

The boys and the dog all got a little hyper when Joel came over. She did herself. He was funny and cute and made her feel young. Pam wondered if he had a crush on her, and she couldn't help but be flattered by his attention. She frequently reminded herself, however, that young men often got crushes on older women, and it was almost always just a passing thing—as it should be. She had absolutely no romantic notions about the auburn-haired college boy with the ready smile and bright green eyes. Absolutely. She just liked him as a human being, as did her sons—and her dog.

Joel tossed a rubber bone across the room for Barney, and he went lumbering after it.

"You don't quite have the knack of this, old boy," Joel said as he tried to pull the bone back out of the dog's mouth. "You're supposed to give it back to me so I can throw it again."

Joel looked over at Pam and grinned. "I'll even throw in fetching lessons at no extra charge."

"Barney's conning you. Normally he doesn't do anything but sleep," Pam said, patting at her hair. She wished Joel would call before he dropped by. She'd have liked a little warning so she could brush up a bit and put on some lipstick.

She was feeling better about her appearance, however, since her new haircut and permanent. Her hair now had a soft wave that framed her face nicely. And after Brenda had brought over some of her cast-off warm-ups, Pam had been able to retire her old gray sweats and threadbare Levi's. She was wearing a terry warm-up set now, in emerald green with a white knit collar. It was a little unkind to her thighs, but the color was good on her.

For some reason, Joel brought out the vanity in her. She knew he admired her, and that made her want to look as nice as she could. It also made her waste too much time standing in front of a mirror.

She even used eyeliner before going to the Food Mart. She usually went in the evening now. It was less crowded then and a better time to shop, and the boys enjoyed an outing before bedtime.

Joel's welcoming smile would warm her.

Last night, she'd gone to the grocery. And after the boys were in bed, she'd taken a glass of iced tea out into the backyard and sat on the back step, enjoying the soft evening air and the moonlight on her wonderful oak tree and thinking about how Joel had come out of the stockroom pushing a trolley full of lettuce, a smile lighting his face when he saw them.

He liked the boys as much as he liked her, Pam reminded herself. Joel was lonely for contact with a family.

Yes, maybe she was a mother figure for him.

Pam had mulled that thought over. Yes, it could be. Maybe it wasn't infatuation with an older woman at all. He just liked her warm and cozy little family.

Or maybe it was a little of both. Whatever, there was no harm in doing her shopping in the evening. And there had been no harm in she and the boys going out to have a hamburger with him.

This was the second time Joel had dropped by since taking her and the boys out last Saturday night. She had enjoyed the evening very much. It was a lovely little familylike excursion with no disasters and a good time had by all. Joel had such a charming way with the boys, and they were so starved for a man in their lives. George was a dear, but he wasn't around them very much, and he was just beginning to understand that children were small people and not household pets.

Joel had come for them in his panel van, which had only two seats in the front and a canvas-covered mattress in the back. The boys thought that was great fun and rolled around on the mattress like playful puppies.

"We used to call vehicles like this 'lovemobiles' when I was in high school," Pam observed.

"They still do," he said without further comment.

They drove to a small café near the DCC campus for what Joel called "real hamburgers." Even the buns were greasy, but the burgers tasted wonderful. The boys were fascinated with French fries cut in spirals instead of strips. Joel cut up a meat patty for Tommy and showed him how to dip his potatoes in ketchup.

"You're so good with the boys. Did you have younger brothers and sisters?" Pam asked between bites.

"No. There was only me. I grew up in foster homes. But the older kids always had to look after the younger ones, and I like little kids. I like to make them happy. I still wonder if I shouldn't have majored in early-childhood education, but teachers are underpaid, and I'm tired of being poor. I'd like to make a good enough living to afford happy kids of my own."

"What happened to your parents?" she asked.

"My dad disappeared from the scene before I remember. My mother left me with my grandmother. When I was nine, Grandma died. No one adopts nine-year-olds, so I went the foster-home route. Not a childhood I'd recommend, but I survived."

Strange how adversity ruined some people and made others stronger. *Joel will make a terrific father,* Pam thought. She hoped his future wife and children appreciated how lucky they were to have such a man.

Pam found herself staring at the college clientele that populated the small restaurant. They seemed so young and carefree, so effortlessly beautiful and slim and sure of themselves. Joel waved to one of the girls, a peaches-and-cream blonde wearing braids.

The girl probably thought that she was Joel's older sister, Pam decided. Why else would he be with a woman who had two kids?

After eating, Joel had driven them down to the West End, Dallas's recently renovated warehouse area that was now full of expensive restaurants and lively night spots. But there were also snack bars, ice-cream and balloon vendors, novelty stores and street performers.

Scott especially was thrilled by the jugglers, who were on every street corner juggling everything from fire to frying pans. Pam found it as much fun to watch Scott's wide-eyed amazement as the performers themselves. Joel apparently felt that way, too. He kept looking at her sons' faces, checking out their reactions to things, smiling at their smiles, enjoying their wonder.

Pam insisted on paying for their ice cream, and the four of them sat at an outdoor table and licked away. She wondered if passersby thought they were a family. Would they notice that Joel was too young, that she was too old?

As usual, both boys got ice cream everywhere. Joel helped Pam wipe at their hands and faces with napkins. She fished a couple of Handy Wipes out of her purse to get off the worst of the stickiness.

"I'll bet you've got Band-Aids and Kleenex in there, too," Joel said, indicating her oversize handbag.

"You bet. And Life Savers, baby aspirin, crackers and a couple of spare diapers. When motherhood enters your life, you quickly learn to travel prepared. I might forget my lipstick, but I seldom ever travel without a pacifier."

They watched an organ grinder and his monkey for a while. Pam gave each boy a quarter to hand to the monkey. It was funny watching the three little creatures regarding each other. Scott stared at the monkey's tiny hands, then looked up at his mother to make sure she saw them, too. Pam wished she had brought a camera.

Next they stopped to watch a surprisingly eloquent violinist capturing a crowd with his rhapsodies. But Tommy began to whimper, his bedtime past. He fell asleep against Joel's shoulder on the way back to the van.

Pam held Tommy on the way home. Scott fell asleep on the mattress. When they got home, Joel helped her carry the boys inside, pull off ice-cream-sticky clothing and prepare sleepy babies for bed.

Then they sat on the back step and had a beer. The moonlight bathed them, and the cicadas serenaded. Barney scratched on the screen door to come out.

"I like being here like this," Joel said, patting Barney's head. The yellow dog moved closer, putting his big head on Joel's thigh.

"Yes, it's nice," Pam agreed. "Peaceful, not too hot."

"No, I mean here with you in your backyard after an evening sharing your kids. Thanks. It felt nice. May I come back again?"

"The boys would be disappointed if you didn't," she said. She wanted him to come back, too, and she wasn't sure why.

They had a second beer. "Say, are you of legal age for this stuff?" she asked, remembering that the legal age for drinking alcoholic beverages in the state had been raised to twenty-one. "Or am I contributing to the delinquency of a minor?"

He laughed. "I was twenty-one last week, and this is the first beer I've tasted in my entire life."

"Sure," she said sarcastically. "Maybe the first *legal* beer."

The step was narrow, and their shoulders were touching. Pam knew she should shift her position, put an end to the touching, but they stayed that way for a while. She was very aware of the point of physical contact. It warmed her like his smile. She was as starved for male companionship as her sons, it seemed. Scott and Tommy wanted to touch Joel, too, to crawl into his lap, to hold his hand.

Pam closed her eyes and thought of his hands. They were strong hands with a sprinkling of blondish hair across their backs. His arms and shoulders were strong, too, from all that lifting at work. Yes, he had nice broad shoulders and narrow hips, like most young guys. His hips were probably narrower than hers, she thought, regretting the extra padding she had accumulated. She wondered if he had hair on his chest, if he had a girlfriend, if he'd ever made love. Probably. Most guys had by the time they were twenty-one.

"Do you know how old I am?" she said finally, shifting her position.

"No. I suppose around twenty-four or twenty-five."

"I'm thirty. When I was graduating from high school, you would have been finishing the third grade," she said, wondering if he really wouldn't have been in the second. The difference in their ages was closer to ten years than to nine, but admitting nine had been truthful enough for one evening.

"That old, huh?"

"Yeah."

Pam thought her confession would put an end to his interest, but Tuesday evening Joel dropped by with a six-pack. He'd worked an extra shift at the store, he explained, and had the evening off. Pam was busy making preparations for a catered dinner the following evening, so he took the boys for a ride in the van to get them out of her way. Again he helped her put them to bed, but she was too busy for a beer. He sat on the high kitchen stool, downing two beers and watching her for a while. She was stewing chickens for chicken tetrazzini and making key-lime pies. It was the kind of meal impossible to do efficiently. The kitchen was a disaster area. She was exhausted. He rubbed her shoulders for a while, but with so much to do, it was hard for her to relax. When he offered to help, she sent him on his way. His presence was distracting her.

Later, after she had finally finished cleaning up, she rubbed her own shoulders, remembering the feel of his stronger hands. Her father used to do that for her mother—rub tired shoulders at the end of a long day at their dry-cleaning establishment. And she used to rub Marty's back and shoulders all the time, but Pam couldn't ever remember him doing that for her—like Joel had done.

And now Joel was here again, sitting in her living room, making her feel just a bit flustered and asking if he could work for her. The idea was preposterous, of course. But he was so sweet and earnest.

Scott was bringing trucks now. Joel accepted each one graciously and added it to the growing collection on the end of the sofa.

"Can you manage your college expenses on what you earn?" she asked, curious to learn more about Joel's life.

"Yeah, just barely. In two more semesters, I'll have a degree in accounting. Now, where else are you going to find an employee who will do your books, take out your trash and amuse your kids?"

"As much as I need help, I really can't afford to hire anyone," Pam admitted. "I can barely pay for baby-sitting the way it is. In fact, I'm starting to read the job openings in the classified ads with ever greater interest. I'm afraid my days as a self-employed person may be coming to an end.''

''That bad, huh?''

''Yes. I work hard, but I just can't earn enough to make it pay.''

''Well, maybe a soon-to-be accountant can find some ways to make the business more cost-efficient. Care if I just sort of hang out some and see if I get any ideas? Maybe you're too close to the operation to see the problems.''

''I see problems all right,'' Pam said. ''I charge as much as I dare the way it is. I just don't have the time to do enough jobs. And sometimes, there isn't any work. It's so unpredictable.''

''You need to schedule farther in advance and make people change dates to adjust to your schedule, not the other way around.''

''That's easy for you to say,'' Pam said, feeling a bit indignant. After all, he was just a kid and she was doing the best she could. She found herself sensitive to his criticism. ''You don't know the Buffy Pattersons of the world.''

Sunday afternoon Joel took them to watch hot-air balloons being launched from a park in Fort Worth. They pulled the mattress out onto the grass and opened cans of pop.

How much fuller their lives had become since Joel entered the scene, Pam thought. And how drab things would seem after he passed on through, but in the meantime, she supposed she'd enjoy the gift of his presence.

She remembered a poem she'd read long ago—something about celebrating the temporary. That's what she was doing today. Nothing stayed the same, but times of happiness were waiting along the way. This day, she was happy. She didn't want worries about tomorrow to ruin it.

The balloons were spellbinding as they made their silent passage across the heavens. "I'd like to do that sometime," Pam whispered, as though she were in church. "It must feel so pure up there, so peaceful."

"I'll take you sometime," Joel said. "I'd like that—to take you someplace you've never been before."

Pam's heart lurched a bit. How lovely. How perfectly lovely.

The sunlight on Joel's auburn hair turned it to bright gold. She wanted to touch it. He was sitting cross-legged, and Tommy had crawled onto his lap just like he belonged there.

Joel stayed for dinner, then helped her stuff creamed crabmeat into eight dozen cheese puffs for a bankers' meeting.

"Did you decide whether you're going to hire me yet or not?" he asked.

She hadn't.

But she had thought a lot about Joel's offer. If nothing else, just having an adult around to run errands and watch after the boys would be wonderful. It was out of the question, however. Totally.

"All I'm asking is the same hourly wage I get at Food Mart," he told her on Tuesday when he dropped by to bring the boys a huge box salvaged from the stockroom. He cut out a door and window, and soon the boys had put their stuffed animals "to bed" in it.

"I've been thinking a lot about your operation," he continued, "and I think that where you've been going wrong is you're doing too many nickel-and-dime jobs that bite into your time and don't reap enough reward. I'll bet you made a whole lot less on that ladies' luncheon the other day with all that chicken-stewing and dessert-making than you made on the assembly-line cocktail tidbits for that bankers' function. You need to specialize. Wedding receptions and cocktail buffets—big bashes where you can offer a set list of prices on certain predetermined items. It simplifies negotiations, shopping, setup, everything. And if crab-filled puffs are too much trouble and not cost-efficient, you take them off your list. You get it down to a science. You know exactly how long it takes you to make one hundred puffs, exactly how much the ingredients cost you, exactly how much profit you make per dozen puffs. You don't make the things—like rolls and little cakes—that you can buy elsewhere cheaper. You buy a big freezer to take advantage of specials and to work ahead when you have a lull." He stopped for breath and looked at her. "Am I making sense?" he asked.

"Yeah," she admitted. "You are. How'd you ever get so smart?"

"I've been poor all my life. That's taught me more than a lot of that stuff I'm learning at college, but don't tell my professors."

Pam wondered if Joel *could* make a difference. Maybe hiring that bright young man would turn things around for her catering service. But was it really just thoughts of improving her business that tempted her? What if she really wanted him around so he'd rub her shoulders and she could brush up against him occasionally? Was she so starved for the male of the species that she'd use him like that? She couldn't decide if she was turning into a dirty old woman or regressing to a lovesick teenager.

"Why would you even want to get involved in such a marginal operation?" she asked, still uncertain as to what the answer should be.

"I'm not sure," he said, his brow creasing. "It just feels right to be here in this house with you and your two kids. And there are some other feelings I haven't sorted out yet."

Joel thought about those other feelings as he lay on the narrow bed in his one-room efficiency. The neon light on the club across the street made flickering shadows on his ceiling, but it was too hot to pull the shade, and to save money, he avoided using the air conditioner as much as possible.

The lady was thirty. That was pretty grim, he had to admit. He had figured with her kids being little like that, she'd be on the good side of twenty-five. Twenty-six max. But she had been married for three years before the kids came along, she had explained. And before that she'd been in the Army. A sergeant. For the past weeks he'd been mooning around over a thirty-year-old former Army sergeant. It'd be funny, if he didn't like her so much.

Every time he got around her, he wanted to kiss her. Even when the boys were around, he'd look at her mouth and think about kissing.

And when the boys weren't around, he thought about other things—the same things his body was reminding him of now.

Stephanie had called a couple of times. They had fenced around a bit, accusing each other of insensitivity, selfishness, stubbornness and other sins. In a challenging tone, she announced that she was seeing someone else, someone more suitable, and it made Joel jealous enough to tell her the same. Or maybe it was just pride. He felt pretty certain it was over between them. Neither one of them seemed able to say the words, however. Stephanie suggested a cooling-off period. He'd readily agreed. In a month or so they'd have a long talk and figure out how they really felt.

"I miss you," Stephanie said. "And I think I still love you, but I see now that love isn't enough. We have to want the same kind of life, and you're a hard guy to get into a tux."

"I miss you, too," Joel had said back. But it wasn't exactly true. He'd cared a great deal for the beautiful young woman, and he certainly admired her zest for life. But lately he'd been thinking more about Pam than he had been about Stephanie.

But Pam was thirty.

There were lots of nice girls his own age in his college classes. He'd taken some of them out before Steph came along, and he wondered if he shouldn't be doing so again. Joel went through a mental list of girls he admired and thought would accept a date with him. He added and discarded and ended up with three names: Gretchen, Barbara and Laura.

Gretchen was blondly gorgeous. Barbara was perky and cute. Laura was bright and sophisticated.

If he had any smarts at all, he'd have a fantasy about one of them. But he wasn't feeling very smart right now—only confused.

PAM TOOK ANOTHER LOAD OF FOOD out to the station wagon and the last of the pies from the oven. Tommy was fussing in his playpen. "Just a minute, honey. I need to take this box out to the car, then I'll come back and feed you.''

But Tommy wasn't hungry, and he kept pulling on his right ear. Pam felt his forehead then took his temperature. One hundred and two.

She gave him two children's Tylenol and a bottle, then rushed off to take a shower. When she got out of the shower, he was crying—really crying. And warmer.

Pam picked him up and carried him to the rocker in the living room. Scott was playing with his cars and watching *Sesame Street*.

While she rocked her sick baby, Pam wondered what in the world she was going to do. Two things were certain, however. This feverish baby had to be checked by a doctor, and she wasn't going to leave him with a sitter. She thought of the food loaded in the station wagon, of how furious Mrs. Patterson would be if her party was ruined.

Pam carried Tommy into the hall. His whole body felt so warm against hers. Nothing frightened her quite like a sick child. She pulled up a chair and sat down with him by the telephone table. He sounded like a little kitten, his mewing pitiful and sickly.

Brenda wasn't at home. Cindy burst into tears at the very idea of assembling a dinner party. And she didn't have a driver's license yet, anyway.

Pam called Joel at the Food Mart and explained her dilemma.

''I'll get Paul to cover for me here, and I'll deliver the food for you.''

Tommy was crying hard now, and it was difficult for Pam to talk. ''It's more than delivering,'' she explained, growing more apprehensive about Tommy by the minute. ''The vegetables have to be cooked. The salad tossed.

The entrée warmed. The plates arranged. There's a maid, but she has to be told to come in out of the rain.''

Joel met her at the P.M. clinic, and they traded car keys. ''Call me when you get there. I'll try to talk you through this,'' she said. ''If Mrs. Patterson gives you a hard time, unload the food and leave. She'll just have to manage the best she can.''

''And you can kiss that account goodbye,'' Joel reminded her.

''Worse things have happened. Thanks, Joel. I really owe you for this one.''

''Sounds like you need a permanent assistant, lady,'' he said.

The nurse called Pam. Tommy was next to see the doctor. She stood. Scott clung to her skirt.

Joel touched Tommy's feverish little face. The concern on his own face was apparent. ''Poor little guy. He really feels rotten, doesn't he?''

Joel patted Scott's head and was off.

The phone was ringing when Pam opened the front door. She put her crying baby down on the sofa and answered it. ''What is the meaning of this, Pam?'' Buffy Patterson's voice demanded.

''The meaning is I have a sick baby.''

''And you send this—this *boy* to manage a sit-down party for twelve!''

''I had no choice. My baby is more important than your party. Take it or leave it, Mrs. Patterson. I really can't discuss it anymore. I have to go take care of my baby.''

She gave Tommy a dose of antibiotic and bathed him with cool water like the doctor suggested.

The next call was from Joel. By this time Pam had moved the rocker to the hallway near the telephone. The rocking distracted Tommy from his pain. She and Joel kept the connection between the Patterson's kitchen and her phone open all evening as she talked Joel through the party. She put the phone down between conversions until she heard his voice again. They never hung up.

Finally he said, "Well, I guess that's about got it on my end. All that's left is cleaning up the demolition zone. What a mess. Incidentally, you're right about the maid. How's Tommy?"

"His fever is still high, but he doesn't seem as restless. Come by when you finish."

"I've got two hours at least here."

"I know. We'll be here."

When Joel arrived, Scott was asleep on the sofa, still in his overalls, the remnants of his "dinner" of cheese and crackers mixed among his Tonka cars.

Tommy had finally fallen sound enough asleep to let Pam put him in his bed. Joel carried Scott to his.

Together Pam and Joel unloaded the station wagon and put the food and dishes away.

It was almost one-thirty before they carried cups of hot tea to the cluttered living room and collapsed on the sofa. "What a night," Pam said. "I guess you know that you're hired, if you still want the job, but be forewarned that you might be signing onto a sinking ship. I've decided that if you're willing, I'll go for broke and see if having some help will turn things around, but if I were you, I'd stay at the grocery store."

"I accept your gracious offer," Joel said, leaning his head against the back of the sofa.

"You're crazy, you know. You may get paid in crab puffs. But seriously, I'll try to pay you the same wage that you make at the store, plus a percentage of the profits when we get some. But let's work that out tomorrow. I'm too tired to think business tonight.''

Pam ached all over from the tension and from carrying around a thirty-pound toddler all evening. She wished she'd thought to take some aspirin, but she was too tired to bother, too tired to do anything but sit there. So why did she want Joel here, too, she wondered. And why did he stay?

He reached for her arm. ''Turn around,'' he ordered.

Pam obeyed and luxuriated in a few minutes of having her shoulders massaged. ''This isn't fair. You did all the work,'' she murmured.

''You cooked the food, which was superb, by the way. I helped myself rather generously to leftovers. And you took care of a sick kid all evening. And besides, I like to rub you, to feel the knots go away under my fingers. There are a lot of them, you know. You work and worry too much.''

''Perhaps. But right now, I have no alternative. I'm all we have.''

''What happened to the boys' father?''

Pam said nothing for a minute, then resumed her place at the corner of the sofa. Her tea was cold.

''He left us,'' she explained. ''Tommy was three months, Scott was a year and a half. I woke up one morning, and there was a note on his pillow. I can still quote it. 'I'm going to miss you, hon, but this isn't how I want to live my life. The kids were your idea. I'm sorry.' ''

''He didn't like the kids?'' Joel's tone was incredulous.

''No. He'd never wanted them, but he had been honest about that. He told me we could get married, but no kids. I talked him into Scott. Tommy was an accident.

Scott had been a pretty easy baby, and we'd managed. But Tommy had colic and cried all the time. By then, Scott was into everything. He got jelly on Marty's guitar. The apartment smelled like dirty diapers and spit-up. Marty is a singer—an entertainer—and kids weren't his style. I should have known better than to think I could turn a rambler into a homebody. He went to Nashville searching for the big time.''

The tears surprised her. She thought she'd shed them all. ''Oh, God,'' she said, wiping at her cheeks. ''I'm so embarrassed. This is all old history. I cried over it quite enough.''

Joel's arms were comforting, but they made her cry more. And when he began to kiss her tears, she found herself lifting her mouth to his.

This can't be happening, she thought. She was the mature person here, and she shouldn't be allowing it.

But his lips were so very sweet, his tongue so very seductive. There was no resistance in the lips that met his, in the mouth that yielded to his eager probing.

Her whole consciousness became focused on his mouth, his kiss. She wanted as much of it as was possible for her to have, for the kissing to continue endlessly. The wetness of their mouths mingled, their tongues touched, and warm exciting signals shot throughout her body.

One of his hands was in her hair, the other stroking the small of her back.

And suddenly the kissing wasn't enough. Her body became demanding. Her breasts pushed against his chest, begging for attention. Joel's hand shot up between their bodies to caress breasts made full and hard with longing.

His mouth was at her throat now. She felt the buttons of her blouse being unfastened, and an image of his mouth at her breast flashed across her mind. He was saying her name. Over and over. "I want you, Pam, really want you. I think about you all the time. It's making me crazy."

And she felt crazy, too. Crazy and reckless. Her body was open and pulsating with desire. "Joel," she heard herself say. "Joel." She wanted to tell him to carry her to her bed like a bride, to pull her clothes from her body, to fill her body and end her loneliness.

She was very close to saying those words when she heard Tommy's cry.

Her baby. Her sick baby.

Joel did not protest when she pulled away. He knew she had to go.

Pam was grateful Joel didn't follow her. She stood by Tommy's bed, patting, finding his pacifier for him. He wasn't as feverish. The antibiotic was working.

She went into the bathroom to splash cold water on her face. It felt as warm as Tommy's. Then she stared at herself in the mirror. She was flushed. Her heart was still pounding. She tried to remember when she had last been so aroused and couldn't.

She took a deep breath and went to unravel the mess she had made.

They sat on opposite sides of her kitchen table. She didn't trust herself on the sofa with him again.

With hands folded in front of her, she said, "We can be business associates and nothing more. And if a businesslike relationship would be impossible for us to maintain, we'd better put an end to the arrangement right now. Any other sort of relationship between us would be unseemly, unrealistic and stupid."

Joel started to protest, but Pam held up her hand. "No. Let me finish. I've had my heart broken once. Getting involved with someone short-term can only end in my getting hurt again. And it would be short-term, Joel. I think you realize that. We are at different places in our lives, have different needs."

"It seemed to me we were needing the same thing in there on the sofa," he reminded her.

Pam felt the flush returning to her cheeks. "Yes. And it scares me to death. I'm glad Tommy woke up. Nothing good could have come of that, and I promise you that I won't allow it to happen again. I have the sole responsibility for two small children. I have no right to do anything that might jeopardize their future. If I get involved with a man, it has to be as much with them in mind as myself. And let's face it, you are a college student who's hardly ready to settle down and be a father for a ready-made family."

Chapter Five

Brenda doubled over with laughter at the sight of her husband wearing overalls with a shirt and tie. The shirt had a starched buttoned-down collar, of course.

"You're too much," she said.

"Well, isn't this appropriate attire for a wallpapering party? They'll never believe me back home in England when I tell them Americans make a social occasion out of papering a room. Are you sure you didn't misunderstand?"

"Positive," Brenda said, adding a paper painter's cap to her husband's head, removing his necktie and kissing his chin. "That awful Mrs. Patterson canceled a dinner on Pam at the last minute, and Pam invited us to help eat the food she had prepared."

"Yes. That part I understood. But the wallpapering?"

"Her living room is drab. She can't afford new furniture or drapes, but she thought wallpaper would be an inexpensive way to liven the room up a bit. And the party part of it is sort of an American custom. In pioneer days neighbors came to help you raise your log cabin or the barn. Now friends and family come to help you move or paint or get married, and you feed them in return."

"I don't know a thing about putting up wallpaper," George protested.

"Neither do I," Brenda admitted. "But she said the young man who's working for her claims he knows how. Just think of it as an educational experience. We'll come home smarter. Maybe we can even paper the spare room. Now, go get the stepladder. Pam said to bring it."

Brenda discovered that Pam's young assistant did indeed know how to paper a room. He organized them into an assembly line of measuring, cutting, pasting. Joel himself did the actual hanging. They finished the living room in record time and decided to eat before tackling the entry hall.

Pam had invited her baby-sitter over to keep Tommy and Scott out of the way. A pudgy friend of Joel's showed up in time to eat, and Brenda found it amusing to watch the two overweight young people eyeing each other, making small talk. Cindy suddenly had lipstick on, and the boy, Paul, kept trying to hold in his stomach.

The teenagers both loaded their plates with Pam's veal scaloppine and potato croquettes but actually seemed more interested in each other than eating. From the looks of their figures, that was a first.

"Looks like you've got something going there," Brenda said, pointing at the two out the kitchen window. Cindy and Paul had taken their dessert plates and were sitting in the shadows of the oak tree. Scott had followed them and was using the last vestiges of daylight to dig in the dirt with a stick. Cindy and Paul seemed to be deep in conversation and oblivious to the busy little boy. "Can true love conquer plumpness?" Brenda asked.

"I hope so," Pam said. "They're nice kids. Cindy's been trying to diet ever since I've known her. Maybe a little attention from a boy will give her incentive."

"But if she starts dating, you may have to find another sitter," Brenda warned.

"She has me now," Joel said as he got up from the table and carried his plate to the sink. "That was terrific, Pam. Have you thought about cooking for money?"

"Oh, do you think I really could?" Pam asked coquettishly.

"Why, shore, little lady, if you had the right strong man to help you."

Brenda was surprised at the informality of their relationship. Pam had just hired the young man. Shouldn't he be calling her "Mrs. Sullivan"?

Joel Bynum was nice-looking and easygoing but just a college kid. Brenda wondered why Pam had hired him instead of some mature woman who would know what she was doing.

"Tommy's looking glassy-eyed," Brenda said. "You want me to put him into his crib?"

"Would you? His bottle's there on the counter," Pam said. "Be sure to check his diaper."

With his fingers in his mouth, Tommy nestled up against his aunt's shoulder as she carried him down the hall. Brenda kissed the top of his head, and wispy, fine hair tickled her nose.

Before putting her nephew in his crib, she stood with him for a while, jiggling the sleepy baby up and down, cooing to him. "You're a pretty little guy. And sweet. I remember when you were little, however, and cried continually, and I didn't think you were so sweet then. I thought you were a diabolical monster put on earth to torture my sister and drive her husband away."

Tommy touched her face with wet fingers and cuddled his body more closely against her breast. Brenda kissed his hand. "Sweet, sweet little Tommy," she crooned. "Go to sleep, sweet Tommy."

She lowered him into his crib and handed him his bottle. The skin on his cheek was smooth and ripe as a plump peach. And unbelievably soft. Brenda leaned over to kiss that soft, sweet cheek. "Sleep well, little one."

She left the door ajar and went back to help Pam finish cleaning up the kitchen. Only Joel and Pam remained in the kitchen. Brenda stopped in the doorway, some instinct warning her she was about to intrude. She backed into the shadows of the hall.

"I can't stop thinking about the other night," Joel was saying.

"I know," Pam said. "Me, neither. Maybe your working here isn't a good idea."

Feeling like a voyeur, Brenda watched in amazement as Joel touched her sister's hair. It was not an accidental touching. He reached up and buried his hand in her thick hair, and Pam leaned into his caress.

Brenda retreated down the hall and leaned against the wall. Was her sister out of her mind? A woman of her age allowing a boy to touch her like that! Pam must be more lonely and desperate than she had ever dreamed.

But if she was so desperate, why had she turned down a date with that attractive Robert Fenwick? Her sister's behavior made no sense at all.

Brenda waited until Joel had gone back to paperhanging before accosting her sister.

"You let him touch your hair!"

Pam looked startled. A blush covered her neck and rose to her cheeks. She turned away from her sister's gaze.

"My God, are you in love with a college boy?"

"No. Nothing like that," Pam said, picking up a plate and rinsing it off. "I'm not that stupid—at least, I don't think I am. He's just so sweet and has been so nice to me and the boys. It's hard not to respond, but it's just a crush—really."

"His or yours?" Brenda demanded, hands on hips.

"A little of both, I guess."

"Pam, I can't believe this! You haven't slept with him, have you?"

"Heavens, no," Pam said too emphatically, still not looking at her sister. She picked up a saucepan to scrub.

"But you've thought about sleeping with him, haven't you, or you wouldn't be blushing like that? Your neck is as red as a lobster."

"Lay off, Brenda. I'm a big girl, remember, and Joel and I work together and have become friends. It's no big deal."

"Sure," Brenda said, carrying a stack of dirty dishes to the sink. "Was that 'friendship' when he ran his hand through your hair like that? And the look on his face! He's after more than your cooking, Pamela Sue. You sure know how to pick short-term men!"

"What do you mean?" Scouring pad in hand, Pam turned to face her sister.

"You can't possibly think that a kid his age—a *college boy*—would enter into a permanent relationship with a woman of thirty with two little kids. He's just bought into the myth."

"What myth?"

"About how the best way for a young boy to learn about sex is at the hands of an older, experienced woman."

Pam rolled her eyes. "I suspect that Joel Bynum doesn't need instruction. He's probably had a whole lot more experience than I have."

"Nevertheless, it's bound to be a sexual thing," Brenda insisted, searching for a place in the refrigerator for the leftover veal. "What else could it be?"

"Yes. You're exactly right. I'm such a femme fatale. I can't walk down the street without men following me, and my phone just rings off the wall. You can't imagine what a burden it is."

"Spare me the sarcasm," Brenda said as she closed the refrigerator door harder than necessary. "You are very attractive when you let yourself be. And I still say young guys think older women have some sort of mystique. I've been reading about it in magazines. Don't let him break your heart, sis," she said, her tone softening. "I couldn't bear to see that happen to you again."

"He's not like Marty. He's really awfully nice," Pam said lamely.

"Yeah. He seems to be. But a young kid like that, when he does get married, is going to want to marry some sweet young thing who's never had children. He'd want his own kids, Pam. You know that. A relationship with him wouldn't last the year out."

Pam nodded. "You may be right. I don't know. But you're way ahead of things. For now, Joel and I are just going to work together."

"You say you haven't slept with him, but he's kissed you, hasn't he?"

Pam turned back to the sink. "I don't want to talk about it anymore."

"Am I interrupting something?" George asked from the hall door.

"No," Pam said firmly. "What do you need?"

"Joel and I need another beer," he said. "I say, Pam, he seems like a rather decent sort of chap. Where did you find him?"

"At the grocery," Pam said flatly. "In canned goods."

"Well, jolly good," George said, looking from one sister's face to the other and sensing that he should make a hasty exit. "I suppose I should take something to Scott," he said. "What do little people drink?"

"Take him a can of juice," Pam said.

George took his cans and left.

With Scott in the middle, the three males sat on the sofa to drink from their respective cans. Scott's sturdy little legs stuck out in front of him. His knees had dimples. His bare feet were fat and silly.

"I say, old man, do you still watch television a lot?" George asked the boy.

Scott nodded.

"What else do you like besides game shows? Do you like drama? Sports?" From Joel's amused look, George gathered he was doing something wrong. "Ah, yes, you little tykes like those animated things. Cartoons. Right?"

"I like ice cream," Scott said, smacking his lips and wiggling his toes.

"I see," George said. "Well, so do I. What about apple pie? Do you like that? I have developed a tremendous fondness for the classic American dessert."

Scott looked up at George, his head cocked to one side. George couldn't decide if the child was amused or confused. George looked to Joel for help, but Joel was leaning against the sofa, his eyes closed, one hand holding his beer, the other resting on the dog's head.

"What do you want to be when you grow up?" George asked, taking a different tack with the boy. "Your mother tells me she thinks your brother will be a veterinarian.

Would you like that, or perhaps law enforcement? Lots of children think they'd like to grow up and be a policeman."

"Joe won a boat."

"Is that right?"

"Tommy's a baby. I'm a big boy."

"Well, yes. I can see that."

"I can count to ten."

"Well then, let me hear you."

Scott forgot four and seven. George had him repeat the count and coached him a bit. "You need to slow down, young man. Do it with me. One, two, three . . ."

Scott held up three fingers. "Three," he said.

"By golly, that's right. Now how many is this?" George held up five fingers.

Scott didn't answer.

"Here. Count with me. One, two, three, four, five. Five fingers. I have five fingers on each hand. You have five fingers on each hand. Baby Tommy has five fingers."

Scott looked from George's big hand to his small one, comparing, the concentration apparent in his expression.

The child was really quite lovely. His skin so perfect, his little teeth so white, his pale hair so shiny. There was a freshness and innocence about the boy that George found rather appealing.

Scott pointed at George's shirt sleeve. "Blue," he said.

"Right-o! Now, what color is this?" George said, pointing to Scott's shirt.

Scott stared down at his front, his chin resting on his chest. "Red!" he said firmly.

"You're doing great, George," Joel said from the far side of the sofa without opening his eyes.

"You really think so?" George asked, pleased.

"Sure. The kid likes you. Why don't you give him his bath?"

"His bath! I couldn't do that."

"Why not?"

"I don't know how."

"Use soap and warm water. You do that while I finish up in here. Then when Pam and Brenda finish in the kitchen, we can have coffee."

George stood and reached a hand out to Scott. Joel watched the two of them solemnly head for the bathroom. Then he allowed himself to smile.

FOR THE FIRST TIME since she'd started her catering service, Pam paid all of the month's household bills and business expenses and had money left over. She rechecked her figures, mistrustful. She was actually in the black. Finally. Of course, it wasn't much, but maybe it was a beginning.

She closed her ledger and folded her hands on it. She needed to sit a minute and gloat.

Joel had made a tremendous difference; there was no question about that. He was full of enthusiasm and ideas. He even had a natural flair with food.

He was at the print shop now having fliers made that advertised catering for wedding receptions. He planned to leave them in church offices and with area bridal consultants. He had taken Scott with him. Tommy was still down for his nap.

It was such a relief to share responsibility, Pam acknowledged as she sipped her coffee. Trying to do everything herself had been difficult. And as much as she loved her boys, she got so hungry at times for adult companionship. For all his youth, Joel was definitely an adult. In fact he was wise and responsible far beyond his years. Pam now had someone to tell things to—she could complain about difficult clients, share cute things the boys had done, discuss the news events of the day.

Having Joel around made her realize how much she'd missed sharing her life with a man. Marty had been far from a perfect husband, but they had had their good times, and while they were still married, there was always the hope that things would get better, that he would come home after the last show instead of carousing, that he would learn to love the boys as she did. And when he walked out on her, it left a huge, gaping hole in her life. In fact, as she looked back over the last fourteen or fifteen months, she could now acknowledge how tough it had been. At the time she had told herself things weren't so bad, that other women had worse. But the continual worry and endless work had robbed her of energy and enthusiasm and spirit.

Of course, she still worked hard, but now that Joel was around, it was shared work, and it seemed to be getting her someplace.

She opened the ledger again to stare at the figures. She was beginning the month in the black, and she'd even paid a hundred dollars on her Sears bill. She felt like celebrating, and she wanted Joel to know he was appreciated.

Since the wallpaper hanging, Pam had carefully avoided any further touching between them. Sensing her feelings, Joel had honored them, but sometimes it happened anyway. Their hands would brush, their shoulders might touch. Pam could tell that he was as aware of it as she was. And he still insisted on massaging her shoulders at the end of the day. "Asexual rubbing" he called it. His hands didn't stray.

She suspected he was as confused as she was with so many facets to their complicated relationship. They were business associates and friends. At times she was the older and wiser teacher and Joel was the eager young student. Often their relationship was that of two family members; sometimes she felt like his sister, other times, his mother. And more and more, he took on a parenting role with her sons.

Now when they accidentally touched, they both looked away, unable to make eye contact, unable to face the emotions buried just beneath the surface.

She wanted him sexually, just as she was sure he wanted her. The kissing on the sofa—how long ago?— almost a month. The vision of those stolen moments still haunted her. Her lips throbbed with the memory of kisses so passionate they seemed to touch her soul, kisses that forced her to acknowledge the truth of her loneliness and her attraction to a man who could not be a permanent part of her life.

In the night she would think of ignoring reality and propriety and having an affair with him. He could come to live here with her and sleep with her in this bed. They would laugh and love abundantly. She longed to lie in his arms, satiated with lovemaking, to know that he would be there when she awakened.

But the day would come when he wouldn't be there. Would he leave a note on the pillow like Marty?

He would go off to find a woman he could marry and start a family with—his own family, not a ready-made one with a wife who would be forever older, graying first, wrinkling first.

Brenda had asked if she was in love with him, and Pam denied it. But sometimes, when she saw him kissing her

sons, her heart would turn over, and it surely felt like
love.

THEY HAD PLANNED TO HAVE a late dinner after the boys
were in bed, then work on a shopping list for the next reception and go through Pam's collection of cookbooks,
looking for additional cost-efficient, time-efficient canapés and buffet fare to add to their list of catered offer-
ings.

Joel helped her bathe the boys and put them to bed,
then she told him to go check the pages she had marked
in the cookbooks. She wanted to freshen up a bit.

"What about dinner?" he asked. "I'm getting hungry."

"It's ready to microwave. I'll be there shortly."

Pam changed into a hot-pink sundress she had borrowed from her sister. With hot curlers in her hair, she
took great pains with her makeup. She even used eyeliner. Brenda would have been proud. Her lipstick
matched the dress. She took out the curlers and put on
white shell earrings.

Not bad, for an old broad, she told her reflection.

She started down the hall, then went back to her mirror for one last look and a bit of lifting and fluffing of
her hair. Well, they wouldn't think she was his mother.
Maybe they'd just think he was a young guy taking out a
woman who was older than he was. Except in this case,
she'd be taking him out.

Amazed at how nervous she was, Pam went down the
hall to the kitchen. Joel, his back to her, was looking
through a cookbook and making notes on a tablet.

"What took you so long?" he said without looking up.
"I looked in the refrigerator, and I didn't see anything
ready for the microwave."

"Don't worry. You'll get fed," she said, taking a bottle of champagne she'd hidden at the back of the bottom shelf of the refrigerator. She got two wineglasses from the cupboard and walked around the table.

Joel's eyes widened, and he let out a low whistle. "My God, Pam, you look beautiful."

"Uncork this, will you?" Pam said, handing him the bottle.

As he worked on the cork, he asked, "What's the occasion, if I may ask?"

"In a minute," she said, feeling strangely shy. "We have to go into the living room."

"Why?"

"Because you don't drink champagne in a kitchen."

The cork popped, and Joel filled the two glasses. Pam picked them up and went into the living room. Joel followed her with the bottle.

He looked around the living room. The books and toys were put away. Sprays of crepe myrtle were arranged in a tall vase on the table behind the sofa. The magazines were stacked neatly on the coffee table.

Pam stood in the middle of the room and handed him his glass. "For the first time in eight months of struggle, the business has shown a profit. You've turned things around for my catering service, and your presence in this house has brought joy to me and my sons."

Her voice choked a bit with emotion as she lifted her glass to him and said, "Thank you, Joel, for more than I can ever tell you."

Joel took a sip then lifted his glass to her. "And I thank you, Pam, for sharing your business and your kids with me. This has been the happiest time of my life."

"Don't say that."

"Why not? It's true."

"It makes my mascara run."

"Can I hug you—as one caterer to another?"

"Please do."

He set the glasses on the coffee table and enveloped her in his arms. Pam returned his embrace, relishing the solid feel of him, this good, young man who had become such an important part of her life. Her head rested against his shoulder, his cheek against her hair. It was a sweet moment, full of emotion and caring. She wanted to say more to him, to ask him to stay with her forever, but she had no right.

"So," she said at the instant of parting, "let's drink our champagne. Then you run home and change."

"Do I get to know what for?"

"I thought we should go out to dinner to celebrate—let someone else do the cooking for a change. Cindy and Paul are coming to baby-sit."

Joel was back in less than an hour, looking older and quite handsome in a muted plaid sport coat and gray slacks. His curly hair was more tamed than usual.

"You got even more beautiful in the last hour," he said. "I knew you were a fine-looking woman, but to see you in full regalia is a little overwhelming."

"Thanks. It's nice to know it hasn't all gone away. Sometimes I get to feeling kind of used up and matronly. Come on out in the kitchen and say hello to Paul and Cindy."

The two teenagers were drinking Diet Cokes and eating unbuttered popcorn over a game of Trivial Pursuit.

"Whooeee! Would you look at Mr. Bynum," Paul said. "Now, explain to me, please. Is this a date?"

"Paul!" Cindy said, giving him a warning look.

"Well, I just wondered," he told her peevishly. "They both look so dressed up, kind of like two people going out on a special date, and I'm just wondering if I missed something. Ouch!" he said, glaring at Cindy. "You don't have to kick so hard. Okay, okay. I'll shut up, but I still don't understand. But then other people probably don't understand why a sweet boy like me is going out with a mean girl like you."

"Is it a date?" Joel asked Pam as they walked toward the driveway.

"No. We're just going out to dinner. A date implies romance."

"And we're just business associates?"

"Right."

"Well, then. Whose car do we take on this nondate, and who drives?"

"We take the station wagon. I'll drive us down. You drive us home."

"Sounds fair to me," Joel said as he opened the door on the driver's side for her.

She drove to Vincenzo's on Lover's Lane, an Italian restaurant she'd read good things about, including the reasonable prices of their entrées. The maître d' seemed to think they were on a date and led them to a secluded table behind a palm. The waiter also seemed to assume they were on a date as he talked to Joel about a bottle of wine, then complimented him on his *"bella amica."* The accordion player and violinist certainly thought they were on a date as they kept strolling by their table playing Neopolitan love songs.

"I think I'll see if I can't turn us a profit every month if it will earn us an evening out like this," Joel said, lifting his wineglass to her.

"Sounds good to me," Pam said, wondering how many months their association would continue.

After dinner they drove to Gershwin's for an after-dinner coffee. The music was mellow, and several couples were on the dance floor. "I'm not much good at that kind of dancing," Joel said, "but I'm willing to try."

Once again she was in Joel's arms. The wine and good food had made her as mellow as the music. They didn't try to be fancy. Joel just sort of improvised around the floor, but it was all right. Their bodies were in tune to the music. The voice that told her not to dance close seemed so far away that it was easy to ignore.

Pam closed her eyes and leaned her head against his shoulder. He was several inches taller than she was, and his shoulders were broad. Maybe if he were small and thin she wouldn't keep forgetting that he was so much younger. Actually, she was tired of thinking about the age difference. Sick and tired. Maybe it didn't matter as much as she thought. It certainly didn't on the dance floor. What made it matter, however, were families. His future family versus her present one. But she wasn't going to think about that now. She wanted to enjoy herself. It was too long since she'd been dancing, and she feared it would be a long time before she would again.

One thing was certain, however. He would not be dancing with his mother like this. Or his big sister. He was dancing like a guy attracted to the woman in his arms.

JOEL GOT UP AT FIVE the next morning to type the final draft of his Business Law paper. He had planned to come home early last night in order to add some extra documentation from a journal article he'd come across. But he'd gone dancing instead—close dancing to old-time music like in the movies. He couldn't believe some of that dated music! Helen Reddy. Frank Sinatra. Mama Cass.

The Supremes. Even Perry Como, his grandmother's favorite. But it had been nice. In fact, he could have danced all night, holding Pam in his arms, humming tunes he'd first heard when he was a kid, responding to corny lyrics that started touching his heart as the evening wore on.

He decided he'd hand in the paper late if need be rather than cut the evening short, and he put all thoughts of school out of his mind. But when your dancing partner has a baby-sitter tending her children, dancing all night isn't an option. And when he arrived home at twelve-thirty, he looked over the paper and decided it was good enough as written. He added a few lines, quickly compiled a bibliography, set the alarm and took his fantasies to bed.

When the alarm went off, he was dreaming about Pam. They were still dancing, but this time in a high mountain meadow to music that seemed to waft in on the night breezes, and he was kissing her, holding her very close, telling her he wanted to make love with her.

Joel groaned and kicked the covers off. Reality came down on him hard. He was in a crummy little room, and there was no Pam in his arms—and maybe there never would be again. He had gotten himself emotionally tangled up with a woman who was at a different place in life than he was. She couldn't back up, and he wasn't sure he wanted to jump ahead. He had to type a paper he really should have spent more time with. And he wasn't really all that interested in business law—or accounting.

His stomach rumbled all through class, and he longed for a cup of coffee. The lecture was about zoning laws, but it was more interesting than he thought it would be. A person would need to know that stuff if he ever started his own business—like a restaurant.

After class Joel went for coffee and doughnuts at the campus coffee shop with a group of kids from his class. A lively discussion about the upcoming gubernatorial election erupted, followed by one about the influence of rock music on contemporary American culture, a subject that really interested Joel. Like most of his peers, he loved the music of his generation. He wondered what his companions would think if he confessed he'd been dancing to Perry Como last night.

After the doughnuts had been eaten and the second cup of coffee lingered over, the group reluctantly parted. He liked that part of college life, Joel thought as he headed toward his car. It was nice to be with kids his own age. He'd even enjoyed Gretchen's flirting.

There was a concert Saturday. Cheap Trick. Gretchen had an extra ticket. Several of the kids were going and planned to meet for pizza afterward.

Maybe he'd just go. Cheap Trick was one of his favorite groups. And he hadn't gone out like that with a bunch of kids since he'd stopped seeing Stephanie.

When Joel walked into the kitchen, Pam was putting away groceries. He could tell by the way she held her shoulders that she was tired and upset.

"Where have you been?" she snapped. "Your class was over an hour ago."

"I do have another life, you know," Joel snapped back.

Silently, they finished emptying the sacks. Then Pam poured two cups of coffee and sank into a chair. "What about your paper. Did it turn out all right?"

"I suppose, considering all the research I didn't do," Joel said, sitting across from her. "I'm really going to have to hit the books in the next few days if I'm going to pass my finals."

"I ruined the quiches," Pam said, rubbing at her temples.

"How come?"

"I forgot the salt," she admitted.

"Pretty flat, huh?"

"Yeah. Not only do I have to make them over, but all those ingredients are wasted. There goes the profit on this gig." There were two little creases between her eyes, and she drank rather than sipped her coffee. Joel suspected she had a headache.

"You okay?" he asked.

"Yes. No. Hell, I don't know. I can't keep my mind on what I'm doing. I snap at the boys. I have a pimple on my nose. The car is acting funny."

"And you can't believe you felt so romantic dancing with me last night," Joel added. "You still think about the time we kissed, and part of you is waiting for it to happen again—and more, but what would be the point? You feel like you're robbing the cradle, acting like a dirty old woman and wonder if you should fire me. Does that about cover it, or have I left out something?"

She almost smiled. "What about feeling foolish? I know there are girls your own age that you go out with. I'm sure you went home last night and wondered why you'd been out ballroom dancing with a matron when you could have been rocking with a coed."

"No, those feelings didn't come until this morning," Joel admitted. "I'm not seeing anyone else, if that's what you're wondering. However, I was engaged until the middle of June."

"You were engaged when we first met? Why didn't you tell me?"

He shrugged. "I was already having second thoughts. Realizing I was attracted to you made me face up to the fact that I wasn't really in love with her. That was good to know, whether anything happened between you and me or not."

"Nothing can happen. I couldn't trust a relationship between us to last."

Joel finished his coffee before responding. And then he spoke very carefully. "There are no guarantees for anything, Pam, and no one can speak past the moment. Not really. As you keep pointing out, I'm young and just finishing school. I'm not really sure what it is that I want out of life. Two years ago I would have sworn I was going to marry a Chinese girl and live in Taiwan. Then all last year I thought I was going to marry a rich girl and wear three-piece suits. All I know at this moment in time is that I want to be here with you and Scott and Tommy."

"That's not good enough," Pam said. She was crying.

Chapter Six

Pam tasted the honey-yogurt dip for the fresh fruit tray, then set the two kettles of stewing chicken breasts off the stove to cool. She was preparing for yet another wedding reception, this one tomorrow evening.

She had wedding receptions scheduled into next year. Joel had been right about specializing, about getting a system.

She wiped her brow and turned up the fan. Her antiquated central air-conditioning unit didn't help the kitchen much when she cooked in the heat of the day.

She took a minute to sip her iced tea and look out the kitchen window at Joel's shirtless figure, all bronzed and muscular, as he worked in the yard. He was ripping the rotten boards from the fence a section at a time and replacing them with new ones. He picked up the hammer and rhythmically began pounding nails into the wood, his muscles flexing and relaxing, his body shiny with sweat, the sun making golden highlights in his dark red hair. Scott had taken his toy toolbox out into the yard and was pounding away in imitation of Joel with a rubber-headed child's hammer. Tommy was sitting with Barney, who had found a cool spot in the dirt under the oak tree.

Tommy was in the process of examining Barney's teeth. The dog was a saint.

Pam's gaze moved back to Joel. How wonderful his body was. In his clothes, he looked thin, but he really wasn't—just tall and lean. With an effortless grace he worked, his movements purposeful and fluid. Such pleasure it gave her to watch him.

A section of the fence had finally fallen in, and Joel decided it couldn't wait for a visit from her father to be repaired. Since summer school had ended, he had been using any spare time to work on the fence or her car or the new bookkeeping system he was setting up for her business. She was depending on Joel too much, Pam cautioned herself for the hundredth time as she took a can of frozen lemonade concentrate from the freezer compartment and put it in water to thaw. He was her only business associate and her most constant companion. She found herself wishing August could go on forever, but she sometimes felt obligated to ask him if there wasn't someplace else he would rather be.

"Like where?" he asked.

"Like Padre Island with those two college friends who invited you to go with them. Like where there are other people your age. Surely you get tired of hanging around two little kids and their mother all the time."

"Not particularly," he said with a shrug. "Scott and Tommy aren't the most brilliant conversationalists I've come across, but they're funny and make me laugh. And their mother, when she isn't moaning around about how I should go off with 'people my own age,' is a lovely woman with beautiful brown eyes to match her rich brown hair. Of course, much as I like her sons, there are times when I would like to ship *them* off to Padre Island and enjoy the company of their lovely mother without them around. If I could ever get her alone, I just know she would not be able to resist my boyish good looks, my irresistible charm, my animal magnetism, my innate sexuality.''

He joked like that a lot. But Pam knew that under the banter was serious intent. He wanted to move in with her. Always speaking hypothetically, he talked about two living cheaper than one, about a woman being safer with a man around the house, about the problem people had sleeping when their one window faces a flashing neon sign, about how the smell of rancid grease coming up from a café below one's apartment could make a person start each day slightly nauseous. He commented on the time and gasoline he was wasting driving back and forth all the time. He quoted psychological studies about the importance of couples living together before any decisions about permanent commitment were made, about children needing parental figures of both sexes in their lives.

The novelty would wear off, Pam told herself. Joel was just playing at family now because he'd never really had one. Without realizing it, he was practicing for the day when he'd be a husband and father, when he'd have his own family and house to look after. But in the meantime, he should be young and see the world first. He could be married and responsible for the rest of his life.

And she told him so. After he talked about the hypothetical advantages of moving in, she felt obligated to speak of the advantages of his moving on.

Pam was trying very hard not to become too attached to him, but she suspected it was already too late for that. If he left now, her heart might not break, but she would be infinitely more lonely than before. Joel had spoiled her. During her marriage, for every hour she had spent with Marty, she had spent ten times that many alone. Whereas, she and Joel were together for large chunks of every day. They took the boys for rides and walks. They grocery-shopped and did assembly-line food preparation. They loaded the sandwiches, blankets, boys and dog for picnics by Lake Dallas. They took the boys to kiddie carnivals and wading pools. They pored over cookbooks and food magazines far into the night. Together, they managed the larger catering jobs, with Cindy taking care of the boys. Other times just one of them would go, and the other would stay home with the boys. Pam found she looked forward to the larger jobs so that she and Joel could work together.

She realized she was setting herself up for a fall, but Pam rationalized that now she at least had the wisdom of age and experience to cushion the landing. She never dreamed that Marty would ever leave her. She knew that Joel would.

She took glasses of lemonade to the three males in the backyard then sat with Tommy for a while and watched Joel work. Tommy crawled into her lap and sucked on his thumb. He seemed lethargic, but then he had been restless in the night, waking up four or five times, and this afternoon he had awakened early from his nap. Pam hoped he wasn't getting another earache. She kissed his forehead. It was hard to tell if he had a fever or was just warm from being outside.

Tommy ate little at dinner. He just sat there sucking his thumb and whimpering when Pam tried to get him to take a bite. She gave him two children's Tylenol and rocked him while Joel did the dishes.

By bedtime Tommy had a temperature of one hundred but no other symptoms. He wasn't pulling on his ear. Pam looked at his throat, but it didn't seem red.

Joel said good-night, always an awkward time for them. It seemed as though he lived with them, yet he went home at night.

"See you in the morning," he said. "Hope Tommy feels better."

Pam followed him to the door with Tommy in her arms. "Well, good night, kiddo," he told Tommy with a pat on the head. "Get a good night's sleep. You, too, Pam."

"Good night."

"You need for me to pick anything up on the way over in the morning?"

"I'll call if I think of anything."

"Well, good night," he said again, touching her arm.

Pam turned on the television and went back to her rocking. The house seemed smaller and drabber when Joel wasn't there.

She watched a Goldie Hawn movie. It was funny, she supposed, but it was no fun to laugh alone. Finally, she turned it off and went to bed.

Tommy slept for a few hours then woke up whimpering. He felt warm. Pam went to the bathroom to get him a drink of water and two more children's Tylenol. He dutifully sat up, chewed the flavored pills and took a sip of water. "That's a good boy," she told him, offering him the glass again, but he declined and lay back down, thumb in his mouth, his arm around his stuffed dog. Pam waited by his bed until she was satisfied he was going back to sleep.

Scott was sitting up in his bed and watching her. "Go back to sleep, honey." Pam sat with him for a while, rubbing his back.

The next time she awoke, it was to a thin, weak wailing.

She was at Tommy's bedside in an instant. When she touched her baby's body, she gasped. He was burning up with fever. Pam put her lips to his forehead. She had never felt such a high fever, and it made her heart go cold with fear.

How had he gotten so feverish so quickly? And why?

She looked at the clock on the bureau. It was three in the morning.

A feeling of panic pushed against the walls of her chest, but she took a deep breath and willed herself to stay calm.

She threw on some jeans and a T-shirt, then jabbed her bare feet in a pair of loafers. She wrapped a blanket around Scott and sat him on the sofa. "Tommy's sick," she explained. "We have to take him to the hospital."

Then she remembered the gas gauge on her car. It had been perilously low, but she'd elected to wait until morning to buy gas. What if she ran out on the way to the hospital?

When she picked up Tommy, he was limp as a rag doll and totally unresponsive. Fear crushed against her chest. Never had she felt so afraid or so alone.

She carried Tommy to her bed and used the phone on her bedside table to call an ambulance, amazed that she could give her name and address in a reasonably normal tone of voice. "Please, tell them to hurry," she said. "My baby is very ill."

It seemed to take forever for the ambulance to arrive, but her watch said it was five and a half minutes. Pam was waiting with Tommy on the porch when the ambulance, lights flashing, pulled into her driveway. Lights were coming on in houses up and down the block, front doors opening.

Pam handed Tommy to a paramedic then raced back inside for Scott.

She sat in the back of the ambulance holding a subdued, wide-eyed Scott on her lap. Together they watched a paramedic administer oxygen to his brother. How small Tommy looked on the adult-sized carrier. How still he was. If only he would cry. Or move. The oxygen mask engulfed his small face.

A second paramedic was talking by radio to someone at the hospital, giving Tommy's vital signs. They were meaningless to Pam, but she understood all too well from the tone that her child was gravely ill. She reached over to pick up a small, clammy hand, desperately needing a physical connection with this child she had given over to the care of others. She held his hand and prayed.

The lights of the expressway went flashing by, and Pam realized they were being taken to Parkland, the big sprawling hospital in north Dallas that was so often in the news with reports on victims of shootings, automobile accidents, suicide attempts. It was the hospital where President Kennedy had died.

Suddenly the paramedic tending Tommy grabbed the mask from his face. Pam watched in horror as the man put a tube down Tommy's throat. A rubber bag was attached to the tube, and the paramedic began pumping the bag manually, using it to breathe for the flaccid child, while the other paramedic talked once again to the hospital. "Code blue!" he said. "I repeat, we've got a code blue on this seventeen-month old baby we're bringing in."

Orderlies, nurses, physicians—all were waiting for the ambulance. Tommy was immediately placed on a portable respirator.

Pam needed to call Brenda—and Joel. But she couldn't bear to leave Tommy's side long enough to use the phone. She asked an orderly to make the calls for her.

Pam, holding Scott, watched from a corner of the examining room while Tommy was given injections, while IVs were started and samples of blood and spinal fluid were taken, while he was examined by a succession of concerned-looking men and women.

Brenda, George and Joel arrived almost simultaneously, just as Tommy was being taken upstairs. The three stared at Pam, waiting for her to tell them Tommy was fine.

"He almost died," she said, her voice breaking as her composure threatened to leave her. "I don't know what's the matter."

Joel took Scott from her arms. "Will you take Scott home?" she asked. "I'll call as soon as I know something."

Joel hesitated. "I guess you know, Pam, that I care more about you and these two boys than anyone else in the world."

She nodded. She did not doubt his sincerity. At this moment in time, she and her children and this young man were very close, very connected to one another.

Brenda hugged her sister. "Tommy's a tough little fellow," George said, patting Pam's shoulder awkwardly. With her sister and brother-in-law at her side, Pam went upstairs to face Tommy's fate.

The diagnosis was meningitis. The physician who gave them the news did not try to gloss over its seriousness. "He's a very sick little boy," she said. "We'll do everything we can."

Like a robot, Pam turned to the pay phone. When Joel's voice answered, Pam tried to tell him what the doctor had said but couldn't. George took the phone and gave Joel the grim news. "Yes, we'll keep you posted," he said.

Tommy had been placed in intensive care, and Pam was allowed in only periodically. The rest of the time, she sat in the lounge with Brenda and George. Other family members of intensive-care patients shared the room with them. A woman in the corner fingered her rosary and whispered prayers. An elderly woman and her heavy, middle-aged daughter clung to each other through the night.

Pam had a hard time dealing with her fear. She wanted to be with Tommy, to hold him and not let him slip away from her. She wanted to do something, *anything*, even yell and scream and beat her head against the wall. "You two may be right about the no-kids routine," she told Brenda and George, her voice lowered for privacy. "Kids make you vulnerable. You spend all your time worrying that something like this will happen, and then when it does, you feel so helpless, so afraid."

Brenda and George exchanged worried glances. "Do you want us to try and track down Marty?" Brenda asked.

Marty. Pam had not given a thought to Tommy's father. "No," she said without hesitation. "He doesn't deserve to know anything about those boys, good news or bad."

"What about the folks?" Brenda asked.

"Let's wait," Pam said. Wait until they knew one way or the other. The foul taste of fear rose in her throat when she thought of the possibilities.

George left periodically to get them coffee, and he located aspirin for Pam's raging headache and a blanket to wrap around her shoulders when she began to tremble.

Pam called Joel again to report no change. "Did I wake you?" she asked.

"No. I'm too scared to sleep. I wish I was there with you."

"Me, too," Pam said, realizing it was true. She would rather have Joel at her side than her own sister. "Is Scott okay?"

"Fine. He's sound asleep."

"Joel, thanks for everything. I've never had a friend like you."

"I'd rather you didn't say thank-you. I'm not looking for gratitude."

Tommy's condition remained the same throughout the day, but there seemed to be some improvement during the next night. He opened his eyes and whimpered when he saw his mother.

When the doctor came for morning rounds, she was encouraged and took Tommy off the respirator. Pam was so overcome with relief, she sank to her knees. "No, I'm all right," she insisted as the woman helped her to her feet. "My knees are just a little wobbly."

"I understand," the doctor said. "I've got a three-year-old."

"This means he's going to get better?" Pam asked the doctor. She needed a promise.

The doctor would give her none. "It means he's breathing fine on his own. But his fever is still too high, and he needs careful monitoring. But I think we can move him to a room so you can stay with him."

During the second day, Tommy slept fitfully. He would wake, take a little water, then fall back into a troubled, feverish sleep.

George left for the night, promising to come back bright and early to relieve Brenda. Pam refused to go home even for a shower.

She called Joel again. "He's better, but far from well," she told him, then asked that he put Scott on the line.

"I'll come home soon, honey. Can you give me a kiss for Tommy?" she said.

Scott dutifully made a kissing sound over the phone.

Pam couldn't remember the last time she had seen her sister looking so bedraggled. And she herself avoided looking at mirrors, knowing she looked worse. "I'll be all right if you want to go home," Pam told Brenda.

"No. I'll stay. I want to." Brenda pulled a chair over by Pam's. Together, they sat by the bed of the feverish child. Tommy would moan in his sleep, thrash out, then be so still that Pam would have to touch him to assure herself he was still breathing.

She felt better when he started opening his eyes occasionally and making funny little mewing sounds when he saw her. Pam would kiss him and stroke his forehead, and soon his eyes would flutter shut again.

"Did you mean what you said the other night about it's best not to have kids because of all the pain?" Brenda asked.

Pam shook her head slowly back and forth, then leaned back in the chair, her body aflame with weariness. "No. No matter what happens, I can't imagine going through life without having known my little Tommy. But with love, any kind of love, you open yourself up for pain and sorrow. The only way to spare yourself from pain is never to love."

"I remember how crazy you were about Marty," Brenda said. "Maybe you wouldn't have lost him if you hadn't had the kids."

"Maybe. But you can't revise history. I love my kids. You win some and lose some, I guess."

"But now, you and I are older," Brenda said. "Maybe we can't revise history, but we can be more careful about working out our future. You can try to find the kind of man who won't walk out on you, and I can do everything possible to keep the one I have."

"I suppose," Pam said. "But sometimes things have a way of just happening in spite of the best-laid plans."

"You don't approve of George and me not having children, do you?"

"If that's what you both really want, then, of course, I approve," Pam insisted as she stroked Tommy's hand. "I'd never tell anyone they should have children if they don't want to. There are enough unwanted children in the world now without adding to the list. But for me, it would have left a big gaping hole in my life not to have children. I always knew I wanted kids. I didn't pay any attention to Marty when he said he didn't. That's where marriages can get into problems—when one partner wants children and the other one doesn't."

George sat with Pam during the morning, and Brenda went home to bathe and take a nap. When she came back midafternoon, she brought Pam a change of clothes. And she brought Puppy, Tommy's favorite stuffed animal.

Brenda burst into tears when she walked into Tommy's hospital room and saw her nephew nursing on a bottle of orange juice. He took the bottle out of his mouth long enough to gurgle something at his aunt. When she handed him Puppy, he clasped the animal tightly against his side.

"Can I touch him?" Brenda pleaded.

Pam nodded with tears in her eyes. Tommy was definitely better.

The two sisters hugged and cried, then hugged some more. The nightmare was over. Tommy was going to be all right.

"I didn't know how much I loved that little guy until he got sick," Brenda said.

"That was nice of you to think of Puppy."

"Joel did that," Brenda acknowledged. "I must admit that's a nice young man you've got over there. You'd think he was Scott's daddy, the way he takes care of him and talks to him. Scott was 'helping' him stuff little tomatoes for a reception tonight."

"Oh, my gosh!" Pam said. "The Quarter Horse Association," Pam said. "I forgot all about their meeting."

"Joel said not to worry. George is going to take care of Scott, and the food is under control. He said he had to cheat a little and buy some stuff at the deli, but he'll disguise it. He and Scott were getting ready to pick up the glassware and wine for tonight."

Pam went to the ladies' room and cleaned up as best she could. When she got back to Tommy's room, he was sitting up in bed with Puppy. "Baba," he said, using his word for pacifier.

Pam picked him up and hugged him. He didn't even feel warm. Patiently, Tommy waited while his mother kissed his face, his ears, his neck, his hands, then he repeated, "Baba."

With a laugh, Pam fished around in her purse and found a pacifier.

At evening rounds, the doctor was pleased. "Kids are like that," she said. "They get sick fast and get well fast. I'll tell you, though, I'm really glad to see this little guy looking so perky after that bout the other evening. It's a good thing you got him to us when you did."

The doctor turned and looked at Pam. "And now, I'm going to prescribe something for Tommy's mother. You go home, take a shower and crawl into bed. Your sister can call you if we have any problem. It won't do this baby of yours any good if you get sick."

Pam hesitated. The thought of crawling into her bed was a seductive one. Every muscle in her body cried out its exhaustion. The headache that had attacked her the first night had never left. She had been too worried to eat, and she felt faint and light-headed. She needed to see Scott, to hold him and reassure him that normalcy would soon return to their lives. But more than anything, even more than sleep, she wanted to be with Joel. She didn't even examine the reasons why. She just felt an almost physical need to see him and tell him Tommy was all right.

She stayed until Tommy seemed settled for the night, then for the first time in four days, she left the hospital. She felt as though she was leaving a prison after a long incarceration.

It had been raining, and the streetlights reflected on the wet pavement. The air smelled crisp and clean, a luxury after the disinfectant smell of the hospital. Pam filled her lungs with it. The world was still here, and her baby was going to be all right. If she wasn't so exhausted, she would have danced across the parking lot. But her muscles ached with fatigue. Even her hands felt tired as she unlocked the door of her sister's car.

Pam drove the BMW home with great care, fearful that her weariness had impaired her ability to drive. She stayed off the expressway and took the side streets, avoiding traffic. Her eyesight was blurry, making halos around the streetlights. In fact, her entire body was beginning to feel blurry and out of focus. She had to think very hard about how to get home this unfamiliar way.

But ahead of her were the lights from Love Field. She was going in the right direction.

And there it was. Her dear little house. Had it really only been four days?

Her station wagon was in the driveway, but Joel's van was gone, and the lights were out in the house. Joel would still be out catering, Pam realized. And Scott was spending the night with George. That made her smile. Scott in the world's most tidy apartment. George would probably try to teach him to play chess.

With a sense of disappointment, Pam let herself into an empty house. She had wanted a homecoming with hugs and tears of relief.

She went straight to her bedroom, stripped, then filled the bathtub and lowered her aching body into the hottest water she could stand. Such bliss. Never had a bath felt better.

Hovering in a suspended state between sleep and wakefulness, she stayed in the water for a long time, then with thoughts of Joel coming home soon, got out and toweled herself dry and put on a terry cloth robe that used to be Marty's.

She couldn't decide what to wear. A nightgown didn't seem appropriate, but she didn't want to get dressed again, either. As she sat on the edge of her bed, her groggy mind pondering, she heard a key in the lock.

''Pam,'' Joel's voice called out.

She walked out of the bedroom and faced him across the length of hallway. Fear was written all over his face. Pam understood. He thought she had come home because Tommy was dead.

"He's going to be all right," she said. And she started to sob, the fear and exhaustion of the last days taking over her body. In an instant, Joel was there, and she collapsed into his arms.

Yes, she thought. This was what she wanted and needed.

Joel was crying, too. "Oh, God," he said over and over. "I was so afraid we were going to lose him."

The nightmare had left her weak, and Joel's young, strong arms felt wonderfully safe and loving. She had needed the comfort of his embrace, and it seemed only natural when their mouths found each other. Yes, she had wanted that, too. The kissing. The wonderful kissing, like that other time when passion erupted within her and her fantasies were ignited. Her exhaustion had stolen away all her resistance, made her honest. Yesterday, tomorrow, she could pretend, but not now, not at this minute. She wanted him to kiss her, to touch her, to make love to her. The arguments why she should not were obscured by the fog that had descended over her brain. All she knew was that for now, this night, she desperately needed Joel's physical nearness and his love. For it was love they shared, no matter how impermanently, no matter if it was just this one night in a lifetime. How could she live and die without making love to Joel?

She touched his hair, allowed her fingers to entwine themselves in soft, clean locks of auburn hair. Never would she see hair that color again without thinking of Joel.

Joel's mouth was soft, gentle, as he kissed her eyes, her ears, her throat, but always returned to her mouth.

"Oh, Pam, are you sure? I don't want to do anything you'll regret."

She wanted to believe it was a beginning, but she did not. But, no, there would be no regret. Deep in the recesses of her soul, she understood they had been presented with the gift of something pure and beautiful. Never had it felt so right to be loved, to love in return. This night had a predestined quality about it, and Pam felt as though she was merely accepting the judgment of whatever forces had brought them together.

She would celebrate the gift of life with this man. Her baby would live. And because of that, because of all she had survived over the past two years, because Joel had filled her house with joy, Pam herself had never felt more in touch with life than she had this night.

"There will be no regrets from me," she promised, "but I also have no promises. I'm not sure what this means, except I care deeply about you and I need so desperately to be with someone who cares about me. And by the same token, if you get up from my bed and go away from me forever, I will remember you with fondness and always know that I wouldn't have missed you for the world."

A moan came from deep inside Joel's chest as his body came to accept what would be. And with such care, he lifted her in his arms. As though in a dream, in a fantasy, she floated in his arms into her room, onto her bed.

Pam watched as he took off his clothes, the light from the hall illuminating his lean body. Suddenly, Pam was embarrassed because she was not lean, because she no longer possessed the sleek, glowing ripeness of young adulthood.

But he took her in his arms and with unbelievable tenderness began kissing her again, stroking her hair and throat with gentle fingers, pushing aside her robe to caress her bare shoulder.

"Ah, Pam, Pam," he said as he moved his mouth over her face and throat, her shoulder. "I'm so in love with you. So in love. I love everything about you, your smile, your voice, your hands, your throat, your face, your body."

Pam smiled. Sweet words from a sweet boy. And she loved him, too, his face, his hands, his body. How could she not? His smile captivated her. His kindness touched her. His young beauty pleased her.

She closed her eyes and inhaled deeply, drinking in all the sensations she was experiencing. But the edge of doubt was there again, emerging from the first throes of passion. Her breasts had nursed two babies and lost their firmness. Her belly bore the scar of Tommy's caesarean birth. Her once-slim hips were fuller. She was a silly old woman about to expose herself to a young Adonis.

She would pay for this. Embarrassment. Remorse. Heartbreak. Somehow the price of loving Joel would have to be paid.

The price might not be worth the ecstasy, but she wanted him too much to stop.

Pam took his face in her hands and forced him to look into her eyes. "I want you to make love to me. And I hope that someday, when we both look back on this night it will be with a sigh and a smile."

And then, there was no going back.

FINALLY, IN THE NIGHT, his arm grew numb, and Joel was forced to relinquish the woman he embraced. He rolled over onto his back, the side of his body still in contact with hers, and marveled at the wonder of what had happened.

After weeks of obsessive longing, after endless nights of mental rehearsal, he had finally made love with Pam.

He thought he had known how it would be, but he was wrong. He had dreamed of lusty passion, of her swooning out of control in the face of his incredible masculinity, the beautiful captive succumbing to overwhelming desire for the swashbuckling pirate, the love-starved woman being reclaimed by her returning warrior, the adoring girlfriend rewarding the football hero for his winning touchdown. But it was none of those things. It was an ordinary man and an ordinary woman rising out of the tediousness of their daily existence to a kindly, golden place full of light and feeling and bliss, a place where the cares of the world faded away and they became lovers.

Their actions were tentative at first, even fearful, as they set about discovering the incredible sweetness and joyous release of giving totally to another human being. Gradually, as shyness fell away, they began exploring with tenderness and longing the mysteries of each other's bodies. And then the boundaries of their bodies became defused as they joined together with such reverence, such awe.

It was the sweetness that surprised Joel. He hadn't known that passion and sweetness ever joined forces. He felt his own youth very acutely, realizing there was much he did not know and understand.

Pam worried so about the difference in their ages. He kept denying its importance, but he hid behind the bravado of his words. Maybe he wasn't ready to feel this deeply. It tore at him, at the same time making him want both to immerse himself more fully into the role of a mature, loving man and to run with haste back into the comforting selfishness of adolescence. Love and commitment didn't come free. He sensed that now. The responsibility of loving someone was heavy and real. What had happened tonight wasn't two lusty kids on a lark with no one to answer to in the morning. This was real life with all its portent for joy and sorrow.

And there was another fear mixed in with all the rest. The lovemaking had taken its own course, but he had followed it well. He'd been pretty damned good and felt smugly proud, having no doubt that he had brought sexual pleasure to this beautiful and responsive woman. But how had he done that? What if he couldn't perform like that again? What if he tried to make love with her a second time and failed?

It seemed, however, as if he was about to find out. Pam was awake. Joel could sense the change in her breathing, in her body. He rolled onto his side to meet her embrace.

Her body filled his arms. Just the feel of her was intoxicating. This was no nubile girl but a real woman who had worked and lived in her woman's body, borne and nursed children with it and now was using it to make love to him. Joel felt honored and found he wanted her more now than before. He felt bewitched, in love and uncertain what it all meant.

Chapter Seven

The knock on Joel's door surprised him. He glanced at his watch. After midnight.

When he opened the door, he was even more surprised. It was Stephanie, looking even more beautiful than he remembered. She was wearing a strapless gold-lamé dress that would have done a movie star proud on Academy Awards night. The smile on her face was tentative, her bare shoulders smooth and alluring.

"Well, aren't you going to invite me in?" she asked, affecting a pretty pout.

Joel stood aside. He caught a whiff of her perfume as she walked by. Expensive, of course.

"I'd forgotten what a dump this place was," she said, circling the room. The contrast between the glamorous young woman and shabby room was marked. "No wonder you're never here. I'd avoid it, too. Where have you been keeping yourself, honey? I keep callin' and comin' by, but you're never here."

"I work for a catering service," he explained. "It makes for odd hours."

"And you study into the wee small hours," she said, looking at the pile of books and notebooks—most of them open—on his table. "But it's August. People don't study in August."

"I'm trying to finish up a correspondence course."

"Don't you ever play anymore?"

"Not much. I'm trying to get enough money saved for my fall tuition."

"And you could have gone to SMU with never a thought for money. You could have had a good time like other college kids instead of always having your nose to the grindstone. You're a strange one, Joel. Not like other guys at all."

She stopped her walking and stood in front of him. He realized she'd been crying.

"The thought of marrying me must have scared you pretty bad that you'd back away from a deal like that," she went on. "You would have been rich someday."

"I felt like I was being bought. It would have been easier to sort out my feelings for you if you'd been poor like me."

"Wow. For the first time, I think I know what they mean by 'poor little rich girl.' I just broke up with fiancé number two tonight," she said, touching her red-rimmed eyes. "I didn't mind paying for everything, but then he decided I should help myself to some of my daddy's money for him—on the qt, of course. Funny, you didn't want to take a dime from Daddy, and this boy wanted to take all he could get. A banker's son. Old Dallas. But you know how things are with Texas bankers these days. His daddy's bankrupt, and my friend wasn't willing to go the poor-but-proud route." She looked around the room again, as though trying to imagine this friend living poor.

Then, quite suddenly, she was in Joel's arms, pressing her body against his, her mouth seeking his.

At first Joel was too stunned to stop her. She was kissing him deeply. Memories came surging back. Sweet memories. For an instant his emotions hovered in the balance. His body responded with immediate wanting, but warning signals went off in his head.

Firmly, he unwrapped her arms from his neck. "Listen, Steph, we need to talk."

She stepped back from him and looked into his face. "You still got another girl?"

He started to correct her and say he was in love with a woman, but decided against explanations. All he did was nod.

"Is she prettier than me?"

"Come on, Steph. You know no one's prettier than you."

"Are you going to marry her?"

"I don't know."

"I'm sorry I broke it off with us, Joel. I'd like another chance. I think I've grown up a lot. I think I understand you better now."

"But do you understand yourself? I think you've been hurt by someone who sounds like a worthless bum. But that doesn't mean you should come running back to me. It probably means you should find someone who will treat you right and enjoys the same sort of life you do."

"I want to move in with you," Stephanie said.

Joel started to laugh. The idea of Stephanie Anderson living here was ludicrous, but he realized that she thought she was serious. "No, you don't. You just need a friend. Sit down, and I'll get you a beer."

Stephanie didn't move. "Let me just spend the night. I need to be with you. All you have to do is hold me. I won't try to seduce you, unless you want me to."

"I don't think that's a good idea, Steph."

"Aren't you even tempted?" she asked.

Joel looked at her flawless young skin tanned the color of ripe apricots, at the full wonderful mouth he used to kiss by the hour. He remembered the feel of those high, firm breasts, of her slim athletic body. And he remembered the carefree days full of sunshine and laughter and lighthearted silliness they had shared. They had been young and in love until the reality of their separate sets of expectations came crashing down on them.

"Yes. I'm tempted," he said, "but I'm obligated to say no."

She took defeat graciously. He had to give her that. She accepted the offered beer and sat at his table, talking longingly about old times. Then she admitted there was another boy she might be interested in dating. A Phi Delt from Tyler. But he was thinking about a military career, and she didn't want to leave Dallas.

"Can I at least call you up sometimes?" she asked after she had kissed his cheek in farewell. "You're right about my needing a friend."

Joel nodded.

"And will you call me if you and your girl split the blanket?"

Joel nodded again.

After she had gone, her perfume lingered in the air. Joel felt like he'd aged ten years.

PAM WONDERED HOW LONG her sister would keep up the almost daily visits. Brenda's mornings were spent working with a Neiman Marcus fashion coordinator, selecting fabulous outfits to model in the store's famous Zodiac Room for the luncheon customers. When she finished at the store, she came to Pam's.

If the boys were still taking their naps, Brenda wanted to wake them. She visited with her sister, and Joel, if he was there, but the focus of her visits was her nephews. She took them to get ice-cream cones and to see boxcars up close. She read them stories. She took them to the zoo to see the bears and monkeys. On her day off, she took them down to Neiman Marcus to show them off to the other models. And she brought them presents. Cute little shirts purchased with her store discount. Toy cars. Books. A set of wooden farm animals.

Brenda had always taken a more-than-polite interest in Scott and Tommy before, but suddenly she had become the adoring, doting auntie whose nephews were the cutest, funniest, most precocious children in the world, and she actually got upset when the clerk at the ice-cream store failed to take note of how cute her little friends were.

"Who's doing the dusting?" Pam asked one day when Brenda returned with the boys at five o'clock and prepared to dash home before George arrived. Her sister's apartment had always been perfectly kept. Brenda followed a careful schedule for her household chores, with George helping on weekends with bigger tasks such as shampooing rugs and washing windows. Pam marveled that anyone cleaned according to a schedule rather than in response to dirt.

"I have time to do all that," Brenda answered with a dismissing wave of her hand. "George doesn't get home until six. He'll help me cook something."

"But someone still has to grocery-shop, and the laundry doesn't do itself."

"You always used to complain that I didn't come to see you often enough," Brenda said. "Now you're complaining because I come too much."

"I'm not complaining. The boys and I love having you, but I was just wondering how you found the time to come so often."

At first Pam was amused at Brenda's newly found enjoyment of aunthood. But then she became worried. Brenda had just had her twenty-seventh birthday, and Pam realized her sister's instincts and hormones were starting to conspire against her carefully thought out and very adult life-style.

Brenda wanted a baby. She might as well wear a sign around her neck to that effect. Suddenly babies had become the most fascinating thing in the world—not only her nephews, but other people's babies. She cooed at them in restaurants, gravitated to them in public places. She asked how old they were, what their names were, if they walked or crawled yet. And she touched them, feeling plump little arms, patting smooth baby hands, smoothing silky baby hair. Babies drew Brenda like magnets.

Poor Brenda, Pam thought, wondering what her sister was going to do.

In September, after Joel had started back to school for his last semester of college, Brenda suddenly stopped coming. Joel had decided to take twenty hours of classes—a killer semester—in order to graduate at midyear and avoid the expense of an additional semester, and there were days in a row when he didn't come. For the first time in months, Pam and her boys were alone more often than not.

At first Pam thought nothing of it. In addition to her Neiman Marcus job, Brenda was modeling some at the Apparel Mart, the city's huge marketing center for the clothing industry, but Pam still visited with her sister two or three times a week by phone like before. And Joel came when he could.

At times, however, Pam wondered if she was destined to raise her sons alone. She even found herself thinking about Marty. Did he ever wonder how his sons were doing or think about seeing them again?

The boys were cranky, and Pam snapped at them too much. Scott asked for Joel. Even Barney seemed to mope around.

In mid-October, after George had left for a Sunday-morning round of golf, Brenda showed up at her sister's house, a sack of doughnuts in hand. When the boys came squealing down the hall to greet their aunt with cries of "Bwenda, Bwenda," she got teary-eyed.

"Oh, you two are *so* sweet," she wailed, falling to her knees and hugging them.

Over coffee, Pam said, "Okay, little sister, it's time we talk. First you hover about this house like a bee over clover, then suddenly you disappear from view. Do you realize this is the first time I've seen you in almost a month, after a month of seeing you almost daily?"

"I decided I was torturing myself," Brenda said, planting her chin firmly in her propped-up hand.

"In what way?" Pam asked, already knowing the answer. She offered Tommy a bite of oatmeal, but he was busy making a pile of crumbs out of an applesauce doughnut.

Brenda touched Tommy's cheek and sighed deeply. "When Tommy got sick, I sat up there at the hospital thinking about how very precious he was. And Scott. They are wonderful little human beings, a part of you. I think I'd just thought of them as cute little nuisances before. Kids were something that were okay for other people, but not for George and me. We were too clever and sophisticated for that. But now—and don't laugh, please—but it feels like I've got a great big empty space inside of me that needs to be filled up."

"Why would I laugh?" Pam asked, patting her sister's arm. "It's not the least bit funny. I do feel obligated to say, however, that when my boys get sticky or cranky or mess their breeches, you give them back to me. And you don't have to hose down their high chairs or clean up the spilled orange juice. You've never walked the floor with them when they had tummy aches or had one of them spit up all over you. Having kids isn't all sweetness and light. And cute little babies grow up into sassy adolescents with pimples and speeding violations. You've got to love them then, too."

"I know that," Brenda said, her tone irritated.

"I knew it, too," Pam went on, putting Tommy in the playpen with his bottle full of orange juice. "But I'm discovering that knowing it and living it are two different things. I learn anew each day that one must pay for the joys of motherhood."

"Don't lecture me, sis."

Pam brought the coffeepot to the table for a refill. If she wasn't supposed to lecture, then she'd just listen. "Okay, sweetie, I can see this is an enormous problem for you. So what are you going to do about it?"

At this, Brenda put her head down on the table and started crying, great gulping sobs that shook her shoulders. Scott came running down the hall and stood in the doorway wide-eyed at the sight of his aunt crying.

Brenda raised a mascara-streaked face and gulped back her sobs. "I'm okay, honey," she told Scott. He came to her and allowed himself to be picked up and held.

"I made a promise to George before we got married," Brenda said, sniffing. "I can't do anything about *it*. I have to go through life *empty*!"

Pam could almost smile at her sister's melodramatics if the subject were not such a serious one. "Maybe George would change his mind if he knew how much you wanted a child. He loves you very much, Brenda. I can't imagine him turning you down."

"Marty went along with your getting pregnant," Brenda reminded her sister. "He didn't want a baby, but you had your heart set on it, and he finally said okay. Right?"

"Something like that," Pam admitted. "He finally gave in and said go ahead, but just not to expect any help out of him."

"And your marriage was never the same again. Marty was resentful. Before, you had doted on him, arranged his life for him, mothered him, never missed his performances. Then suddenly, you threw yourself into motherhood, and he was playing second fiddle. I think he felt terribly left out."

"I know that now. I should have been more sensitive to his feelings. But in my own defense, I might add that part of the problem was that Marty was immature, a spoiled baby himself. I think a mature man like George could adjust. And I think you would do a better job than I did making your husband feel that he was still very important to you and that you needed him more, not less."

"I don't know, Pam." Scott was starting to squirm, and Brenda allowed him to slide from her lap. "I'm frightened that a baby would ruin a really good marriage. I made a bargain with George, and it would be unfair to him after I promised."

"Can't you just talk to him?" Pam asked, taking a piece of doughnut from the high-chair tray and nibbling on it.

"Then he'd know I was having second thoughts if I wanted to discuss it," Brenda said. "What if he said it was all right when he didn't really mean it?"

"The big sister has no answer to that one," Pam confessed. "I don't want you to end up like me—a single mother raising a kid or kids alone. But it seems that at some point, you and George have to talk it out."

"Maybe so. But in the meantime, I'm going to try to stop thinking about babies all the time. I'm going to make George a pie this afternoon, fuss over him, be grateful I have such a loving husband. Did you know that he's always leaving me little love notes? I find them in my lingerie drawer, in the sugar canister. Can you believe a man like that? He's started having his business lunches at the Zodiac Room so he can show off his wife."

Pam had to agree. George did indeed love his wife. He was a prince among men. And she thought he might even have the makings of a father, but who was to say? A child would certainly disrupt his carefully ordered life.

"Do you have to rush off? Can't you stay and talk while I clean some shrimp?" Pam asked. "You could even help."

"Yuck," Brenda said. "Seafood should only be ordered in a restaurant and never viewed in its natural state." But she got up and tied on an apron. "Isn't Joel coming today? You haven't mentioned him much lately. Is he still working for you?"

"Yes, but not as much. He's taking a heavy load this semester, and it seemed like he was here too much anyway."

"Oh? And what made you come to that realization?"

"Nothing special," Pam said, getting the pan of boiled shrimp from the refrigerator, searching for paring knives. Then she stopped and took a sip of water to wash down the lump in her throat.

It was Brenda's turn to pat. "You're doing the right thing, sis. Nothing could be accomplished by letting yourself get more involved with him. It was keeping you from getting on with your life."

"You mean going out?"

"Yeah. Meeting men your own age."

"I don't have time for that," Pam said, handing her sister a knife.

"One always makes time for the things one really wants. You're just hung up on the kid."

"And just who would I go out with anyway?" Pam picked up a shrimp and peeled off its shell.

"Robert Fenwick still asks about you."

"I'm sure he's just being polite."

"Are you in love with Joel?"

"A little," Pam admitted. "I don't know what to do about it. I think about him constantly, and I don't want to talk about it because I cry these days at the drop of a hat. Peel, Brenda."

"Why don't you go out with Robert, or some other man?" Brenda picked up a shrimp and made a face. "Get some perspective, sis. You've all but lived with Joel this summer. Find out what it's like to be with your peers again. Why don't I see what Robert is doing next weekend? We can all celebrate your birthday together."

Her birthday. Thirty-one years of age. A notch on the march toward forty. Joel didn't know she had a birthday next week. She had let him think there was nine years difference in their ages rather than closer to ten. She was sensitive even about an extra eight months.

"I don't feel like celebrating," she told her sister.

Pam spent the afternoon making quiche, something she felt she could do in her sleep. She didn't forget the salt anymore, and her crust was flaky enough to win a prize. And she took pride in a job well done, but her catering business didn't have much meaning without Joel around to share in decisions, triumphs and failures.

Things had not been the same after they made love, however, even though making love to Joel had been wonderful beyond belief. Pam wasn't just a little in love with him, as she had told her sister. She loved Joel with a deepness and a purity that was both dazzlingly beautiful and exquisitely painful. She loved him enough to back away. Her presence in his life was confusing him. He thought he wanted to move in with her and bury himself in the bosom of a ready-made family. Joel had been a homeless, unwanted child, and he gravitated to her house, her family like a starving man to food. But someday Joel would be just like Brenda was now—overcome with an incredible biological and emotional urge to have a child of his own. He would look at the fading woman at his side and the children fathered by another man and wonder what the hell he had gotten himself into. When she was menopausal, Joel would be at his prime. It was only to be expected that he would someday want his own family, his own children, a wife his own age.

It was best to stop things before she again faced total devastation in her life.

"Why can't we just ride with things and see where we end up," Joel had argued the morning after they made love, after Pam told him no, he could not give up his apartment and move in with her.

"Because I'm too old and have too much responsibility to take risks," she answered.

"I think you're just gun-shy," Joel had said, hands on boyishly slim hips. He was standing in the middle of her bedroom, chest and feet bare. She was sitting on the bed, the sheets and blankets tangled from lovemaking. "If I was a thirty-five-year-old divorced man with children of my own, you would say that you couldn't get involved with me because extra children would make your life too complicated."

"Perhaps," Pam admitted, tugging to wrap the sheet more tightly about her. Last night she was delighted to be unclothed in his presence. Now she felt shy. She ran her fingers through her hair, knowing she looked like a wreck.

"And you're being sexist," he challenged. "You wouldn't think anything about a man nine years older than his lady love."

"That's different."

"Why?"

Pam struggled for an answer. "I can't deal with hypothetical," she said. "I can only deal with myself and how I feel."

"Can you deny what happened in that bed was something special?"

"No. But I don't trust anything that wonderful. I can only trust hard work and guarded feelings. Last night was very out of character for me, so don't be misled. And if the boys had been in the next room, it would have been different. And the boys will be in the next room for a number of years." She dried her stupid tears on the corner of the sheet.

"Life itself is a risk, Pam," he challenged, apparently unmoved by her tears. His beautiful hair was mussed, but on him it looked adorable, like the boys when they woke up in the morning. His body was so lean, Pam doubted if she could get his jeans over her hips. "Put your money on life," he said. "The worst that can happen is you stumble and fall. Then you get up and try again."

"I fell once. It nearly killed me."

"You want a sure thing, and there's no such thing out there."

"Yes, but there is such a thing as hedging your bets."

"Why are you so mistrustful of feelings? Why can't you follow your heart?"

"I did once. It got broken. Can you promise me you won't ever break my heart, Joel? Can you?"

"Hell, Pam, I might walk out the front door and get struck by lightning or run over by a truck. We live in an imperfect world without a single fairy godmother or gilt-edged guarantee."

"See," Pam said, taking perverse pleasure in proving her point. "You can't promise. You aren't sure yourself. You just want to try it on for size."

"And what's the matter with that?" he demanded.

"Nothing," she had said, "if you're young and resilient and only have yourself to worry about."

But, oh, how she wanted to follow her heart, to throw caution to the wind and bring him into her bed and her life for as long as it could last.

Every night she faced the same struggle. If he knew how close she came to telephoning him in the night, saying, "Come to me, please, and stay for as long as you will," if he knew that, maybe he wouldn't have finally shrugged his beautiful shoulders and allowed her to back away into "friendship." But then, maybe he was afraid of getting what he asked for. As kind and loving as he was, the prospect of living with her and the boys must surely raise all kinds of doubts in his barely adult mind.

Living together was a way of putting off a decision about marriage, and he had been around them enough to see how difficult it was conducting a business among young children. And in the future, did he really want to use what money he made with his hard-earned college education to help support an inherited family? Guys his age bought fast cars and stereo equipment. Would he really want to put money away for Scott's and Tommy's education? Buy life insurance? Make car payments and house payments? Pay the orthodontist's bills? Real life wasn't lived in a bedroom under a blanket of passion. That was only a small part.

But, oh, such a lovely part, such a seductive part that interfered with perception and made you think life would be exciting and rosy if only you could go to bed every night of your life with that one special person. Part of Pam felt that way, just as she was sure part of Joel did, too. If the lovemaking hadn't been so special, so infused with such a meant-to-be quality, maybe they could have kissed and said goodbye—or had a small affair, then kissed and said goodbye—and gotten on with their lives relatively unscathed.

PAM LET BRENDA TALK her into going out with Robert Fenwick again. "But it absolutely is not to be a birthday celebration," Pam said. "If a horde of waiters and waitresses bearing a cupcake with a candle gather around our table singing 'Happy Birthday to Pam,' I will never forgive you if I live to be a hundred."

"I promise," Brenda said. "Get a sitter."

Pam arranged for Cindy to come—with Paul, of course. She'd have to remember to buy Diet Coke and microwave popcorn. Both teenagers had lost a notice-able amount of weight but seemed to have reached a plateau, seemingly content to be not-too-fat as long as they had each other.

Joel and Pam spent Saturday afternoon preparing for an engagement party the next evening and going over the calendar for the next month, arranging their work schedule around Joel's classes and study time.

At five-thirty Pam started looking at the clock. She needed to get ready for her date.

Joel noticed. "You got plans for the evening?"

"Oh, I'm just going out with George and Brenda," she said.

"You want me to stay with the boys? I can study here after they're in bed."

"That's awfully nice of you to offer," she said nervously. "But I've already arranged for Cindy and Paul to come over."

"Oh? How come you didn't ask me first? I work for nothing."

"I thought you might have plans for a Saturday night. You know, a date or something."

"I don't, but I'll tell you, Pam, I may next Saturday night. I'm getting tired of being kept at arm's length. I wish we hadn't ever made love if this is how it's going to be. I go home to that barren one-room apartment and lie on that narrow bed and remember, and it's making me crazy. It's torture for me to be around you and not be allowed even to touch you, and I'm not sure how much longer I can stand to be such a masochistic fool, sticking around here and torturing myself, wanting you, getting more involved with Scott and Tommy." He pushed his chair back. "Well, have a nice evening. I'm leaving."

Pam dialed her sister's number.

"I have a headache," Pam said.

''Take two aspirin and get dressed. You're not getting out of this date, Pam. I've made reservations at Alexander's. Robert broke another date to join us. Does my blue silk dress fit?''

''I haven't tried it on yet.''

''Well, if it doesn't, I know that white outfit will.''

''Brenda, I'm just not up for this.''

''Please, honey. Just see how it feels to be courted by a mature man. You might discover you've really been missing something. Please, as a favor for me.''

Her sister's blue silk was too tight in the hips, but the white knit was quite flattering. It had a full skirt and draped top that made her waist look smaller than it was. That cheered her a bit, but she couldn't stop thinking about the hurt look on Joel's face. She believed him when he said he would have a date next Saturday night. And she was having one this Saturday night. It was all for the best, but she wanted to throw herself onto the bed and cry.

''Are you and Joel going someplace special?'' Cindy asked when she saw Pam.

''I'm going out with my sister and her husband,'' Pam said.

But it was Robert who rang the doorbell, looking darkly attractive, mature, elegant, rich.

''You're even lovelier than I remember,'' Robert said smoothly, handing her a single, long-stemmed rose with a courtly little bow.

Pam was terribly aware of Cindy and Paul staring from the living room. What if they told Joel? But then, that shouldn't matter. She wasn't engaged to Joel. She should have told him herself this afternoon that she was going out with a man. There was absolutely no reason for this subterfuge—except she was hopelessly in love with Joel and more confused than she had ever been in her life. And if he knew about tonight, he most assuredly would get himself a date next weekend. And Pam hated whoever that date might be. She would be a pretty, fresh, unencumbered young thing with slim hips and firm breasts. She would charm Joel into forgetting about that thirty-year-old woman and her two sons. Thirty-*one*, Pam silently corrected herself. She was a mixed-up idiot of a woman.

Robert glanced around her small living room without comment. Barney looked up from the sofa and wagged his tail. A row of stuffed animals lined the coffee table. Pam thought of Robert's designer-showcase apartment and wished she had at least put the toys away.

Pam introduced Robert to Cindy and Paul. Cindy took the rose and put it in water.

As they walked out to Robert's sleek Chrysler, Pam could feel Cindy's and Paul's watching eyes. She felt like a despicable traitor going off with the enemy.

Robert caught her up on his life as they drove to George and Brenda's apartment. He had followed her suggestion and hired the incredible Miss Duff to work for him.

"I can't tell you what a difference that woman has made in my life. The girls adore her and are better-behaved than they've ever been. She helps them with their schoolwork and helps me keep my life in order."

Brenda and George had cocktails and canapés ready to serve. Brenda gave Pam an approving wink. The borrowed dress looked good.

The two couples seated themselves on matching white sofas and sipped their drinks from handsome gold-rimmed glasses. They discussed the gubernatorial race, world hunger and the acting ability of Meryl Streep.

George told a droll joke about a politician and the Pope. It was all very adult, very sophisticated.

Pam called home. She'd forgotten to tell Cindy and Paul where she would be.

Over dinner later at the restaurant, Robert was attentive, asking Pam about her business, her sons. "Brenda tells me you've hired an assistant."

"Yes. He's a very clever young college boy," Pam said, "and like your Miss Duff, he's turned my life around. The boys love him, and I'm actually making enough money to support myself. I don't know what I'd do without him."

Brenda frowned and looked across the table, her eyes issuing a warning. *Don't get maudlin. Don't ruin this evening that I planned for you.*

"I know what you mean," Robert was saying. "I depend so much on Miss Duff, it scares me. She even has entertained for me a couple of times."

The meal was good, the wine perfect. Pam knew she should pay more attention to the ingredients of the excellent veal, but she was too distracted. She shouldn't be here. She and Robert were beating a dead horse.

At the end of the meal, a lovely little pastry bearing a tiny lighted candle was placed in front of Pam. There was no singing.

"Happy birthday, sis. I had to have a little something to mark the occasion," Brenda said, handing Pam a small gift-wrapped box.

Pam blew out the candle. The gift was a pair of lovely gold earrings. Pam kissed her sister, then her brother-in-law. They were both dears, and she was lucky to have them.

Robert handed her a birthday card. Enclosed were two adult and four children's tickets to the Greater Dallas Professional Rodeo Round-up.

After they dropped George and Brenda off at their apartment building and drove north toward Pam's house, she asked Robert if he was in love with Miss Duff.

"Why, are you in love with your assistant?"

"Now, wouldn't that be a stupid thing for me to do—fall in love with a college boy?"

Robert glanced at her face. "Do I sense a problem here?"

"We were talking about Miss Duff," Pam reminded him.

"I think about Miss Duff a lot—you know, look forward to going home at night because she's there. When her hair is not in the awful bun, she looks rather lovely. She has smooth skin and wonderful green eyes. But she's careful to maintain an employer-employee distance between us. And besides, she's older than I am."

"How much?"

"I don't know. At least seven or eight years. Maybe more. I suppose if it weren't for that, I'd try to court her. But I'd be afraid someone would think she was the twins' grandmother instead of my lady friend."

"Don't flatter yourself," Pam said dryly. "You don't look *that* young."

"And you don't look *that* old," he said.

"I'm not sure about the rodeo," Pam said. "The boys might like it, but I think it's pointless for us to pretend that we want to go out with each other."

"Or maybe we need to get the stars out of our eyes and look at things more realistically."

Pam invited him in for a cup of coffee. When they walked in the front door, Joel was stretched out on the sofa.

Joel stood and politely shook hands with Robert as Pam somehow managed to introduce them. The two men eyed each other, Joel taking in Robert's elegant attire, Robert taking in Joel's jeans, ratty athletic shoes and T-shirt with its Budweiser crest.

Joel could have passed for eighteen.

"I think I'll pass on the coffee," Robert told Pam. "I'll call you about the rodeo."

"What rodeo?" Joel said after the front door closed.

"He's offered to take the boys and me when he and his daughters go."

"How sweet."

"Where are Cindy and Paul?"

"Her dad got sick. Her mom got scared and wanted her at home."

"Nothing serious, I hope."

"I just talked to Paul. He was checked at the emergency room and sent home after a lecture on stress and smoking."

"That's a relief. Well, would *you* like a cup of coffee?"

"No. Are you going out with that guy again?"

"I don't know. Are you going out with someone next Saturday night?"

"I don't know."

Chapter Eight

When Pam answered the door, she was a bit shocked to see her brother-in-law standing on the front porch.

"Why, George, what a surprise. Come in."

"Thank you. I hope this isn't too much of a bother. I know I should have called first, but I was sitting there in my office thinking about things, and I thought, by golly, maybe Pam is the person I need to talk to about this. I was halfway here before I remembered I hadn't called. I'm afraid if I don't talk to someone soon, I may go a bit daft."

"No problem," Pam said. "We'll have coffee. Or would you rather have tea?"

"No, no. Coffee's fine," he said, standing awkwardly in the middle of the entry hall, looking impeccable, as always, in his gray pin-striped suit and carefully knotted tie.

What could he want, Pam wondered. She couldn't remember George ever coming to see her without Brenda. And to arrive in the middle of the afternoon, unannounced—well, it was peculiar.

"Go sit down," Pam said, gesturing toward the living room. "I'll put the coffee on."

"Oh, if you don't mind, I'll just sit with you in the kitchen. That's one of the things I like about your household, sitting in the kitchen with the boys' high chairs and the good smells, cookies in a jar, drinking coffee out of mugs instead of china cups. You even have a window with a tree outside. One feels rather cozy and comfy. I've sat in living rooms and dining rooms all my life, now I'm wondering if Brenda and I shouldn't put a table in our kitchen—a round one like yours—and buy some mugs. Coffee gets cold so quickly in china cups."

"I'll send Scott and Tommy over to supply the crumbs for the floor," she said, smiling over her shoulder.

"Where are the boys?" he asked, looking around the empty kitchen.

"They're still taking their naps," Pam explained, surprised to see the disappointed look on George's face. "Scott ought to be awake shortly. He's getting to be such a 'big boy,' he only stays down an hour or so."

"I'd enjoy seeing the little chap," George said, taking off his coat and carefully hanging it over the back of a chair. "He and I have become friends. I gave him his bath once, you know."

"Yes," Pam said as she measured the coffee. "I remember. The night we hung the wallpaper."

"The little tyke just stood there and let me take off his clothes and lift him into the tub. And we counted his rubber toys and decided what color they all were. I think the boy's bright. I've discussed this with some very knowledgeable people, and it's quite clever for a child under three to be able to count like that—I mean not just by rote but to understand that four means four objects and five means five and so on. Then after we did the counting and color bit, Scott started getting silly and splashing and laughing. A rather funny sight, you know, to see this charming little naked creature, all rosy and wet and totally unembarrassed to be bathing in front of another person, sitting there having a lovely time making the water splash.''

"Yes, children usually love bath time,'' Pam said, slipping into the chair across from George. "Of course, Scott's not supposed to splash in the bathtub, and he was taking advantage of you. Kids get smart in that way, too.''

"Oh, no,'' George protested. "It was no trouble to wipe up the water with a towel, and the little fellow was having such a fine time. We poured in some bubble bath, and I helped him make bubbles. Then when I got him out of the tub, he was very patient about me drying him off and putting on his pajamas.''

Surely George had other things more important than sitting here discussing the joys of giving Scott a bath. She certainly did, Pam thought with a glance at the clock. She tried to take advantage of the boys' nap time to get her work done. When they woke up, she needed to run errands, and right now, she should be stuffing mushrooms.

Pam pushed the cookie jar in George's direction. It was full of chocolate-chip cookies, Joel's favorite, except Joel hadn't been around to have any of them.

"My, but these are good,'' George said, examining the cookie he had just bitten into. "I say, does Brenda know how to make these?''

"Sure. You could, too. The recipe's on the back of the chocolate-chips package.'' How funny, Pam thought. Brenda had been making scones and tea biscuits, when George loves good old chocolate chip.

"Why, there's little Scott!'' George said, his face lighting up.

Scott was standing in the doorway, still clutching his favorite 'blankie,' a former crib blanket that had once been a fluffy yellow with satin binding and now looked like a dingy rag in spite of regular washings.

Still groggy, hair mussed and with the marks of his pillow on his cheeks, Scott padded across the floor to his uncle. With great uncertainty, George held out his arms, indicating that the boy would be welcome on his lap. Scott looked at his mother. Pam nodded, and he presented himself to his Uncle George for picking up.

Looking as though he had just been granted an award, George lifted boy and blanket onto his lap. He smoothed Scott's hair, then took one of Scott's bare feet in his hand and held it out for examination, as though he had never really looked at a not-quite-three-year-old foot before. Scott looked up at his uncle's face then apparently decided some action was required on his part and wiggled his toes.

Pam got two mugs out of the cupboard and poured the coffee. Then she got Scott a glass of apple juice.

"So, to what do I owe the honor of this visit?" Pam asked, reseating herself.

"Well," George said, clearing his throat, "I am sure you are aware that Brenda and I agreed during our courtship that, given our respective ambitions and desired life-style, children would be an intrusion. We have both been fairly adamant about this decision, and it has been reinforced over the years of our marriage when we have been around small children and seen the havoc they bring to homes and schedules and even marriages—including your own."

Pam took a sip of her coffee. "Yes, I know you agreed not to have children," she said, "and that it was a mutual decision."

George absently patted Scott's thigh. Scott was holding his Tommee Tippee cup in both hands, downing his apple juice with gusto.

"And our life has been so perfect," George went on in his verbose British way. "We have a tastefully decorated home, a circle of interesting friends, satisfying careers. We travel, play tennis and handball with a vengeance, are involved with the Theater Guild. And I hope I don't sound immodest when I say that Brenda and I are considered to be an attractive couple and admired for our style. I take great pride in having one of the most beautiful women in Dallas as my wife, and I am still captivated by her beauty, her..."

Pam held up her hand. "Yes. I get the picture. Life is perfect. So, what's bothering you?"

"Well, perhaps it has to do with getting older. Maybe it is my friendship with young Scott here. But I have become increasingly aware of this...of this yearning to...I think rather frequently of late about..."

"You've changed your mind and want a kid," Pam said, helping him along.

"Well, not exactly," George said, wrinkling his high, aristocratic brow. "I'm not completely certain that is what I really want. Perhaps it's just a passing biological urge—you know, some sort of despicable macho desire to see my wife pregnant just to show the world I am capable of such. And I worry a bit about what might befall the white upholstery in our living room and our collection of Waterford crystal should a child enter our lives. I even wonder if Brenda would recoup her lovely figure should she carry a child. But I also wonder if perhaps I was hasty in making a commitment to a childless marriage and not holding the door open to renegotiation at a future date."

"So what's the problem?" Pam asked. "Talk to her. Ask Brenda if she still feels the same way. You might be surprised."

George added sugar to his cooling coffee and took a sip. "I know that's what I should do, but I'm full of doubt. I love Brenda so very much, and I don't want her to think that I am in any way unhappy with our life together, that I am not perfectly content having just the two of us. Wanting a child implies I'm dissatisfied, don't you think?"

"I'd never thought of it that way before," Pam said. "Most people think of marriage and family in one breath. You and Brenda are unusual in that you've separated the two processes. All I can say, George, is that wanting children is a perfectly normal desire. Not wanting them seems stranger to me."

"But I look at you, dear Pam, and see the hardship two youngsters have brought to your life, and I am rather ashamed that I might wish such on my wife."

Pam shook her head. "Oh, come off of it, George. Don't overanalyze. People have been having kids since day one. They're no picnic, but my boys are precious beyond belief. And I would hope that Brenda's situation would be drastically different from mine. I hope she wouldn't wake up some morning with a note on her pillow and no husband to help her raise this hypothetical child."

"Oh, good heavens, no," George said, appalled. "You know I would never leave Brenda. She is my life. I love her so much that I'm desperately afraid of doing anything to upset the life we have created together. Our life could not be improved upon, and I feel somewhat ashamed that I'm even thinking about changing anything. A baby might ruin everything."

"Well, babies are never perfect, that's for sure. But if your life 'could not be improved upon,' why are you sitting in my kitchen having this discussion?"

Scott squirmed around on George's lap and touched his uncle's necktie. "Yellow," he said.

"Yes, by golly, it's yellow," George said.

"Give your Uncle George a hug and a kiss, Scott." Pam watched as her son obliged, putting his arms around George's neck and offering a puckered little mouth for kissing. George kissed Scott with a smack, then touched his nephew's smooth cheek, gazed at his perfect skin and the rim of dark lashes around large curious brown eyes. Poor George, Pam thought. That was unfair of her. Nothing was more seductive than a sweet, loving child.

"You know that sometimes he can be a real terror, don't you?" she felt obliged to add. "His latest trick is putting everything in the toilet, including an almost-full bottle of the only good cologne I own. There are moments when I'd like to send him back."

She could save her words. George wasn't listening.

"Do you remember how many this is?" he asked, holding up four fingers.

Scott held up four fingers of his own. "Four," he said triumphantly then added eagerly, "I can jump real high."

Pam wondered what her role in all this should be. Should she tell George that Brenda thought she might want a baby? Should she tell Brenda that George thought he might want a baby? The whole thing was so ridiculous that Pam wanted to laugh out loud. It read like the script of a bad television soap opera.

But then, Brenda and George had both come to her in confidence. It was not her place to interfere.

"Talk to her," she told George. "Maybe Brenda is just waiting for an opportunity to reconsider the baby issue.

She has spent a lot of time with Scott and Tommy, and perhaps she realizes that children are an important part of married life and is having some of the same kind of thoughts that you are.''

"You really think so?"

"Sure. Why don't you stop by a florist and buy her some flowers. Take her out tonight to a lovely restaurant. Wine her and dine her. Then, when you make love to her, look into her eyes and ask her if she's ever wanted a baby to grow out of your shared love."

"But what about our bargain?" George asked helplessly as he gave Scott's thigh more pats.

"Good grief, George! You're being tiresome. Just ask her! The worst she can say is no."

IT WAS HOT FOR OCTOBER, even a Dallas October. Joel had tried studying without the air conditioner, but even at eleven o'clock, it was too hot in his small apartment without it. Unfortunately, when it wasn't ovenlike outside, the unit made the room so cold that Joel was forced to put on a sweater.

Wearing a sweater and running the air conditioner was stupid, but that was just one of the things about this place that annoyed him. The walls of the small, drab room seemed to be closer and drabber than they used to be. The smells and sounds from the restaurant below were more distracting than before. It was harder than ever to ignore the blinking neon light across the street.

His chair scraped against the bare wooden floor as he pushed it back from the table. He stretched then got up and walked around the room a few times to revive himself before stopping in front of the kitchen cupboard to scrounge around for something to nibble on. The crackers he found were stale, but he ate them anyway. Then he forced himself once again to pick up his economics text-book and began rereading segments in the chapter on entitlement programs that he had underlined in previous study sessions. It was heavy going.

This entire semester had been heavy going. At times, Joel wondered if he had overstepped himself in signing up for twenty college hours. Never had he been forced to study so much and so hard. And never had studying been more difficult for him to accomplish.

Studying at Pam's kitchen table was no longer possible. The boys were a distraction, but he could manage that, and besides they were usually in bed by eight-thirty or nine. It was the presence of Pam herself that caused his mind to wander out of accountancy and finance and into all sorts of other places, including the double bed in the room at the end of the hall. He had spent one night there and every other night since reliving it.

But after they made love, Pam had backed away from him. At first Joel wanted to believe it was Tommy's illness that made her so uptight. She had thrown herself into nursing her younger son back to health, sleeping with him at night, hovering about his crib in the day-time, rocking him by the hour. Joel had gotten behind the first couple of weeks of the semester and never really caught up because he had been so busy keeping the catering service going, allowing Pam to cling to her baby and convince herself that he was alive and well and going to stay that way. How it had pleased Joel to be able to do that for her. He felt like the man of the house taking care of his little family.

And he had convinced himself that Pam would eventually change her mind about his moving in with her. After they made love, Joel had gotten out of bed that morning thinking he would pack up his few possessions and move in with her and the boys that very day. But she had put a stop to that notion, sitting up in bed, a sheet modestly wrapped around her body, informing him that, no, he was not going to move in with her and that she cared too much for him ever to allow him back in her bed.

Women! Were they all as confused as Pam, he wondered. But then he really didn't care about the state of other female minds. It was Pam and Pam only he was obsessed with. And part of the obsession was his overwhelming need to move in with her, to *live* with her, to shave in her bathroom, wake up in the morning in her bed. But he, too, had his doubts. At the same time he stood in her bedroom arguing with her, Joel wondered if Pam wasn't right about everything. Maybe they were worlds apart in what they wanted and needed out of a relationship.

Pam wanted promises, guarantees, happily ever after. Joel was too much of a realist to believe that anything was forever. He had spent his young life staying for a time at a place then moving on. He had lived in more than a dozen foster homes after his grandmother died and soon learned to consider each new home temporary. The time of parting didn't bother him so much when he knew it was coming.

And Joel had learned about the wisdom of not counting on things even earlier from his mother. Each time his mother called him or came to see him, she would promise to send for him as soon as she was on her feet financially, as soon as the new man in her life had gotten used to the idea of having her kid with them. Joel always enjoyed seeing her or talking to her on the phone, but he learned not to count the days until they would live together again. He still remembered how his mother always smelled of gardenias and how wonderful it felt to sit in her lap there in his grandma's living room and listen to her soft, Southern voice telling him how it was going to be someday.

Someday. It had been a long time since he had believed in someday.

Of course, his mother did send for him once, when she lived in Shreveport and worked in a shoe store. But she had gotten sick, and his grandmother came to get him. Grandma was sick, too, and had died not long after that, and Joel had only heard from his mother a few more times. He didn't know where she was now or even if she was alive.

What Joel did believe in was living for the moment. He wondered if his willingness to assume a parenting role for two little boys had something to do with the fact that they weren't really his, and if he needed to walk away, it wouldn't matter quite as much as if he'd fathered them himself. That thought scared him. That was the thing Pam was most afraid of, and with good cause, apparently. While Joel did indeed want to move into her house and love her and her two children, he did not know if he'd still want to be there a year from now, five years from now. But he remembered how horrified he had been when he learned that her ex-husband had walked out on his own two kids. On Scott and Tommy! Joel didn't understand how the guy could ever look at himself in the mirror again. And, intellectually, Joel could see that a lifelong commitment to a relationship was the ideal. Could it be he was changing, or was the terrible need he felt to be with Pam giving him fuzzy vision?

His thoughts went round and round, and his desire for Pam sexually had kept him on a nervous high the whole semester. It was hard for him to concentrate, and cold showers didn't help a bit. He wondered how that myth ever got started. The fact that he still had his head above water scholastically was a minor miracle. The discipline that had come so easily before Pam arrived in his life now continually eluded him. His thoughts wandered like someone demented. Images of making love to her would flash across his mind in the middle of the night and make him groan out loud. And there were other images—of funny little boys with sweet-smelling skin who loved to roll around on the floor with him in mock wrestling matches. There had been other little kids before, in that long succession of foster homes, and he had liked them, too. What made these two different was they were *her* kids. Yeah, he thought too damned much about her kids, her house, her bed, her body, her soft voice and sweet sighs.

She was too old, just like she said. He should marry a younger woman and have children of his own.

Stop it, man, he told himself and went to get a beer out of his refrigerator. A beer would calm him.

He managed to go over two more chapters before the solution to all of his problems appeared to him in a blinding flash.

Joel paced the room again, examining his idea for flaws, warming to it.

He looked at the clock. It was past midnight, and he still needed to read three more chapters. He got another beer and seated himself at the table.

But he couldn't stop thinking about his brilliant idea. He wanted to share it with Pam, see her smile, feel her arms around his neck as she thanked him. He wanted to carry her back down the hall to the bed. The boys would be long asleep. He would close her bedroom door, and they would make passionate, beautiful, soul-searing love.

Then he would have to get up and study a couple more hours, but his mind would be clearer. Everything would fall into place, and he would march into that classroom and make a solid A on that test.

He dialed Pam's number.

"Hello," her sleepy voice answered.

"Can I come over? I need to talk to you in the worst way."

"Joel! It's late. Is something wrong?"

"No, something's right for a change."

"And it can't wait until morning?"

"No. I'll flunk my economics test if it does."

"Have you been drinking?"

"Naw. Well, just a couple of beers. How about it? I can be there in fifteen minutes."

Joel turned off the air conditioner. It could get hot as Hades in here for all he cared. He would be with Pam.

PAM TOOK THE NIGHT LOCK OFF the front door and let him in. She had dressed in a loose-fitting T-shirt and jeans and had put on a touch of makeup. Joel felt disappointed. He wanted a bathrobe-clad Pam, like before.

"It's too late for coffee," she said. "You want cocoa or something?"

"I just want to talk." He took her hand and led her into the living room. Scott's cars were lined up on the windowsill. A Dr. Seuss book was open on the coffee table. *Green Eggs and Ham.* Joel had read it to the boys so many times, he could almost recite it from memory.

"You want guarantees," Joel began in a rush as they sat down. "You've been walked out on before, and you worry about being hurt again, and you worry about the future—taking care of your family, making your business prosper. Right?"

"Yes," Pam said suspiciously.

Her eyes were exactly the shade of brown as her hair. Brown eyes had always been Joel's favorite. They were so expressive, so sensual. And Pam's were rimmed with thick lashes with high-arched eyebrows. And when such rich brown eyes and hair, such thick, dark lashes were combined with a fair, smooth skin, the results were lovely beyond words.

"Yes?" Pam said again.

"I'm a terrific business partner, aren't I?"

This time she just nodded.

"In time, we can rent a building, set up our own catering kitchen, bakery, own our own glassware, punch bowls, plates, silverware, tablecloths, the works. Right?"

"Perhaps."

"In fact, I think we eventually should buy a wonderful old mansion and restore it, operate our business out of it and rent out the home for meetings, weddings, parties—which we cater, of course."

"You're way past me now," she said.

"But it sounds like a good idea, doesn't it?"

"Yes, I suppose. But I doubt if we could swing a deal like that. Is this why you came here in the middle of the night, to talk about buying punch bowls and an old house?"

"No. I got sidetracked. I came here to propose."

Pam blinked. "Do what?"

"Propose—marriage. I want you to marry me. Will you marry me?"

Joel got down on his knees, took her hands in his and said it again. "I love you, Pam. Will you please marry me and put an end to all this agony?"

Pam pulled her hands away. "What in the world brought this on? A week ago all you wanted to do was move in. Where did *marriage* come from? And get up off your knees to answer me. You're making me very nervous. How many beers did you have anyway?''

"You want commitment," Joel said, pushing Dr. Seuss aside and sitting on the coffee table in front of her and reaching again for her hands. "A marriage license is as close as I can come to that gilt-edged guarantee."

"I had one of those once, remember? The commitment comes from the man himself, not from a piece of paper."

"And you don't think I'm ready to make that sort of commitment?"

Pam shook her head slowly back and forth. "It would never work. You don't know what you're saying."

"Do you love me?" he challenged.

Pam started to get up, but Joel pulled her back. "Well, do you?" he demanded.

"Damn you!"

"Is that a yes?"

She was crying. Joel wanted to take her in his arms, to comfort her, to kiss her tears. But he had to get all this said first, and he settled for kissing her hands, her palms, her wrists. This whole scenario was coming out all wrong. He had rehearsed it on the way over, but Pam wasn't saying her lines right.

"Pam," he repeated gently. "Do you love me?"

"Of course, I love you," she said angrily, jerking her hands away and rubbing away her tears. "I love you more every time I see you, every time I don't see you. Being with you now makes me hurt with love. But I'm thirty-*one* years old. I had another damned birthday, and I'm not even thirty anymore. But I was doing just fine until you came along and made me feel older. Just think, when you're thirty, I'll be *forty*!"

"And when you're fifty, I'll be forty. When you're sixty, I'll be fifty. Shall I go on?"

Pam held up her hands for him to stop. "No. I feel old enough the way it is. But more is at stake than love. You'd be crazy to marry me. The novelty of all this would wear off eventually. Then you'd end up feeling like a cad when you left me, so spare us both the pain, okay?"

"I admit that I'd prefer living together first in a trial relationship to make sure we're both as in love as it seems, both willing to hang in there for the long term. But I can understand your reluctance to get involved with a man who has thoughts like that. So I asked myself, what would make me feel totally committed and what would make you believe in me? Part of the reason you think that I'll leave you is because you assume that I would want to have children of my own someday. Right?"

"It's only normal," Pam agreed with a sigh. "Even Brenda and George, who have sworn for years that they didn't want kids, are both having second thoughts."

"Well, then, you marry me," Joel said with a big smile. "I'll adopt Scott and Tommy. Then we'll have a baby of our own."

Pam's mouth actually fell open. She stared at him, the strangest expression taking over her face.

"We'll do *what*?" And she all but leaped from the sofa and backed across the room. "You've got to be crazy. There's no way this tired old body is going to have another baby. Two is my limit."

No, she definitely wasn't saying her lines right, Joel thought as he followed her across the room. "We can wait a couple of years until the boys are older and your 'tired old body' has time to rest up. But the more I think about it, the more I know this is the answer. Surely you realize *I'm* not the sort of man who would abandon my own kid. Having my baby would bind you to me like burned beans to an iron skillet. The more I think about it, the more I think this is the solution. Your guarantee, my commitment. And besides, when you love someone, it seems kind of like the next step. I know now that I don't want to go through life without having a baby with you. You're the only woman I'd ever want to have a baby with. Really, Pam.''

Pam backed into the hallway. What was the matter with her? Did she think she was going to get pregnant just being in the same room with him?

''This would be funny if it wasn't so stupid,'' she said, her head shaking back and forth. ''You want a baby. Brenda wants a baby. George wants a baby. Everyone wants a baby but me!''

''You just need time to get used to the idea,'' Joel said hopefully.

''I've had almost two years to reinforce my decision that two were all the children I can handle. Good God, what a mess I've gotten myself into,'' she said, alternating between holding her face between her hands and waving her arms. ''I've fallen in love with a *boy* who wants to father a child with me! Well the answer is no. Absolutely no. Love does not conquer all, Joel Bynum. Another baby means more money, more stretch marks, more worry, more years invested in child-rearing. Life is supposed to come in stages, and there's a time for child-rearing and a time for enjoying life without little kids influencing your every decision. I want to get married again someday, and I want to have some time with my husband like my parents are having now—just the two of them. I waited too long to have children the way it is. I'm already going to be one of the older mothers when Scott starts kindergarten. If I had your baby, people would think I was its grandmother. No way, Joel. No damned way. I'm not tough enough.''

Joel felt a rush of disappointment and the anger of rejection. God damn it, he'd asked her to *marry* him. "You exaggerate," he said, following her into the hall. "Why do you keep trying to make yourself out to be so damned old? It's really boring.''

"Well, *excuse me*. And I never said I was old—just older than you. If I were in love with a man my own age, I wouldn't feel old at all. But I'm older than you by a whole decade. I remember things that happened before you were born. My era is different. My music is different. My favorite movie stars. My political views. Everything. And we are at different stages in our lives. You've got to accept that and stop trying to make yourself believe it doesn't matter. If I didn't already have children, maybe I'd throw caution to the wind and have them with you, but I have Scott and Tommy. And I love them to distraction, but they make me tired. Very, very tired.''

Joel had used up all his words. He felt like a balloon that had lost its air.

They were both crying now and hugging each other. His idea had been a disaster. He needed to read three more chapters of economics. And he was beginning to understand that love could hurt like hell.

Chapter Nine

Not a hair out of place marred the sleek perfection of Miss Duff's smooth, blond hair and its precise bun on the nape of her neck. Her oxford shoes were carefully polished, and her gray twill dress would have looked like a uniform if it were not for a red belt and gold buttons. Miss Duff could have passed for a proper English nanny until she spoke in perfect, unaccented American English.

"I really can't thank you enough for coming to baby-sit," Pam said, balancing Tommy on her hip, as she showed Miss Duff into the living room. Scott was riding his kiddie car up and down the hallway, but he parked his car by the telephone table and followed his mother. "I guess you remember my boys," Pam said. "Tommy is twenty-two months now, and Scott is almost three."

"How do you do?" Miss Duff said, touching Tommy's arm and bending to take Scott's hand and shake it as though he were an adult. "Do you boys have any teddy bears?" she asked.

Scott nodded.

"Would you show them to me?" she asked. "I like teddy bears very much."

Pam put Tommy down, and Scott led his brother down the hall to fetch teddy bears for the lady.

"We'll get along just fine," Miss Duff assured Pam as she seated herself on the sofa.

Miss Duff may have looked like a nanny, but she had the bearing of a duchess. Pam wondered why such a handsome woman insisted on dressing in such matronly attire. Miss Duff's wonderful hair shone like spun gold, her eyes like rich green emeralds. Her skin was smooth and youthful, her body tall and pleasingly mature. Brenda would have pointed out the need for mascara on the woman's pale lashes and a bit of blush on her pale cheeks, but there was a dignified beauty about Miss Duff that, having escaped first perusal, became all the more remarkable when one realized it was there.

"I hate for you to spend your Sunday afternoon baby-sitting," Pam said, seating herself in the rocker. "When I called, I really just wanted you to recommend someone from your agency."

"Since I've gone to work for Mr. Fenwick, I've lost touch with the agency," Miss Duff explained, "and with him and the girls gone for the day, I was only too happy to help you out."

"My regular sitter and her boyfriend want to go to the commencement ceremony, too," Pam explained. "They're friends of the young man who is graduating."

"You said the graduate is your assistant, I believe," Miss Duff commented as she smiled at Scott and accepted a one-eared brown bear from him.

"Yes, my assistant. A really fine young man. I'm going to miss him," Pam said with more of a sigh than she intended. "And the boys will, too. Joel's been like a member of the family."

"Yes, sometimes it's difficult to keep from getting too attached to people," Miss Duff said, accepting an over-size panda from Tommy. "I've found that when that happens, it's best to move on."

"Oh?"

"Yes. I've been taking care of other people's children for years, and when I start to like them too much or start feeling like I belong with that family, I know I'd best pack up and leave. The children are not mine to love, and leaving saves greater pain on down the road."

"Unless I'm mistaken, it sounds like Robert may be losing a housekeeper," Pam said.

It was Miss Duff's turn to sigh. Her face lost its controlled expression for an instant and drooped a bit. "Probably," she allowed. "I like being in his home too much. A man as kind and generous as Mr. Fenwick will certainly remarry soon, and then I'll be left out in the cold. Even if his wife wanted me to stay, I couldn't, not after these months of running the household like my own."

"I think Robert would court you if you'd let him," Pam said, wondering if she was betraying a confidence. "At least, that's the impression I got the last time I saw him. We were supposed to be on a date, but neither one of us had the heart for it."

Miss Duff accepted two more teddy bears, asked their names and seated them alongside the other two. Then she asked the boys if they had a dog.

Scott and Tommy went scurrying down the hall calling for Barney.

"I'm older than Robert...than Mr. Fenwick," Miss Duff explained, "and that makes me very uncomfortable. If I were to become involved with him, I'd be afraid the day would come when he was sorry."

"But you care about him?" Pam prodded.

Miss Duff looked away, composing herself. "Yes. I like him and those two little girls, but *c'est la vie*," she said with a small shrug.

Pam could understand the woman's reservations, but she suspected Miss Duff was closer in age to Robert than she herself was to Joel. "Somehow, it seems wrong for you to deny a relationship with a man you really like because of a few years' difference in your ages."

"But I'm forty-one years old, and turning forty altered my perception of myself, forced me to acknowledge the narrowing of options. My life has not been an easy one, and at times I feel every one of those years. I'm not inclined to pretend I'm younger than I am. Mr. Fenwick is thirty-four and is as youthful and vigorous as a twenty-five-year-old, and I have been in his household long enough to witness the attraction he has to and for younger women. I know he thinks I would do a fine job raising his girls and running his household, but I would be a fool if I thought he could ever fall in love with me."

Scott and Tommy came charging down the hall, herding Barney between them. The dog had probably been asleep on her bed, Pam thought. And no wonder Miss Duff knew the boys had a dog. She surely noticed the dog hairs all over the sofa.

She watched as Miss Duff petted Barney, asked Scott his name, asked Tommy if he loved his dog. The older woman laughed when Tommy hugged Barney's neck and planted a kiss on his head. Barney wagged his tail, obviously enjoying the attention.

Pam admired the nice way Miss Duff had with children. In fact, she admired the woman herself. Surely Robert found his housekeeper a refreshing change from the glossy young women he had been dating. Or maybe not.

Who was to explain why people were attracted to each other? Obviously, logic didn't always prevail.

She certainly hadn't planned to become smitten with a man totally inappropriate for her. It had just happened. Joel had grinned at her, and suddenly she found herself wishing she'd washed her hair. She played games with herself for a while, but she could admit now that almost from the first minute she saw Joel, she liked him more than she had liked other males at first sight. And he had noticed her. They had started sending out glances, sparks, chemistry, mutual admiration, whatever one wanted to call it, while they were picking up cans of chili.

"Now, why don't you let me feed the boys their lunch while you're getting dressed," Miss Duff said. "Then, by the time you're ready to leave, maybe they'll be accustomed to me."

"It's none of my business," Pam couldn't resist saying, "but I think you're exactly the sort of woman Robert Fenwick needs for his daughters, his household and himself. And haven't you reached a time in your life when you would like to stay put instead of moving on?"

"I'm not sure," she said, pulling Tommy and a teddy bear onto her lap. "I've always worked hard and depended only on myself. And the few times I thought I was in love, it didn't work out. I guess I've come to the age where no risk sounds like the best course. And now, my dear Mrs. Sullivan, what about you? I detect a note of genuine sadness when you talk about the young man who is graduating today. I suspect we are sailing in the same boat."

Pam nodded. "Yes, but it seems more appropriate for you to stay in the boat than me. Robert is a grown-up man who's old enough to know what he's getting into. With Joel, I'd feel like I was robbing the cradle. He's only twenty-one.''

"A lot of young people are quite mature by the time they are twenty-one," Miss Duff observed. "I had been on my own four years by the time I was that age, but I can certainly sympathize with your reservation. Robert's so youthful-looking, and I have this horrible fear that the day would come when I'd be mistaken for his mother.''

Then why are you dressing the part? Pam wanted to ask. But that would be rude. She herself had worried that someday people might make the same mistake about her and Joel, and she wondered how much of a disaster that would be. Would Joel be able to laugh about it? Would Robert, if people thought Miss Duff was that much older? Maybe both men would obligingly lose their hair, get a paunch and solve the problem by looking ten years older themselves.

"I wonder if we could drop the 'Miss Duff-Mrs. Sullivan' routine," Pam suggested. "I'd like for us to be first-name friends.''

"My name is Jessica.''

When Jessica Duff smiled, Pam felt like it was entirely possible for Robert Fenwick to be in love with her, housekeeping skills and child-rearing aside. She was a gracious, beautiful woman.

"Why don't you stay and have dinner with us after the ceremony?" Pam asked.

"I wouldn't want to intrude on . . ." Jessica started to say, then stopped and smiled again. "I'd like that very much.''

Pam put on her old standby blue gabardine dress and decided it looked like something Jessica Duff would have worn to baby-sit. She pulled out a white wool skirt she seldom wore around sticky-fingered children and added a pink silk blouse and a black tweed jacket. She stared at herself and tried to think what Brenda would do to jazz up the outfit, then added oversize pearl earrings and a sheer black scarf. Not bad for an amateur, she decided.

She took Joel's graduation gift out of her bureau drawer. The gold watch was engraved on the back, *Love, Pam, Scott and Tommy.*

The watch had cost too much. The whole Joel episode in her life had cost too much. She now conducted her days under a mantle of sadness.

She wondered if the time was close at hand for a final parting. The father of Greg Williamson, one of Joel's classmates, had offered him a clerical job for the winter at a Colorado ski resort, and Pam had encouraged him to go. "Get away from me for a while. Hang out with other young people and then see how you feel."

She wondered what Joel's decision would be. At one level, she was sincere when she encouraged him to leave. At another, deeper level, however, her heart cried out for him to stay. She wanted to give in, to promise to marry him, have a dozen kids for him, if that was what he wanted. She'd starve and exercise herself to a more youthful figure, try to dress in with-it fashions, turn her radio from mellow to rock. Whatever.

Jessica had said she was not inclined to pretend she was younger than her age. Pam admired the older woman's wisdom but knew if there was any reasonable way she could look five years younger, she would take advantage of it.

Pam met George and Brenda, Cindy and Paul in the lobby of the college auditorium, and they all went inside together. How sad, she thought, that Joel had no family of his own to attend the ceremony. She thought of her own and Brenda's growing-up years in the bosom of a close and caring family that celebrated special days with love and thoughtfulness. Pam's heart ached to think of Joel facing life alone and unloved since the age of nine. He was a remarkable young man to have accomplished a college education alone and unaided and to have come out of such a childhood the kind, gentle human being that he was. She felt honored to have known him.

Dallas City College was a small school, and fewer than a hundred seniors were graduating at the small, midyear ceremony. As a result, the auditorium was only half full of relatives and friends.

From her seat in the balcony, Pam watched the black-robed graduates march into the auditorium to the dignified strains of "Pomp and Circumstance" played by a string quartet of earnest young musicians. And most of the graduates were young, their lives an empty book yet to be filled. She wondered how many of them would soon marry and start families. New lives, new marriages, new babies. She envied them a bit, having all that in their futures.

There was Joel, looking up at her. Pam waved. How serious he looked in his cap and gown. Dear, sweet Joel. Would she ever again find a man she could both love and adore?

The commencement speaker was an illustrious graduate who told his rags-to-riches story and instructed the graduates to set their sights high and learn from their failures. The president of the college turned his remarks into an appeal for contributions to the college. And the president of the alumni association welcomed the new alumni.

Cindy and Paul held hands throughout the ceremony. Brenda and George did not. In fact, they seemed to avoid touching at all. Pam wondered if they'd had their talk about a baby and hoped she hadn't given bad advice. However, they couldn't just go through life never discussing such a landmark issue.

She and Joel had had no further conversations on the topic of babies or marriage proposals since their disastrous confrontation three weeks ago. They had circled warily through a few catering jobs, but as Joel plunged himself into studying for finals, Pam had seen less and less of him.

When Joel's name was called, the five of them clapped loudly. He saluted in their direction and marched across the stage to receive his diploma.

At the end of the ceremony, Joel did not throw his cap jubilantly into the air like the other graduates. He looked up at Pam again, his eyes questioning. What now?

Their little group went to find Joel among the mingling graduates, families and friends. "Congratulations," Pam said. "You should be very proud." And she leaned forward to kiss his cheek, but suddenly his arms were around her and the kiss became something else.

Breathlessly, she stepped away from him. All around them, people were giving the unlikely couple puzzled looks. The kiss had been too romantic for an older sister—or for a young-looking mother.

"I say, old man, congratulations," George said. "Good show."

Brenda took charge, herding them out to the cars, reminding George they needed to stop for beer and wine on the way to Pam's house.

In honor of the unseasonably warm weather, George decided to grill the chicken breasts in the backyard while Pam tossed a salad. Brenda had brought a broccoli-and-rice casserole and French bread. Cindy had baked a chocolate cake, with Paul's help, she assured everyone. Joel seemed overwhelmed that they had gone to so much trouble for him.

Scott and Tommy were so glad to see Joel, they followed him around like two little puppy dogs. Finally, he shed his sport coat and tie, took them into the living room and, in spite of his good trousers and starched shirt, stretched out on the floor for a wrestling match. The boys squealed with delight as they crawled all over him. And, of course, Barney came to join in the melée.

Pam was aware of Jessica assessing Joel. At one point during the evening, she looked at Pam and offered a small, knowing smile that said, "I understand why you might love such a man."

George pumped Joel about his job plans, but Joel was evasive. "I need to take the CPA exam before I can expect anything permanent. Some of my classmates have already taken the exam, but I haven't had time to prepare for it. However, I have interviewed for a few jobs, contingent on certification. Somehow a position with an accounting firm doesn't seem as wonderful as I once thought it would be. Working with Pam has started me thinking about the food-service business. I may use my accounting skills for my own business someday."

Later, after everyone had gone and the children were in bed, Joel went out in the backyard to roll the grill into the garage. Pam followed him outside with two jackets. The night sky was sparkling clear with stars by the millions and an almost-round moon that looked like it was cut from bright orange cardboard. They both breathed deeply of the crisp air and sat down on the back step for a minute, unwilling to give up the beauty of the night. "Déjà vu," Pam said, remembering the night when she had sat here with the grocery-store boy. That had been in June. Now it was December—almost Christmastime.

"Yeah, that seems like a hundred years ago," Joel said. "Or at least I feel a hundred years older."

"I would think you'd feel young and eager and pretty damned proud of yourself and what you've accomplished," she said, pulling her jacket closed. They should have gone inside, but inside another awkward time of parting awaited them, and she felt weak tonight.

"Oh, I guess I'm proud, but mostly I feel relieved that I finally made it to graduation, except that means I have to face the future. For three and a half years all I thought about was keeping my nose to the grindstone and getting to the next semester, but now there aren't any more semesters. You know, in spite of all the bad stuff that happened in my life, I always thought that, if I worked hard and stayed out of trouble, someday I'd find my way to a contented, satisfying life with lots of love and kids and money in the bank. Now, I'm not so sure."

"No, don't lose faith. You're..."

Joel put his hand on her arm. "If you're going to tell me how young I am, I don't want to hear it."

"Are you going to Colorado?" Pam asked.

"Do you want me to?" he asked.

"It's not for me to say."

"Yes, it is. All you have to say is don't go, and I'd stay here with you."

"For how long?" she asked.

"For as long as we both wanted it."

"One of us would get hurt, and I have a feeling the one would be me."

HOW STRANGE LIFE COULD BE, Pam thought as she stared at the man standing on her front porch. After longing with all her heart and soul, then gradually losing faith that this day would ever happen and finally deciding—intellectually, at least—it would be best if she never saw Marty Sullivan again, then suddenly, with no warning, there he was, his smile oddly timid, but his cowboy hat at the same old rakish angle.

She had been expecting her sister, who was coming to spend the night while George was out of town. But there was her ex-husband instead, suitcase in hand, a taxi pulling away from the curb.

She was stunned, but then the day was bound to come, she supposed. Someday, surely, Marty would remember he had two sons.

Pam had wondered how she would feel if she ever saw him again. Now she knew—curious, apprehensive, sad.

He was a few pounds heavier, but, then, so was she. His sideburns were unstylishly long—like a character actor in an old movie—and his flashy Western clothing looked like a costume.

How long had it been? A year and a half? No, longer. Twenty-two months, she calculated, almost two years. It seemed like another lifetime ago when she woke up husbandless. Tommy had been three months old when Marty left, and last month her younger son had his second birthday with his mother, aunt, uncle, brother as well as Cindy, Paul and Joel in attendance, but not his father. But then Marty never remembered birthdays. Pam had always reminded him to call his mother on hers. She would even remind him of her own birthday, and he'd tell her to go buy something pretty for herself, then he would dedicate a song for her that night at the club while she pretended she was married to a thoughtful and romantic man.

"Aren't you going to ask me in?" he asked. He even took his hat off. *My, my,* Pam thought sarcastically, *the courtly routine.*

"What do you want?" she asked.

"To see my wife," he said.

"I am not your wife," Pam said.

"What do you mean? Of course, you're my wife. I never signed any papers."

"You signed that note on my pillow and walked out. That was enough for the judge."

"Hell, Pam, I was really down when I wrote that note. You know that. I wanted to be big-time and was tired of singing in second-rate clubs and tired of living with a wife who took better care of babies than she did of me. How did you know I just wasn't trying to teach you a lesson?"

"That note sounded pretty final to me."

"My mom said you wanted me to come home," Marty said.

"That was a year and a half ago. I was lonely and scared and hadn't yet come to the realization that I was better off without you. I was down, too, especially after you took the money out of my purse and left me with an overdrawn bank account and two babies. But then I finally saw you for what you are—a selfish jerk who doesn't deserve a family or even a passing thought."

"Now, wait just a minute," he said, holding up a hand in protest. "You make it sound like I left you at the door of the poorhouse, and that's not so. I left you my truck and my guns. Those guns were worth at least a couple of thousand. And I didn't touch that savings account."

"Only because you couldn't find the passbook! You looked though, didn't you, in the dark, going through my purse, digging in all the drawers, throwing stuff out of the closet before you sneaked out the door? The only reason you hadn't already spent the money I'd saved while I was in the Army was because I kept it hidden. I knew if I didn't, you'd probably gamble it away in Vegas. Why are you here, Marty?''

"I missed you, and I wanted to see you. Come on, Pam, how long are you going to make me stand on the porch? It's cold out here, and I want to talk to you."

"What about?"

He said the only answer that would make her step aside, and then with only a small uncertain step. "About my little boys, among other things," he answered. "How are the kids? Is the baby walking yet?"

"He's two years old."

"Is that right?" Marty said, slipping past her.

He stood in her entry hall, taking in her house. The furniture was mostly the same—pieces she had bought secondhand when she and Marty married, a few things from his mother and her parents.

Marty had aged too much for two years. His hair was a little thinner, he was getting a bit jowly and his skin was taking on the leathery look of someone who'd baked too many hours beside motel swimming pools. But he still swaggered when he walked. She wondered if he still called every woman he met "honey."

"How come you moved out of our apartment?" he asked. "I had to find you through the telephone book."

"I couldn't afford the rent," she said angrily. Did he really expect her to still be sitting there, waiting for him to show up? "My parents helped me buy this house at a government auction. It was a wreck, but with a hell of a lot of hard work, we made it fit to live in."

"Well, you did a fine job," he said, walking into the dining room, peeking in the kitchen, giving the living room a quick perusal. "You've made a nice little home here that I'll bet you could sell for a nice profit. And you must have a good job to be able to afford that station wagon in the driveway."

"I bought it used, and I still owe on it. Your derelict truck brought two hundred and fifty dollars as a trade-in. They had to come haul it off."

"Well, I'm just real proud of how well you've done for yourself," he said. "I'll bet that passbook is all full of deposits. I knew a good-looking, smart, hard-working woman like you would get a good job at a bank or a fancy dress store."

"I cater parties," she said flatly. "It allows me to work out of my home."

"Well, you always were a fine cook. I never appreciated that before. It was hard, learning to live alone again. Real hard. I missed my wife's cooking and lots of other things, too. I realized how many bookings I'd gotten because you'd sweet-talked the club manager. I'll be the first to admit I didn't appreciate you like I should have, Pam, and I'm really sorry about that."

"I am your ex-wife," Pam reminded him.

"You mean we really are divorced?" Marty looked hurt—deeply and profoundly hurt. He should have been an actor.

"I sent a copy of the decree to your mother since I didn't know where you were."

"Well, Mom and I had a bit of a falling out over my dad's estate," Marty said. "Maybe you can help me patch things up with her. I tried to call her, but a telephone company recording says it's no longer a working number."

"She got married and moved to California over a year ago."

"Married? You mean she let some man get his hands on my dad's insurance money?"

"I'm sure your mother can take care of herself." Pam wished she hadn't let him in. Marty's presence in her house was an intrusion.

"You're probably right. Mom is a smart woman, just like you." Marty took Pam's arm and said, "Now, why don't we sit down and figure out how you can straighten out this mess we've made of our lives."

Pam pulled her arm away.

Marty shrugged and sat on the sofa. Warily, Pam sat down in the rocking chair.

"I made a real bad mistake, honey," Marty said, leaning forward, his elbows on his knees. He was using his sincere voice now. "I didn't know how much I counted on you to get my bookings, make all the calls and write the letters. Club managers ask about you all the time. Hell, if I'd had you with me when I went to Nashville, I bet I'd still be there. If I was to go back now and take you along, things would be different. I know a guy whose cousin has a really important job at Ace Records, and with you hustling up some club dates for me and getting me some exposure, it wouldn't be like before. I want to go back, Pam, more than anything, and try for the big time one more time before I give up and sell horse trailers for my uncle out in Lubbock. But I need a grubstake, and I need my wife at my side where she belongs. I know if we get together again, the breaks will come. I just know it."

He was still handsome, with the same cocky lift to his chin, the same smooth charm. Marty used to be able to look at her with those blue eyes, smile at her with that sensual mouth, soft-talk her with a sexy voice calculated to melt the hardest female heart, and she would give in or forgive—whatever it was he wanted of her.

But she was remembering only the worst about him, and that wasn't fair. When it had been just the two of them, when they were living only for themselves, they laughed and loved like two beautiful children with no thought of tomorrow, and it had been fine. Mighty fine. The carefree time in her life had passed, however. The time had come when she wanted to face tomorrow with all its grown-up demands.

Marty came over and knelt in front of her. She wouldn't let him have her hands, so he clung to the arm of her chair, looking a bit like an overgrown altar boy. "I need you, darlin' Pam, more than you'll ever know. Just think how great it would be, making our mark in Nashville. I'll bet your folks would look after those two boys for us—at least for a while. You might have to work for a time, until I got into some big money, but not for long. Pretty soon everyone would turn and look at you when you walked in a club and tell everyone that pretty woman is the wife of the one-and-only Marty Sullivan."

Pam leaned back in the rocker and closed her eyes to accommodate the heavy sadness that descended over her. The man she once had loved so desperately now stirred only pity in her breast. It made her mistrust her own emotions. Maybe she didn't know what love was. Maybe she was one of those women who only picked men who would hurt them.

"How about it, honey? No woman ever loved me like my Pam. I want you to love me like that again."

Yes, Pam thought. He needed a woman to love him, to facilitate his life, to mother him, to make him feel good about himself. Poor Marty. Poor baby boy. He needed the woman she used to be.

"I can't," she said.

"What do you mean you can't? This is Marty you're talking to. Open your eyes and look at me. Marty, your husband. Remember how good we were together, how we danced and laughed and made love? Remember how proud you used to be when I introduced you during my act. You used to blush a little, then wave and smile at the folks. From now on I'll do that every time. I'll say, 'And now I want to introduce my beloved wife, Pam, who made me what I am today.' And it would be the truth. I need you, honey. I'm willing to admit that now. I really need you."

"It's too late," Pam said.

She heard the car drive up, then her sister's voice at the front door, and there was Brenda standing in the entry hall, holding an overnight bag, staring.

Marty scrambled to his feet. "You're looking good, Brenda," he said.

Brenda looked at him, then at her sister. "Sis, are you all right?"

Pam nodded. "Marty was just leaving."

"I'm not finished talking to you, Pam," Marty said, his voice stern.

"Yes, you are," Pam said firmly. "If you need money, I'll give you what I can spare, then I want you to go away."

Later, after she had cried in her sister's arms, Pam said, "He didn't even ask to see the boys. Can you imagine? He didn't even ask to tiptoe into their room and look down at the sons he fathered. Poor Marty. He's missing the whole point of life, and I feel so sorry for him."

"You don't still love him?" Brenda asked.

"No. The love is dead. It feels now like it never was. And that's so sad. Once, Marty was my life."

"And now you love Joel," Brenda said flatly. "At work today, I met the new assistant manager of menswear. He's newly divorced, single and lonely and seems like a real nice guy. But as I started to tell him about my sister, I thought, 'Forget it, girl. She's a hopeless case.'"

"I told Joel to go to Colorado."

"Why?"

"Because I'd rather lose him now than later."

Chapter Ten

A strange male voice asked for Pam, and Joel handed her the phone. She dried her hands on her apron before accepting it.

"Hello," she said into the receiver, listened for a minute, then looked at Joel and gestured wildly toward the stove.

Joel set the boiling shrimp off the burner just before the pan overflowed.

Then she turned her back to him. "Why are you calling?" he heard her ask.

"He's a friend," she answered. "No, I don't have to tell you who he is. I don't owe you any explanations about anything."

Pam went into the hall, trailing the telephone cord behind her, but Joel could still hear her.

"I can't stop you from seeing a lawyer," she was saying, "but if you do succeed in having the decree set aside, I'll get another one."

There was silence for a time, then Pam said, "Don't make more trouble for me, Marty, please." Her tone was pleading. "No, I haven't forgotten how it used to be. I haven't forgotten anything."

Joel held his breath, waiting for her next words. He shouldn't be listening, but he stood rooted to the floor, his hand holding on to a chair.

"I know you're down, Marty. I know you need someone, but there's too much water under the bridge, too much mistrust for me to be that someone."

When she hung up, Pam leaned against the wall and put her face in her hands. The man had made her cry. Joel hated him for doing that, but the fact that her ex-husband still touched her enough to bring her to tears only added to Joel's feeling of defeat.

"So that's what's been making you so edgy," he said. "Your ex is back in town. Have you seen him?"

"Yes. He came over last night."

"Just in time to be reunited with his family for Christmas," Joel observed wryly.

Pam shook her head. "It's not like that."

"Well, obviously you still care about him," Joel challenged, "or he couldn't make you cry."

"I was married to the man for five years," Pam said, her tears changing to irritation. "He's the father of my children, and I can't imagine not caring about him. He's been a big part of my life, and it will always upset me to see the worst in him come out, because I can remember Marty at his best."

"I thought you were over him." Joel sat down, then got up again. "My God, Pam, the man walked out on you and his own children. How can you have any regard for a bum like that?"

"You don't understand, do you?" Pam said, shaking her head. "The fact that I was once married to Marty and he fathered my children makes him a part of me, like an arm or a leg or a child. I can't make that feeling go away. And there will be times, I suppose, for the rest of my life when a certain song or a smell or a place will take me back to a special time with him, and I'll think good thoughts and long a little for what might have been.''

''I wouldn't want to be in love with a woman who thought about another man,'' Joel said. ''I want the woman I end up with to think just about me. It sounds like you're still carrying a torch for the guy. Maybe you should just go back to him like he seems to want.'' Joel knew he sounded like a spoiled little boy, but he couldn't help it. He was saying what he felt.

Pam went back to the sink, picked up a potato and began to scrub. ''The only women who don't think about past loves are the ones who married the first boy they ever fell in love with and never have cause to change course, and I suspect men are the same way. I am sure there are times when you think about the Chinese girl or the rich one.''

Her voice was condescending, big sisterish. It made Joel feel angry and defeated. She was wrong. The other women in his life now seemed like adolescent crushes. Even Stephanie. They hadn't caused world-class pain and suffering. They didn't make him think he never wanted to fall in love again.

Stupid as it seemed, this was the first time the knowledge that Pam had truly loved another man became a gut-felt reality. He had wanted to believe her first marriage had been a mistake from the beginning, that Scott and Tommy were the only good that had come out of it, that the boys just somehow miraculously appeared without benefit of serious sexual involvement. And any sex that had taken place between Pam and her ex-husband certainly could not have been the beautiful, heartfelt, almost spiritual lovemaking he had experienced with her. Surely she had never given herself as completely to another man as when she had come to his arms that one glorious night. Surely she had just tolerated sex during her marriage.

Apparently it had not been that way at all. Joel was forced to face the fact that Pam had really loved the guy, that she had enjoyed a sexual relationship with him, and Joel didn't like it one bit. He wondered if the man was handsome, if he was passionate, if that bed back there had been *their* bed.

But then, what the hell difference did it make anyway? Only the man who became Pam's second husband had any real reason to be jealous of number one. Only the guy who was going to spend the rest of his life with her needed to confront the ghost of husband past, and that future husband wasn't going to be Joel Bynum, it seemed. Pam didn't want a young husband. She didn't want to have another baby. She wanted some used-up old guy who had ghosts of his own.

Well, so be it. Joel was tired of the role of lovesick kid. Sick and tired. Falling in love was more complicated than he had ever dreamed it would be, and it made more problems than it solved. He had assumed that one of the functions of the phenomenon was to make the future crystal clear. Wrong. He was in love with Pam, but he couldn't envision a future, only an illusive present with him living in this house, enjoying those two little kids and their mom. Even that baby he claimed he wanted her to have was only a vague romantic notion wandering around on the road to someday.

"My first *serious* involvement? Hell, no," he said in answer to Pam's question. "I've been in love dozens of times before, and I think it's time for me to find a woman to hang out with who wants me to be there, and not one who's always telling me to go away and leave her alone.

Your ex-husband was angry to hear another man's voice on the phone, wasn't he? Well, next time you talk to him, tell him the voice is moving on. The voice finally got the message.''

''Joel, no,'' she said, reaching for his arm. ''Don't be angry.''

He pulled away. ''You can laugh about it with your sister, about the kid who fell in love with Pam, when Pam was too mature, too wise, too afraid of what other people would think to take a risk. She wanted everything nice and tidy and safe.''

''That's not fair,'' Pam said indignantly. ''I want to do what is best for both of us and for my children. Face it, Joel, the cards are stacked against us. Getting involved in a relationship with so little chance for success can't do any of us any good.''

''Unless it should happen to work,'' Joel tossed out angrily. And it could, he told himself, at least for a year or two anyway. Maybe forever. They wouldn't know unless they tried.

''Believe me,'' Pam said, ''I wonder all the time if it might work and try to convince myself that it could. I even think about having that baby with you in an effort to keep you around permanently, but then I'd feel like I was cheating you. You should marry someone who can experience parenthood for the first time with you, not some woman who's reluctantly agreed to one last child before she closes the factory only so the man will marry her. I don't want to trap you with a baby. And I don't want to be twice divorced with children by *two* previous husbands.''

''Forget the baby,'' Joel said, exasperated, running his hand through his hair. ''It was a bad idea. Forget about marriage. That offer was premature. All I want to do is move in with you and see how it goes. That seems like the sane, *adult* thing for two people like us to be doing, to give it our best shot. We work together, and we love each other. It seems so stupid for me to be going home at night and not sleeping with you in that bed, making love to you, waking up with you. Then, if we find out the arrangement isn't what we both want it to be, I leave. If it's terrific, we reopen negotiations.''

Pam stabbed the potato with a knife, wrapped it in foil then picked up another one to scrub. ''I'm the daughter of two very conservative people who would have a hard time understanding their daughter living with a man she wasn't married to. But even more than that, I am the mother of two children. Don't you think that it's a bit unseemly for me to cohabit with a young guy who isn't their father?''

''It's done all the time, Pam. I hardly think your neighbors will take out a petition. And you might be surprised about your folks.''

''What happens if the boys someday ask about the man who *used* to live with us?''

Joel threw up his hands. ''I can't figure out why in the hell I'm in love with you. You are the most exasperating woman I've ever known in my life. How am I supposed to know what you should tell the boys *if* I move in with you, *if* I move on, *if* they even remember, *if* they bother to ask? Tell them I was a foundling you took in. Tell them I was your long-lost kid brother. Tell them we were married and it didn't work out. Tell them we weren't married and it didn't work out. Tell them I died. Tell them it's none of their business. Maybe they won't be asking. Maybe they'll be out in the backyard with me playing catch. When are you going to figure out that nobody in the whole damned world can make you an iron-clad promise about anything? How can you be smart about some things and so stupid about others?''

''Since you brought it up, why the hell are you in love with me?'' Pam asked, eyes blazing, her hands on her hips. She was wearing jeans and an oversize pink sweater that emphasized the darkness of her eyes. Her milky skin was unrouged, unpowdered, but there was a touch of color on her lips. Her hair was longer than it had been last summer and made a thick mane of deep chestnut brown about her face. Her clothing, her sneakered feet, her jutting lower lip made her look almost childlike, but the fullness of her breasts under the loose sweater, the weariness around her eyes, the hint of creases between her eyes and on either side of her mouth denied first youth and spoke of the middle-aged woman she would become.

He had seen her looking as beautiful as a woman could look and seen her looking careworn and bedraggled. He had seen her cry and laugh, be angry and mellow, sad and happy. When he graduated, it was her eyes he sought out of all those people, and only her presence made the event meaningful for him. He liked to steal looks at her when she was watching her children and see the radiant look of motherly love on her face. She was the sister and mother he had never had. She was his friend and, ever so briefly, his lover. Never had his life been so entangled with another human being.

Why did he love her? How could he possibly explain that to her?

''Because your mouth is the most lovely in the history of the world,'' he began, ''and you like to kiss your children's necks. Because you make mistakes and aren't afraid to cry and laugh. Because you never once called me

'Red' and will drink beer out of the can. Because when I'm with you, I feel whole.''

"Thank you," Pam said. "Now if you don't mind, I need a hug in the worst way."

Joel took her in his arms. Her smaller size made him feel older and stronger than he really was. He put his face against her hair and drank in her aroma. Another reason why he loved her—her shampoo smelled like coconut.

"I'm throwing in the towel," he said into her hair. "I'll help you with the holiday party stuff, then I guess I'm heading out."

Pam started to say something, then stopped herself. She took a breath and started again. "I think that's probably for the best, but I'll miss you like hell."

A VISIT TO THE DOWNTOWN Neiman Marcus had always been a trip down memory lane for Pam. She, her mother and sister used to drive downtown from their home near the Southern Methodist University campus for a day of shopping. One of the times they always went was the last week in August when they shopped for school shoes and clothes. Her daddy went along on those occasions. Other times, it was just the three "girls," browsing their way through the huge downtown department stores—most of which had long since moved to shopping malls. They seldom bought anything at Neiman's, but, rather, wandered through the store to stare at the riches, to see blouses that cost five hundred dollars and art objects that cost thousands. They often rode the elevator up to the sixth floor to indulge themselves in one of the less expensive lunches in the Zodiac Room, where they could watch exotic models parade the finery from the floors below up and down the runway that jutted into the middle of the huge decorous room. Then the models would circulate among the diners, telling them the designer and price of their outfit and where it could be found in the store. Pam and Brenda would go home and play "model" by the hour, dressing up in their mother's clothes and swishing down imaginary runways. Brenda could walk like a real model even then. Pam frequently tripped over her own feet.

Neiman Marcus had changed over the years, but the downtown store still retained many of its opulent trappings reminiscent of a bygone era when Texas's own brand of royalty reigned supreme and the wives of fabulously rich oil barons needed someplace to spend their husbands' serendipitously acquired wealth. One could still find overpriced treasures among the famous store's merchandise, but now there were also departments that at least acknowledged that not everyone in Dallas was rich and spent money indiscriminately.

Neiman's still went all out for Christmas, Pam thought, as she wandered through a store-turned-fairyland with a forest of ornate silver trees covered with thousands of twinkling lights and with Christmas angels and huge shimmering snowflakes suspended from the ceiling. A string quartet serenaded the first-floor shoppers with traditional Christmas music.

Pam and Brenda's mother liked to tell about the times when women still wore hats and gloves to town, and even now the Zodiac Room at Neiman Marcus managed to cling to some of the old standards. The jeans-clad crowd didn't ride up to the sixth floor for an elegant luncheon served by uniformed waiters.

It had been almost a year since Pam had dressed up and come downtown to watch her sister model. How strange to be going someplace in the daytime without her children, Pam thought, feeling light and unencumbered as she browsed, stopping to buy her favorite brand of makeup in the first-floor cosmetic department and two small chocolate Santas for the boys at the candy counter. She checked out "moderate" blouses that still seemed expensive to her, then rode the escalator up two floors to visit the shoe salon. The shoes were fabulous. She always loved new shoes and started to ask the price of a pair of red lizard pumps, but saved herself the trouble, wondering if she'd ever be able to afford shoes from anyplace but Kinney's or Sears.

By noon, she was seated at a tiny table near the runway and ordering the least-expensive item on the menu, which was, now as before, a plate of assorted finger sandwiches.

Wearing an outfit that looked straight out of the 1940s, Brenda appeared on the runway and winked at Pam. The vivid yellow, peplumed suit had exaggerated shoulders, a short skirt, wide black belt and huge black buttons. Brenda carried a long-handled umbrella in one hand and a jeweled cigarette holder in the other. She stopped in the center of the runway and affected a Bette Davis-like pose. Her abundant blond hair looked as though she'd been riding in a convertible. Her body was wonderfully slim, and her elongated legs were curvy and sexy.

Pam couldn't keep the proud smile from her face. She wanted to lean over to tell the table of blue-haired matrons sitting next to her, "That's my sister."

When Brenda made her way through the tables, giving the patrons a closer look at the outfit, she stopped at Pam's table. "Shall I put you down for two, sis? It also comes in orange."

Pam saw the women watching them. When Brenda had gone on to the next table, Pam did turn and nod at one of the women. "My sister," she confided.

The woman turned to one of her companions. "Victoria, the model is that woman's younger sister," she said, pointing in Pam's direction.

Pam felt her smile freeze a bit on her face and took her mirror out of her purse. Actually, she looked pretty damned good today. She had done full makeup, and her hair was behaving. The soft coral of her sweater was becoming, the silk scarf looked smart. She looked like a reasonably attractive, thirtyish woman, and of course, the woman at the next table would realize Brenda was her *younger* sister without being told.

The finger sandwiches were artfully arranged around a cup of sherbet. Planning to keep her table throughout the lunch service, Pam nibbled, trying to make the food last a long time and analyzing the ingredients. The delicious tuna salad had curry powder and raisins. She'd have to remember that. When she had finally finished the last sandwich and eaten the melted sherbet, she ordered coffee.

Pam sipped her way through two refills, watching Brenda model four attractive outfits, including a bathing suit and cover-up from a famous designer's cruise-wear line. Brenda was bronzed from regular tanning-salon visits and sleek from careful dieting. Sandals revealed perfectly pedicured toenails. Pam knew that part of a model's life was to spend inordinate amounts of time grooming and preserving face and figure. Her sister had developed a regimen of exercise, skin care and diet that she followed religiously. Pam wondered what would happen to both face and figure if Brenda had a baby. Things would change, that was for sure. Perhaps she would still be able to accomplish perfection, but she'd have to be far more clever and organized than her untanned, nonsleek sister to do it.

Pam couldn't remember the last time she put polish on her nails. With her life-style, to do so was an exercise in futility. She promised herself facials but never got around to them. She never used hot-oil treatments on her hair and waited until a haircut was an emergency. Someday, she realized, there would be time again just for her, but that day was a long way down the road. For her, Scott and Tommy were far more important than glamour.

When Brenda's duties at the store were finished, the sisters drove their respective cars to the Anatole for a cocktail in the hotel's lobby bar. The bar was in a spectacular atrium filled with tropical trees and plants. Incredible tapestries of heroic dimensions hung from the glass roof ten floors above them. The piano player was fingering his way through Broadway show tunes. Pam sank into a comfortable lounge chair. *Nice,* Pam thought, as she gazed about her. Brenda looked like she belonged in such elegant surroundings. Pam wondered if she looked like a mommy who'd been let out of the kitchen for a day. She took out her compact again to discreetly freshen her lipstick—and to reassure herself.

Brenda ordered them both frozen margaritas—her treat, she insisted.

"That gorgeous man over there is looking at you," Brenda said.

"Don't be ridiculous," Pam said. "He's looking at *you*."

"No, he's not," Brenda said, smiling mischievously. "Take a look."

Pam couldn't resist. Three men were sitting across from them. The one with hair raised his glass to her and smiled. *How about that,* Pam thought, feeling pleased.

"You're supposed to smile back so he'll come over and introduce himself," Brenda explained. "Or have you been out of circulation so long you've forgotten how it's done?"

"I have no desire to pick up a man in a hotel bar," Pam said primly.

"You don't have to pick him up. But there's no law against being friendly."

"I can be friendly with my sister," Pam said, "but I must admit, it does boost my morale a bit to have a man notice me."

"I keep telling you, Pamela Sue, that lots of men would notice you if you'd give them a chance. Have you heard any more from Marty?"

"No. That business about hiring a lawyer and setting aside the divorce was a bluff. I feel so sorry for him. He's desperate to get his life back on track, but I'm not the answer. Even if I could get back some of the old feeling for him, I could never trust him. I'd always be afraid of waking up in the morning and finding him gone again. I want a man who's solid as rock, one who will stay put forever."

"Speaking of men going, when's Joel leaving?"

"Soon."

"That's what you said last week."

"He's leaving soon," Pam repeated. "Can we talk about something else?"

"Sure. I'm sorry. I just hate to see you unhappy. I'll be glad when Joel is a memory. Did you enjoy your lunch and the modeling?"

"Yes. It made me think of when we were kids, and you were fabulous," Pam said. "I had forgotten what a terrific model you are and how glamorous you look up there on the runway."

"Thanks. You could do it, too, if you worked at it. That's what it takes—working at it."

"Even if I had your natural attributes, I think it would be very difficult for the mother of young children to keep herself up like you do."

Brenda took a sip of her drink and looked at her sister over the glass. "In other words, my modeling days might be over if I have a child?"

"I didn't say that. I said it would be difficult. I couldn't manage it, but you probably could."

"Well, I think the whole question of 'to have a baby or not to have a baby' has become a moot one," Brenda said. Her lower lip quivered just a bit, but she lifted her chin and stared impassively at her long, red ceramic fingernails.

"Oh? Have you and George discussed it?"

Brenda shook her head back and forth. The lip still quivered, and her eyes filled with tears. She took another sip of her drink. "I think he's going to leave me."

Pam stared at her sister then replayed Brenda's last sentence in her mind to see if she had misunderstood.

"George? Leave you? Whatever makes you think a thing like that? George adores you."

"He's acting so strange," Brenda said, taking a tissue from her purse and looking around to make sure no one was noticing her distress. "He keeps starting to say something and stopping in the middle of a sentence. Last night he said, 'Would you be terribly disappointed if I...' And then he stopped and said to forget it, that it was stupid. The other day he started saying something about realizing he'd made a terrible mistake, then refused to continue. He looks at me so funny and keeps telling me I'm too good for him. Then when we make love, he gets all choked up and, well...quite frankly, we're having a terrible time in that department. I have the feeling he'd rather talk in the dark than be romantic. You know how it is—sometimes it's easier to say difficult things when you don't have to look at the person. But then I get so afraid of what he might say that I pretend like I'm feeling real romantic and try to seduce him to shut him up. Some reason to make love, huh?''

"That's the stupidest thing I've ever heard!" Pam said in disbelief. "Let the poor man have his say."

"I'm afraid he knows I want to have a baby," Brenda said, sniffing miserably. "He keeps asking me what I think of Scott and Tommy. I bought a maternity dress and was trying it on a couple of weeks ago when he came home an hour early. I quickly grabbed a belt, but what if George knew what kind of dress it was? Oh, sis, I'm afraid I've really messed up. My marriage to George is the most important thing in the world to me, and we agreed to live our lives just for each other, to put all our energy into having the best marriage and the fullest love possible. I wish I could get all this baby business out of my mind. If I had to choose between George and a baby, I'd take George. My husband is my life."

Pam put down her drink and took her sister's hand. "And you're his. But you don't have to choose," she said. "George wants a baby, too."

"We have a different kind of marriage," Brenda went on, almost by rote. "We want to travel, collect art, study French, have intimate little dinner parties with clever, interesting people. Our lives—" She stopped and looked at her sister. "What did you say?"

"I said 'George wants a baby, too.'"

Brenda cocked her head to one side and regarded her sister suspiciously. "How do you know that?"

"He told me. It seems Scott had a tremendous influence on him, and his nesting instinct is nagging at him as much as yours is."

Brenda stared across the table at her sister. "Why didn't you tell me?"

"I told him to tell you," Pam said. She wanted to laugh, except that would make Brenda mad. The whole situation, however, was too ridiculous for words. Her two young sons communicated with each other better than Brenda and George.

"But he didn't tell me," Brenda said. "Surely you figured that out. So why didn't *you* tell him I wanted a baby, too?"

"I practically did, Brenda. Really. I stopped just short of hitting him over the head with it, but I didn't say the actual words because I thought that they should come from you. After all, you two are grown-up people and shouldn't need an intermediary. George kept going on about how he just couldn't disappoint you like that and that he was a really terrible person to want more out of marriage than perfection. He was on a real guilt trip over his change of heart. I'm sorry, Brenda, I thought George would run right home and you two would laugh and cry and get pregnant."

Brenda shook her head in amazement. "You mean all these weeks when we've been hemming and hawing around, we've both been trying to find a way to say the same thing."

"So it would seem. Sounds like you two need to make up for lost time."

"He really wants a baby?"

"Last month he did," Pam said. "You're going to have to find out his present state of mind on your own. And for heaven's sake, stop the hemming and hawing."

"We have to go," Brenda said, grabbing her purse.

"May I finish my drink first? I don't have many opportunities to go on outings with my sister and to drink frozen margaritas in a piano bar."

"Well, hurry up," Brenda said impatiently, finishing her own drink with one hard sip on the straw. "I want to stop at North Park Mall. You can help me pick out a nightgown. Black lace, don't you think? Or should it be white? And then I need to buy a bottle of champagne. Oh, sis, give me a hug. I feel like a one-ton weight has just been lifted off my shoulders."

Pam hugged her sister. "You're sure now? Remember, kids are for life. You can't divorce them. They rob you of sleep and add inches to your waist, and you'll never be your own person again—at least not for a long, long time. You'll end up with your white brocade sofa covered in brown vinyl. Your BMW will have ketchup stains on the back seat."

Brenda smiled. "I know. I've seen your sofa and car. I've seen you exhausted and at your wits' end. But I've also seen the way you hug and kiss those two little boys. I saw how scared you were when Tommy got sick, and I got pretty scared myself. You've taught me well the meaning and realities of motherhood, sis, and I thank you for the lesson. I love my husband, and because I do, it makes me want very much to have children with him. It makes *baby* just about the sweetest word I've ever heard."

"Go for it," Pam said, giving her sister the thumbs-up sign. "I need to get home and shell yet another batch of shrimp, but I'm sure you can manage to find the sexiest nightgown at North Park. And don't forget romantic music and candlelight.''

''What if he's changed his mind?'' Brenda asked, perched on the edge of her seat, ready to go.

Pam laughed. ''I think it's out of his hands now, if I know my sister. George will be a father, it seems, and I think a rather splendid one.''

Chapter Eleven

Joel took Scott and Tommy with him when he went to pick up the smoked turkeys, rental glassware and wine fountain and deliver them to the Pattersons' house in preparation for their annual Christmas open house that evening. Pam doubted the wisdom of taking the boys to a mansion, but she was too rattled to protest. Scott and Tommy had been wild all day, cooped up in the house because of the nasty cold rain that was threatening to turn to sleet. They insisted on playing chase with Barney, and the continual squealing, yelling and barking got on Pam's nerves.

With forced patience, Pam tried redirection, searching for a game for her children to play, a television program for them to watch. She didn't have time to read stories but suggested they color a picture for Santa Claus. Then, out of desperation, she brought the Tinkertoys out of the hall closet and suggested they see how long a snake they could make with them. Her ideas only worked momentarily, however, and she was on the verge of losing her temper when the boys knocked down the Christmas tree while racing through the living room with Barney.

She stood in the entry hall, viewing the disaster in her living room, too stunned to speak.

"Come on, guys," Joel had said, getting their coats from the closet, "I think in the interest of your health and your mom's sanity, I'd better get you out of here for a while."

Sudden peace descended on her house like a blessing. She sighed, then began the thankless job of righting and reassembling her poor Christmas tree. "Bah, humbug," she told Barney. "Whoever invented Christmas trees anyway? And I thought dogs were supposed to have a calming effect on children. You're as bad as they are." Barney misunderstood her displeasure and decided she had reinstated the sofa rule. He reluctantly jumped off and lumbered down the hall toward her bedroom.

Trying a bit of rationalization to cheer herself, Pam decided it was a good thing she had economized and bought a small tree or she would have been facing an even worse mess. As it was, getting the ornaments back on the tree and sweeping up the broken ones took the better part of an hour she couldn't spare.

Pam would have loved to take a break, put her feet up and have a cup of tea, but she could do that next week when she was with her parents in Santa Fe. She would have the Pattersons' open house out of the way, have managed somehow to get packed and on her way and be able to turn into a daughter again with loving, indulgent parents to fuss over her a bit. When she opened their letter last month and found airplane tickets inside, Pam was overjoyed. Her parents lived in a different house in a different town, but it would still seem like a return to her childhood with much of the same furniture, the same pictures on the walls, the same Christmas goodies and the same mother and father.

Brenda and George were already in Santa Fe, having decided to leave a few days before Christmas since both needed to be back at work the Monday following.

There was so much to do before she and the boys could get on that plane Christmas Day. Pam had wanted to say no to the Pattersons' Christmas Eve open house, but she couldn't afford to turn down that much money. Santa Claus would have a real struggle without the Pattersons. As it was, Pam had charged a shiny red tricycle for Scott, a red wagon for Tommy, a swing set Joel promised he could put together and a pair of talking teddy bears. She told her boys they were very lucky to be having two Christmases—one in their own home on Christmas morning, when they would see what Santa had left, then another that evening after they had flown on an airplane to Grandma and Grandpa's house in New Mexico. Tommy still wasn't quite sure what Christmas was all about, but he knew it was something special. Scott, however, had climbed up on Santa's lap at the mall like a real pro and announced that he was three now and didn't Santa think he was old enough for a trike. "I can give my kiddie car to my brother," Scott said. "Tommy's only two. He's still little."

Pam dismantled the "snake" and put the Tinkertoys out of sight on the top shelf of the hall closet. She turned on the kitchen radio and found a station playing Christmas music, then went back to stuffing a lobster mixture into mushrooms. She couldn't decide if she hoped Joel stayed away with the boys all afternoon or hurried home to help her.

She wondered if Joel had put off going to Colorado just to help her with the holiday-season catering. He knew she would be hard-pressed to do it alone, especially this open house. In fact, she would be hard-pressed to continue her catering service alone. It had expanded into a two-person operation, and when Joel left, her problems would increase and her income would lessen. But he didn't owe her anything, and he should be studying for his CPA exam right now instead of helping her. He should be in Colorado starting a new life. But she didn't push him anymore. Although they didn't discuss it, she sensed the day of his leaving was close at hand, and now she wished she had some way to postpone it—indefinitely.

Joel's hair was longer now, as though he were already preparing for the more liberal environment of the Colorado ski slopes. His beautiful auburn locks curled about his ears, making him look even younger. Last Wednesday, when they stopped off to have a beer after catering a Christmas party for the library board, the bartender didn't believe Joel was over twenty-one and asked to see his driver's license. It had created an awkward moment, and she and Joel had sipped their beer in silence. The bartender knew without asking that Pam was old enough to drink, the difference in her and Joel's ages being all too apparent. Until Joel came along, Pam hadn't thought much about age. Thirty had been a temporary downer but no big deal, but now Joel's youth made her older by comparison.

She suspected Joel was ready to be off but continued working with her out of a sense of obligation. And while she sensed he was growing accustomed to the idea of leaving her, Pam was certain he would feel bad about leaving Scott and Tommy without a male influence in their lives once again. When Joel left, there would be no one to rough-and-tumble with them on the living-room floor, no one to toss them into the air and make them squeal with delight. And there was a tender side to Joel.

He kissed away the boys' "ouchies" and rocked away their tears. Joel was born to be a father, and she hoped he had children of his own someday.

She thought of the day when Joel would proudly hold his own newborn child in his arms, and she felt sad for her children, whose father did not love them. And she felt jealous of the woman who would bear Joel's child.

Joel was more honest with her now, admitting that while he had never been more smitten with a woman than he had been with her, that he did indeed wonder how much difference age made. He had been caught up in a romantic dream and refused at first to deal with the question. Now he faced the fact that a difference of almost ten years was a lot, that it could cause problems, that it could make a permanent relationship between them less likely.

And he had other reservations.

He admitted that as much as he cared for Tommy and Scott, the idea of a ready-made family was disturbing. Following in another man's footsteps was not what he had envisioned for himself.

And if he and Pam had ever married, he would have felt their union tarnished somewhat by the fact that she had had another husband, been wife to another man.

He had asked her if her present bed had been the one she shared with Marty.

"Yes," she said. "I didn't buy a new bed."

"Does it bother you that you've slept with two men in the same bed?" he asked.

"No," Pam had said, trying to control her anger. "Marty left me. I didn't leave him. And buying a new bed wouldn't change the circumstances of my life. You're a baby, Joel. A romantic baby who wants purity and new mattresses and an innocent wife. I hope you find one who lives up to your expectations."

Strange how Joel's newly-found honesty meant it was somehow all right for them to touch again. When Pam needed a hug, she could ask for one. He rubbed her shoulders again, and they even held hands sometimes. The sexual tension that had so dominated the summer had been stored away like summer frocks in a wardrobe chest.

Only in the night did the old longings attack her, reminding her she was a woman in her prime who had much love yet to give.

Intellectually, she knew there would be another man in her life, that most likely she would fall in love again and eventually remarry. But her heart was more fickle. In her heart, it felt as though there would always be a big hole where Joel was supposed to be.

"*RUDOLPH THE RED-NOSED REINDEER* comes on television at six-thirty," Pam told Jessica Duff, after explaining to her about the boys' dinner. "After they watch it, I'm sure they'll want you to read the book to them. They know they're supposed to go to bed early because Santa needs to come, but I'm afraid they're so wound up, you might have a hard time getting them to sleep."

"I'm sure we'll manage somehow," Jessica assured her.

Jessica was wearing a gray skirt and lavender sweater. Her hair was brushed softly about her shoulders. Without her bun and stern clothing, she looked less formidable than usual and decidedly prettier.

"I really appreciate your coming," Pam said. "My regular sitter had family plans this evening. Are you sure you're not missing something with Robert and the girls?"

"They are at his parents' home in Houston for a few days," she explained.

"And you have no family? It seems a shame to be alone at Christmas."

"Oh, I'm rather used to it," Jessica insisted. "I used to alternate Christmases between my sister's family in Waco and my brother's in Des Moines, but the last few years, I haven't had the heart for it."

"You're welcome to spend the night and be with us tomorrow," Pam said.

"Thank you, no. I'd feel like an intruder, and besides, it's more difficult for me to be with other families than to be alone. I plan to go to church in the morning and enjoy the music. And then I'll help serve Christmas dinner to the homeless at one of the downtown missions."

Pam knew the woman didn't want her sympathy, so she didn't offer it. But she felt incredibly grateful that she herself had children and probably would someday have grandchildren to fill her life. Christmas sometimes seemed like a hassle, especially when Christmas trees got knocked over by hyperactive children, but to be alone on that day of all days seemed especially sad.

Joel had already loaded most of the food into the station wagon. Pam helped him finish up, and they were off. "Terrible way to spend Christmas Eve," Pam said. "I wish I weren't poor."

"I wish I had that damned swing set put together," Joel said. "It's going to be a long night."

Behind locked garage doors, Joel had been working on the project, but apparently swing-set assembly was not his forte and he had run into problems getting the screws A to match up with holes B.

The Dallas traffic was almost bumper-to-bumper—last-minute shoppers, Pam presumed, trying to finish up before the stores closed. She hoped they all got home before the storm worsened and streets froze over. It was only three o'clock, but already it was growing dark.

Both the inside and the outside of the Pattersons' mansion were bright and warm and lavishly decorated for the season. The roof and windows were outlined in thousands of twinkling white lights, and a huge evergreen in the yard was aglow with larger multicolored lights. A twelve-foot tree dominated the two-story entry hall, and festive garlands were draped over mirrors, mantels, doorways and banisters. Exquisite arrangements with candles and greenery decorated every table. The smell of bayberry and pine wafted throughout the house.

By the time the guests began to arrive, the dining-room table was laden with the foodstuffs Pam and Joel had taken a week to prepare. Joel had already assembled the wine fountain on the round glass table that stood in the dining room's huge bay window. Pam poured eggnog made from her mother's recipe into Buffy Patterson's silver heirloom punch bowl.

The bad weather did not seem to have deterred the Pattersons' guests, but then an invitation from Buffy Patterson was akin to a command among Dallas high society. Buffy looked magnificent in a jeweled hostess gown that looked as though it cost a king's ransom. A tuxedo-clad Philip Patterson was his usual haughty self, always a marked contrast to his gregarious wife. "His expression always looks like he's offended by a bad smell," Joel whispered.

"Warm and cozy is not his style," Pam whispered back, giving the uniformed maid a supply of cheese balls with which to replenish the platter on the buffet table.

Joel dropped his voice still lower. "Do you suppose he and Buffy still . . ."

"I haven't the faintest idea," Pam said, cutting him off and sending him to check the fountain. But she had wondered the same thing herself. The Pattersons seemed so remote with each other. Was their marriage simply a facade?

At the evening's end, Buffy—as usual—found things to complain about. The cheese fondue wasn't spicy enough. The pâté was insipid. They had run out of mincemeat tarts. The chocolate torte didn't have as much Grand Marnier as last time. But she finally admitted they had done a good job with the food. And when she wrote their check at the end of the evening, she was generous with a Christmas bonus.

"Pam tells me you're planning to leave the business— and the state," Buffy said to Joel. "I'm sorry. Since last summer, I've watched the two of you working together, wishing I could be young again and have something to work for and a person in my life that I couldn't go fifteen minutes without touching. I thought you two had something really lovely."

On the way home, Joel said, "I hadn't realized Miz Buffy was human."

"I hadn't realized she was unhappy," Pam said. "Strange, isn't it? I guess I made the mistake of assuming anyone who lived in a mansion and had all that money had to be happier than other people."

A worried Jessica met them at the door. "The dog is missing," she said at once. "I let him out earlier, and he never came back. Then I realized the back gate was open.

I looked up and down the block some but didn't dare leave two sleeping children alone.''

"Barney doesn't wander off, does he?" Joel asked.

"Not usually," Pam said. "But he has been known to chase cats and get lost. He's not the smartest dog in the world."

But he was a dear one, Pam thought. It wasn't going to be much of a Christmas if Barney was lost. "I'll go look for him while you work on the swing set," she told Joel.

"The hell you will," Joel said. "I'm not going to have you driving up and down back streets and alleys by yourself at this hour. You unload the station wagon, and I'll go look for Barney."

Pam paid Jessica and couldn't resist giving the woman a hug. "Please, come to see me when I get back from my trip—just to visit and not to baby-sit."

"I'd like that. I'm so sorry about the dog. I should have checked to see that the gate was closed."

"No, *I* should have checked to see that the gate was closed. But he usually stays pretty close to home. I imagine Joel will find him."

Joel took off in his van, and Pam began unloading the station wagon. If it weren't for the swing set, she would have put the car in the garage and carried things in through the kitchen door. The drizzle was finally turning to sleet, as the weatherman had predicted. Dallas didn't have much snow, but the city sometimes had crippling ice storms.

Little pieces of ice bit at her skin as she made a dozen trips back and forth across the driveway. Barney didn't like the cold. *Please,* she thought, *please let Joel find him.*

Every muscle in her body ached by the time she had finished putting pans, platters, food and utensils away. She looked at the kitchen clock. Midnight. The wind even sounded cold.

With dragging footsteps, she carried a basket of folded clothes from the laundry room down the hall to her bedroom and pulled the suitcases out of the closets. One was already packed with gift-wrapped Christmas presents for her parents, Brenda and George. Pam packed two others with hers and the boys' clothing, hoping she wasn't forgetting anything important. It was hard to think about anything but a big old yellow dog.

It was one o'clock.

She filled the boys' Christmas stockings with Life Savers, tiny plastic cars and new crayons. Since there was no mantel, they had pinned the stockings to the back of the sofa.

She put big red bows on the tricycle, teddy bears and Tommy's new wagon, then wrote a note from Santa Claus, explaining that he hadn't had time to finish putting the swing set together because he needed to get toys delivered to other boys and girls and that he hoped Joel would finish the job for him.

Then she stood looking out the window for car lights. Sleet beat a steady tattoo against the windowpane. She wondered if her flight to Santa Fe would be canceled, and images of a cold, wet, frightened dog kept flashing across her mind.

It was past two.

She took a quick shower and got ready for bed. Finally she had her cup of hot tea and a chance to put her feet up, but she couldn't enjoy it. She pulled her rocker in front of the window to keep her vigil and wrapped herself up in a quilt.

Poor Joel. He must be exhausted. By now Barney had probably crawled into a protected place and gone to sleep. Joel would never find him. Maybe in the morning. "Come home, Joel," she whispered. "Give up."

She jumped when the phone rang.

"I found him," Joel's weary voice said. "I'm at the vet's. Barney's foot was cut pretty bad, but the doc's stitching him up."

"What happened?"

"I don't know. I found him huddled in between a couple of trash cans half frozen, and his foot's a mess. He looked like he'd lost a lot of blood. There was a number in the phone book for emergency vet service, but the vet on call has his office out in Richardson on a street I'd never heard of. I had a terrible time finding it."

"Joel, thanks. I guess you know how important that dog is."

"Yeah, he's a good old dog. I'm just glad I found him, and he was plenty glad to see me."

Pam went back to her rocker and shed a few tears of relief. And then tears of sadness. She wanted Joel for the rest of her life. He was so good, too good to be true for someone like her.

At three-thirty Joel's van pulled into the drive behind her station wagon. She opened the front door, and Joel carried the whimpering, bandaged animal inside. Pam had already put an old blanket on the sofa, and they wrapped Barney up like a baby.

Pam stroked the big dog's head. "Don't you do that anymore," she told him. "Those boys need you."

"He'll be fine," Joel told her. "The doc gave him a shot that should knock him out for the rest of the night. He said for me to bring him back next week and get the stitches out. His foot was sliced up pretty badly."

"He would have frozen to death by morning," Pam said.

"Oh, I don't know about that, but he was probably lost and was suffering a lot, weren't you guy?" Joel said, petting the groggy animal. "I kept thinking about how good he was with those boys and couldn't stop looking. You know, one more street, one more alley, one more parking lot. I found him behind the Food Mart."

Joel rose to go and began buttoning his coat.

"Don't go," Pam said, reaching for his hand. "I want you here in the morning when the boys wake up, and I want you to hold me. I want one last time."

IN THE MORNING, Joel rose quietly from Pam's bed, zipped up his coat and carried Barney out onto the frozen grass. The dog was shaky but obligingly lifted his leg. Joel carried him back inside, offered him a drink of water and a bit of food then put him back on the sofa and covered him.

Joel put on the coffeepot, turned up the thermostat then got two sleepy little boys from their beds and carried them down the hall to their mother's room. "Merry Christmas, guys," he said.

Pam opened her arms to them, Joel watched as they burrowed up against her like two little puppy dogs seeking their mother's warmth. Pam laughed. "Hey, you guys slept kind of late this cold winter morning. Don't you two want to see what Santa Claus has brought?"

Scott picked up on it first. "Santa Claus?" he said, sitting up and rubbing his eyes. "Did he bring me a trike?"

"I don't know," Pam said. "I guess we'd better go have a look."

Scott jumped on top of his brother. "Tommy, c'mon. We gotta go see!"

Pam pulled on her robe as she and Joel followed two pajama-clad little creatures racing down the hallway.

"A bell!" Scott said gleefully. "My trike has a bell. Look, Mommie!"

"I told you that bell was a mistake," Pam told Joel over the din.

"Hey, Tommy, look what Santa left for you," Joel said, showing him the little red wagon filled with wooden blocks.

After the boys had tried out the talking bears, answering questions about their age, name and sex and listening to the bears recite nursery rhymes, Joel set Scott and Tommy down on the sofa beside Barney and explained that their dog had had an accident and had a very sore foot. "He can't play with you today, but maybe he'll be feeling better by the time you get back from your trip."

"We're goin' in an airplane," Scott said excitedly.

"Yeah, I know," Joel said. "That's terrific."

Tommy leaned close to Barney to demonstrate his talking bear to the dog. Barney watched with droopy eyes.

After the boys had examined the contents of their stockings and been told about the swing set, Pam went off to cook breakfast. While she was mixing blueberry muffins, Jessica called to ask about Barney.

Joel dressed the boys and took them to the garage to show them the half-assembled swing set. He assured them it would be standing in the backyard when they got back from their trip.

After breakfast Joel and Pam lingered over coffee while the boys ran to play with their toys. "Be careful of Barney," Joel called after them.

With the buffering presence of the boys removed, Pam felt shy in Joel's presence, the memory of their lovemaking lingering in her mind, on her skin. She supposed she should examine the morality of making love with a man she might never see again, but she was weary of self-examination. Last night it had seemed like the thing to do, and she was not sorry this morning. What she did feel was womanly, warm, beautiful, sad, hopeless.

Joel had a Christmas present for her—a silver-framed picture he'd had Paul take of the two of them on graduation day. He was holding his mortarboard but still wearing his gown, his arm was draped around her shoulders.

"Someday, you might want to remember what we looked like back then," he said.

Pam smiled. Her present for him was also a picture, of her and the boys sitting on the back step with Barney. "Cindy took it," she said. "We explained that it was for you. That's why the boys are grinning like that."

Pam went to get dressed and add last-minute items to the suitcases. She called the airport to make sure the runways were open and her flight was still scheduled.

Joel dropped them off at the terminal entrance then went to park the car. When Pam checked the bags, she discovered the flight was delayed a half hour.

The half hour grew into an hour, and the boys grew more and more restless. Joel watched them while Pam went to call her parents and warn them about the delay. Then she held Tommy and tried to get him to take a nap, while Joel walked up and down the concourse with an energetic Scott.

Tommy refused to sleep, so they all walked a bit and bought ice-cream cones. Tommy was getting crankier and crankier, and Pam made a pillow for him out of his coat and insisted he stretch out on two chairs to sleep. Once he knew she meant business, he fell asleep almost immediately. She sat with the sleeping child while Joel managed the now-surly Scott, who was demanding another ice-cream cone. "Hey, man, that was the world's most expensive ice cream, and you can't have another one," Joel said. "You'll have to settle for a stick of gum."

Scott slapped the gum from Joel's hand.

"Pick it up, buddy."

"No," Scott said.

Normally Joel would have said there would be no more wrestling matches unless Scott behaved, but Joel just looked down at the boy, his eyes sad, then turned and walked away. Scott picked up the gum and scurried after him.

After two hours the gate agent announced it would be at least another hour more. They were having trouble with the machine that removed the ice from the wings.

Tommy was awake now, and Scott decided to stretch out on the vacated chairs. Pam rubbed his back, encouraging him to take a little nap, and Joel took Tommy's hand and started down the concourse again. Pam wondered how she would have managed her two little barbarians without him, wondered how she would manage all the times in the future without him.

Finally the gate agent announced boarding would be imminent. Joel picked up Scott and hugged him. "I'll take the rental stuff back on Monday," Joel told Pam, "and see about Barney's stitches..."

"Then you're leaving, aren't you?" she asked.

"Yeah. Paul said he'd look after the dog."

Pam didn't trust herself to speak.

"It's been the sweetest and the most bittersweet time of my life," Joel said. "I think a part of me will always love you, Pam, and I'll always compare other women to the loveliest woman I've ever known.'' He was crying. Scott touched the tears on his face, and Joel buried his head against Scott's chest.

Pam's chest hurt with the pain of parting, and with tears streaming down her face, she bent to pick up Tommy.

The agent announced preboarding for those traveling with small children, and Joel helped her take the boys and hand luggage onto the plane. Then there was just time for one last hug.

''Take care of yourself,'' Pam said, and he was gone.

She struggled to control the sobs that shook her chest and to get seat belts fastened. The boys were subdued now. They didn't often see adults cry.

In spite of all their individual and mutual reservations, Joel would have moved in with her. He had withdrawn his briefly tendered offer of marriage, but he would have been her live-in, with the decision about marriage put on hold until some unknown future date. She could have had him for a time at least, she reminded herself.

Had she done the right thing? If only there was a way to know.

Chapter Twelve

Pam, loaded with her purse and two carry-ons, Scott and Tommy running ahead of her, was the last person off the plane. At the end of the hallway, her parents and Brenda and George waited for her. Knowing they would be there at journey's end had helped. Joel was gone. In so many ways, she wasn't sure how she would manage without him, but she kept telling herself that coming home to her family would help heal her.

In spite of an embroidered Mexican shirt, George in his precise haircut, wing-tip shoes and gray flannels managed to look terribly British, and in spite of her denim dress, Brenda looked like a fashion model. Pam's parents, looking robust and well in their matching velour jogging suits, were their same timeless selves with salt-and-pepper hair, clear-rimmed glasses, ruddy cheeks and ready smiles.

Pam hung back a bit and let two sturdy little boys be scooped up by their eager grandparents. "Would you look how these two have grown?" Sam Hunter said to his wife.

"I got a new trike," Scott told his granddaddy, "and Tommy's got a wagon."

"Is that right?" Sam said with a laugh and a hug. "Do you still like to watch the game shows? Did you see Linda win a car yesterday?"

Scott nodded excitely. "It was blue."

Everyone laughed, and Scott looked pleased with himself.

"What about you, Tommy?" Mavis Hunter asked her younger grandson. "Do you like television?"

But Tommy was bashful and wouldn't take his fingers out of his mouth.

"Hey, don't I get a hug?" Pam said. "I think I feel jealous of my own sons."

Sam and Mavis handed their grandsons over to Brenda and George, then turned their attention to their daughter, embracing her in a three-way hug. "Merry Christmas, Pam, darling," Mavis said. "The turkey's in the oven. Brenda and I have been cooking for days. We're going to have the most wonderful Christmas ever, and you don't need to lift a finger. Daddy and I will look after the boys, and you can just rest. You look like you need it, honey."

Pam knew she looked worse for wear. The flight had been rough, and Tommy had fussed. Scott had spilled his Coke on her slacks. And the past days, weeks, months had taken their toll. She was physically and emotionally exhausted, and now that she was here in the protective presence of her parents, she could acknowledge that was so. She would gratefully let her parents look after the boys and rest.

She allowed her father to take her bags and walked arm in arm with her mother down the concourse.

"I'm glad to be here, Mom. I need a little TLC."

"I can see," Mavis said. "We've been so excited about you and the boys coming, but you know, I was hoping you'd surprise us when you got off that plane and have Marty at your side.''

"Marty!'' Pam would have stopped in her tracks, but her mother propelled her along the concourse toward the baggage-claim area.

"Yes, Brenda told us he's back in Dallas. How is he? Is he ready to settle down and do his duty by his family? I always had a feeling he'd get his head on straight and come back. I think deep inside he loves you and the boys.''

"Oh, Mom, don't be so naive! Marty didn't even ask to see the boys. He's broke and wants me to help him get back on his feet—but 'do his duty by his family'? I'd laugh if it didn't make me want to cry.''

"I always liked Marty,'' Mavis said defensively. "I didn't think you had any business marrying an entertainer, and remember what I told you? I said you couldn't expect as much out of him as a solid man like your father, but if you went ahead and got married, your father and I expected you to stay that way. Of course, I could see why you wanted to marry him. He's irresponsible but such a sweet boy. And a voice as pretty as Elvis's.''

" 'Sweet' is not the word I'd use,'' Pam said, irritation apparent in her voice. "More like con artist, albeit a charming one.''

"Would you like your daddy to talk to him?'' Mavis asked. "Maybe man-to-man they can get this thing straightened out.''

"Mom, I'm going to get right back on that airplane if you don't shut up about Marty! He's history.''

"Well, you know how your father and I feel about divorce, honey. And when Brenda told us you weren't interested in getting back with Marty because you were seeing someone else, we were very disappointed in you.''

Pam pulled her arm away from her mother's waist and glared over her shoulder at her sister. "Thanks a lot, Brenda! You really set me up, didn't you? This sure isn't the homecoming I've been getting teary-eyed over for weeks now."

"I didn't say it like that," Brenda said. "I said you weren't interested in getting back with Marty *and* you were interested in another man."

Pam didn't trust herself to speak. She was sorry she had come. Never had she felt so alone in the world. Joel would be gone when she got back. Because they didn't believe in divorce, her parents wanted her to go live with a jerk who hadn't seen his children in almost two years and probably didn't even remember their names. Brenda should have known better than to tell them about Marty.

Pam wished she was back in her own little home with her boys and Joel. Joel cared more about her boys than Marty ever had.

She had kidded herself into thinking this was going to be a homecoming, that she could crawl back into the bosom of her family and be a little girl again. The only place that was home to her was a modest little house in Dallas.

"Wait," she said, stopping at a pay phone. "I need to make a call."

Pam called Joel's number first, then dialed her own phone number and let it ring for a long time. He wasn't there, but she couldn't bring herself to hang up the receiver. She imagined her empty house with the sound of the telephone ringing throughout the rooms, past the lonely, unlit Christmas tree and the seldom-used dining room, past a kitchen oddly tidy and bereft of activity, past the boys' bedroom with a new wagon and tricycle parked in the corner. The phone on her bedside table would be ringing. She could see the bed. It was made now, its J. C. Penney's floral bedspread smoothly in place, but last night she and Joel had been in that bed, making love. Their exhausted bodies had reached out to each other and for a time given sustenance and tenderness. The cares of the world had fallen away, and it hadn't mattered that she was on the brink of poverty and that she was farther down life's road than he was. They had lost themselves in the feelings of love and, for that magical time, become all things to each other. He was both boy and man to her. They were as innocent as newborns and as experienced as the most worldly-wise, their voyage one of discovery and rediscovery. And finally, when they had fallen into the satiated sleep of lovers, that was fulfilling, too, with moist bodies clinging under rumpled covers, sinking into a warm, dreamless sleep, reviving only enough from time to time to touch the other's sleeping form and take exquisite comfort in that physical presence before sinking again into sweet slumber.

Mentally, Pam closed the door to the bedroom. She felt the questioning eyes of her relatives grouped around her, heard their thoughts. *What in the world is the matter with Pam?*

Hang up, she told herself. *Go eat your mother's turkey and celebrate Christmas. Act normal.* But just as she was about to replace the receiver, a voice answered.

"Paul?" Pam said, puzzled. "Is that you?"

"Yeah. How's it going? Are you in Santa Fe?"

"Yes. Is Joel there?"

"No. Cindy and I are over here picking up the dog. We'll get all that rental stuff returned for you on Monday. And I promised him I'd put that swing set together before you get back."

"He's gone? Already?"

"Yeah. He said it was too depressing for him to hang around. He's left for Colorado."

"Do you have an address or a phone number for where he'll be up there?"

"No. He said he'd get in touch one of these days."

Pam hung up the telephone and leaned her head against the side of the cubicle. He was really gone. But then, what had she expected? She had told him to go. For all the right reasons, she had told him to go.

She felt a hand on her shoulder. "Sis, you okay?"

"Sure. I'm great. Just great."

THOUGH TARNISHED, HER VISIT had settled into warm, comfortable patterns. Her parents fussed over her and relieved her of what mothering chores they could. But Sam and Mavis became baffled when the boys got cranky or got into fights, and Pam had to step in. "Two little girls were easier to raise," Mavis admitted.

The day after Christmas they all went to nearby San Ildefonso Pueblo to watch ceremonial Indian dances, which Pam found to be a strange mingling of ancient Indian rites and Catholicism. Fascinated, George took three rolls of film. The boys were astonished to see Indians in traditional dress outside of a television set. George posed them with three Indian children in traditional dress in what Pam knew would be a charming photograph. And an Indian youth obligingly took a family picture of the seven of them with the pueblo in the background. George promised Pam copies of both pictures.

Her mother cooked all her daughters' favorites, and her daddy showed home movies so the boys could see their mommy and Aunt Brenda when they were little. Scott understood, but Tommy obviously did not comprehend that those flickering little girls splashing in a kiddie pool were the two grown-up women sitting on the sofa beside him.

And there on the screen were her parents, younger, waving to an unsteady camera. Had she been taking those pictures or Brenda? Pam couldn't remember. Her parents weren't as timeless as she had supposed, realizing they had done twenty-plus years' worth of aging in twenty-plus years. But that was the way of life.

Grow old along with me! / The best is yet to be. Her parents' marriage had fulfilled the Browning couplet. They were growing old together, enjoying years made rich and full with their mature love, their shared interests. They bargain-hunted at garage sales and antique stores. They enjoyed the crafts and lore of the unique city they had chosen for their retirement. They traveled in their motor home throughout the state, going to the horse races, fiestas, rodeos and visiting their favorite fishing holes. They took an active role in their church and the local senior citizens' center, where they played bridge two evenings a week and attended monthly dances. The simple events of their lives were made meaningful because they shared them with a beloved person. They still touched, held hands, and Pam was quite certain they enjoyed a physical relationship. Her mother's look could turn quite coquettish at times when dealing with her still-handsome husband. And her father loved to come up behind his wife while she was cooking and nuzzle her neck with his end-of-the-day whiskers. She would feign displeasure and announce that a woman wasn't safe in her own kitchen. If Sam thought no one was looking, he would pat her fanny, and she would turn her face to be kissed.

All Pam wanted out of life was a marriage as strong and true as her parents' and for her boys to grow into healthy happy young men. She didn't care about riches or social position. Even when she had been married to Marty, fame and fortune had been his dream, not hers.

Grow old along with me... The verse haunted her throughout the week, taunted her. She didn't want to grow old alone. She wanted the best that was yet to be in her life.

But in a way, the success of her parents' marriage made them believe too strongly in the institution. They had had problems and overcome them. Others should be able to do the same, they thought. It was hard for them to accept a daughter who turned a deaf ear to a seemingly repentant husband.

Her father waited until Brenda and George had departed to have his go at her. Pam was curled up on the sofa, reading a magazine and enjoying the beautiful view out the picture window of the splendidly rugged Sangre de Cristo Mountains.

"You know, your mother and I just want what is best for you," he began, handing her a cup of tea and pulling a side chair close.

"I hope so," Pam said, tossing her magazine onto the coffee table. "But if you're going to tell me Marty is what's best for me, forget it, Daddy. I will not let him destroy my life a second time."

"People change," Sam said, sipping his tea.

"Not the Martys of the world," she insisted. The tea was too hot. She put it down on the magazine.

"I think in his own way that Marty loved you, honey, and maybe he still does."

"Yes, as much as a self-centered person like Marty can love another person, I think you're right. And that makes me sad, but I will not sacrifice myself and my boys to a life with a man who's only capable of a very incomplete sort of love."

"It's hard for your mother and me to accept the finality of your divorce now that we know Marty is willing to make amends."

"But it is final, Daddy, and you have to accept my judgment on this one. I'm a grown-up woman, and I will do what I believe is best for myself and my children. And I don't want to discuss this again. It's really over."

"Yes, if you feel that strongly, I think it's best that we not talk about Marty again. So what are you going to do, honey? You need a man to support you and help raise those boys."

"That would be nice, Daddy, but as difficult as my life is at times, I can manage on my own. I will not marry any man because I have to be supported and can't take care of myself. If I marry again, it will be because I want to be with one certain man for the rest of my life. In a way, I guess I should thank Marty. By his leaving me, I've learned that I'm strong and can do what needs to be done for myself and my children. I'll wait until I can have a marriage like the one you and Mom have. You help each other and lean on each other and love each other. I won't settle for less again."

JOEL SAT ON THE TERRACE, looking up at the famous Mary Jane ski run. He shaded his eyes from the brilliant sunlight and watched the skiers navigate the hair-raising upper slope. Mary Jane was too much woman for him; he had found out this afternoon the hard way. A few weekends' worth of instruction on lesser slopes had not prepared him for her treachery. Finally, after a wipe-out that shook him pretty badly, he admitted defeat, scooted on his bottom to a protected place under some trees, removed his skis and hiked down. Now he watched in amazement as skiers flew down the face of the mountain like colorful birds, skillfully navigating moguls, leaping inclines, challenging Mary Jane and winning.

Maybe skiing wasn't his sport. It was too damned expensive anyway. He could work all week busing tables then empty his pockets with two days of equipment rental and lift tickets. Of course, he would be making a little more now that he was moving up to morning-shift short-order cook in the Winter Park restaurant where he had found work. And he hated to give up. There had been exhilarating moments on other runs when he felt reasonably competent and almost under control.

He had decided not to take Greg Williamson's dad up on his job offer as assistant comptroller at the lodge in Aspen. Joel didn't want to feel obligated, preferring to drift for a time. His first couple of weeks in the state he'd signed on short-term with a road crew out of Fort Collins. If he walked out of his present job tomorrow, the surly proprietor would have a new kid by sundown. And while he felt a bit guilty about not using his hard-earned college education, Joel didn't want office work, not yet, anyway. After his push to get out of school, he was burned out on accountancy and tax codes. He knew eventually he would light someplace, take his CPA exam, hang out a shingle and settle down to responsible citizenhood. Or maybe he'd have his own restaurant or catering service. The food-service business interested him, even as conducted at Shorty's Bar and Grill. But right now he just wanted to enjoy the scenery and see if there was a skier lurking someplace in his lean frame.

Joel found the incredible winter beauty of the Rockies to be therapeutic. Beyond his small life and problems, there was a big, beautiful world waiting for him, and he was determined to enjoy it.

Part of the beauty of Colorado rested in its inhabitants. Attractive, athletic people were everywhere, seemingly the norm, at least in the ski communities. He watched a shapely young woman in a tight hot-pink-and-black Lycra ski suit that showed her every comely curve to great advantage as she came to a smart stop at the bottom of the run. She poled her way over to a ski rack and unhooked her skis and the top buckles of her boots. By this time, she had felt his gaze.

She smiled in his direction as she clumped up the steps in her heavy ski boots, her teeth dazzlingly white against smooth, tanned skin. She pulled off her cap and shook loose a mane of sun-streaked hair. She was, in a word, gorgeous, probably the most gorgeous of the hundreds of gorgeous women Joel had gazed at this day. If she wasn't a movie star, she should have been. If he were a producer, he would sign her on the spot.

She reminded him of Stephanie. He'd called Stephanie last week. She was getting married. When he sorted out his feelings, he discovered he was relieved. He really didn't want to take up with her again; he was just lonely.

The glamorous skier could have sat alone at any of a half dozen empty tables, but she stopped at Joel's table. "Hi," she said brightly. "This place taken?"

"No, have a seat," Joel offered. Her eyes were an arresting shade of turquoise. Her voluptuous, hot-pink bosom was framed by the scooped-out top of her skin-tight black-and-pink-striped overalls. *Amazing*, Joel thought, and the sun suddenly felt a bit warmer.

"Have a good run?" she asked, propping her feet on a nearby chair and dabbing sun screen on her nose, then closed her arresting eyes and turned her perfect face to the sun.

"Yeah, I lived to tell about it," Joel said sarcastically.

"She's a dandy, all right," the girl said. "If it weren't for Mary Jane, I wouldn't bother with Winter Park. I like

Aspen and Snow Mass better. You ever skied Purgatory? They had great powder last week. Think I'll go back.''

"Do you do anything besides ski?" Joel asked.

"Sure. I play tennis, scuba, sky dive, hang glide, go to college when it's absolutely necessary. How about yourself?''

"I turn eggs over-easy without breaking them.''

She opened her eyes and turned to look at him.

"I'm the breakfast cook at Shorty's Bar and Grill out on the highway," he explained.

She smiled, revealing once again her Farrah Fawcett teeth. "You're cute. How's about ordering me a Coors?''

Her name was Missy Milan, and she was from Denver. She was a junior at Colorado State College in Greeley. After leisurely enjoying their beer, they rode the lift to the top, and she tried to talk him into trying Mary Jane again, but when he refused, she accompanied him down the lesser slopes on the back side of the mountain.

As she flew ahead of him, the sight of her shapely rear was like a seductive beacon as he tried to keep up.

"Say, are you on the Olympic ski team or something?" he asked as he skied up beside where she was waiting at the entrance to the next run.

Missy only smiled, apparently thinking his question didn't deserve an answer. On the next run, she slowed down and stayed at his side, offering him a few tips. "Bend your knees and put more body in it. You don't need to snowplow—keep those knees together. That's better, Joel, go with the mountain. Hey, there's hope for you even if you are from Texas.''

As she skied to a stop at the bottom of the slope, she asked, "You want me to give you a lesson tomorrow afternoon after you finish with the eggs?''

The top of the world was revealed in sunny, panoramic splendor behind this beautiful creature of the mountains. Joel could see his own distorted image reflected in her ski goggles. That distorted person was being offered a friendship and perhaps more by the prettiest girl on the mountain. And she'd even teach him to ski. He had a sense of the evening ahead. They would drink too much, laugh too loudly, sit naked in a hot tub someplace and end up in bed together. If he played his cards right, he could probably have a succession of afternoons and evenings with her. Her smile was inviting, her body ripe and luscious. A man would have to be out of his mind not to want to bury his face between Missy Milan's wonderful breasts. A part of him wanted to do that, to see her naked, to feast on her body. But the rest of him didn't have the heart for it.

She sensed his indecision. "You got a lady?" she asked, still smiling, but the smile was changing. It was saying, *Hey, it's all right. I understand.*

"Not really, but I'm hung up on one."

"Gotcha. I know how it is."

"I wish I could say yes. You're pretty terrific, Missy, pretty damned terrific."

"And you're so cute and sad looking, you make me want to be your mommy. Take care, Texas. See you around." And she took off in a spray of snow, leaping off the edge of the path to the run below.

Joel skied carefully down the mountain and turned in his equipment. Then he went to Shorty's to listen while the foul-tongued Canadian cursed him out for quitting, and he went to his room to pack his few possessions. He'd heard there was a little town above Loveland where the leftover hippies, misunderstood artists and other misfits of the world hung out. It was called Peace. Surely someone needed a short-order cook in Peace. And maybe he'd get out his books and start brushing up for that exam. Or maybe he wouldn't. He'd seen towns like Peace before, with their scattering of wooden houses tossed in no discernible pattern across some high meadow, with no curbs or sidewalks alongside meandering gravel streets, maybe even no names on the streets—towns populated by weathered men and women who were running away from something.

"HOW LONG DID IT TAKE YOU to get pregnant with Scott once you'd made up your mind to get pregnant?" Brenda asked as she put sweetener in her coffee and pushed a plate of sugar cookies out of temptation's way.

"A couple of months," Pam said. She leaned over and opened the window. "Scott, don't come down the slide until Tommy's out of the way. You're going to hurt him. And keep your coat on. It's chilly out there."

"Are you sure?" Brenda asked, examining the calendar in front of her. "It didn't just happen right away?"

"Relax, Brenda," Pam said, sliding the window closed. "You're too uptight about all this. Give nature a chance to take its course before you resort to temperature charts and fertility workups. I imagine that doctor got a good laugh over a couple coming to him after trying to get pregnant for two whole months!"

"We'll adopt if it doesn't work out," Brenda said, absently fluffing at her hair.

"Fine," Pam said, tapping on the window pane at Scott. Barney looked her way. Scott didn't.

"Did I show you our list of names?" Brenda asked, reaching for her purse.

"You read it to me over the telephone," Pam reminded her. "And if you name a nephew of mine Nigel, he and I will never forgive you."

"It's George's middle name and very distinguished," Brenda said indignantly. "George's great-uncle Nigel was a lord or a baron or something important."

"Well, I hope young Master Nigel won't want to do sports. I can assure you that in all the history of the Lone Star State, there has never been an athlete named Nigel."

"You don't know that."

"Well, it's a pretty good bet," Pam said, breaking off just a tiny bite of sugar cookie. "Being married to a Brit and living in London have caused you to lose some of your Texas savvy, so you'd better take my word for it. Nigel is no name for a Texan. Neither is Cedric. You did better with the girls' names. I'd love to have a niece named Cassandra. Of course, I'd call her Cassie. I hope it's a girl, anyway, to balance out the two boy cousins. But now I sound as bad as you do with all this speculating. Let's forget about babies and names and pregnancy. Why don't you two just concentrate on romance and see what happens? Go on a second honeymoon and leave your temperature chart at home! In six or eight months, if nothing happens, then you can get clinical about it."

"Maybe you're right," Brenda admitted. "I think George is feeling terribly pressured by it all."

"I can imagine," Pam said dryly. "Getting pregnant is all you ever talk about. It's enough to give a husband performance anxiety. And poor George is going to feel left out in the cold before the kid is even a reality."

"You don't think we should turn the spare room into a nursery yet? I brought all these magazine pictures I wanted to show you."

"Absolutely not. Go to Bermuda and take long, romantic walks on the beach. And don't mention pregnancy one single time. You're playing like a broken record."

Pam refilled her sister's coffee cup, then went to the door to ask Scott and Tommy if they wanted some hot cocoa. Both boys made a dash for the back door, with Barney bringing up the rear.

So beautiful, her rosy-cheeked sons, Pam thought as she pulled off their jackets and wiped their runny noses.

"Tommy can slide on his stomach," Scott said.

"On my stomach," Tommy repeated, patting his little round belly.

"The boys are getting big," Brenda said. "Scott looks like such a little man, and Tommy's starting to lose his baby fat. Doesn't it make you sad for them to grow so fast?"

"Yes and no," Pam said, smoothing Tommy's hair. "They're so much fun now, and they still let me cuddle. That's what I'll hate—when they get so big they won't let their mother cuddle them."

The boys had their cocoa and a cookie, then tolerated their mother wiping off their chocolate mustaches before hurrying off to watch *Sesame Street*.

"I understand Jessica Duff helped you at that reception the other night," Brenda said.

Pam rinsed the boys' cups and put them into the dishwasher. "Yes. How did you know?"

"Robert and George had lunch. Robert's dreadfully upset over Miss Duff's decision to leave."

"Then why doesn't he do something about it?"

"Like what?" Brenda asked, carrying the coffee cups to the dishwasher.

"Court her. Treat her like a woman instead of a valued employee. He tells her he wants to marry her, but he's never asked her out on a date."

"A date? Goodness, sis, they live in the same house. Dating seems a little irrelevant. And they'd have to hire a sitter."

"Is that an excuse? He needs to make her feel special or he'll never get to first base. He needs to create opportunities for her to dress up and feel feminine and alluring instead of professional and competent. He needs to buy her flowers, send the children to their grandparents in Houston for a weekend and cook for her instead of her always cooking for him. He needs to sweep her off her feet and not take no for an answer. Make her feel like he can't possibly live without her."

"Is that what you wish Joel had done with you—not take no for an answer?"

"Yes, damn it," Pam said, slamming the cupboard door closed. "Why did he let me be so reasonable and responsible and analyze myself right out of a chance at love? Maybe I should have just lived with him for a while and seen what happened—like he wanted. I wish I'd come home one day and found his clothes in the closet and his toothbrush in the bathroom."

"You would have thrown him out. You guys just weren't in sync, sis. He wanted an escape hatch from commitment, and you were afraid to give him one. I think you both had reservations big enough to drive a Mack truck through."

"But I miss him."

"I know," Brenda said, putting a sympathetic hand on her sister's arm. "Have you ever heard from him?"

"Just a couple of postcards from several different places saying Colorado was beautiful. The last one was from someplace called Peace."

"And you called information in these various towns to see if they had a listing for Joel Bynum?"

"Yeah, I guess I did," Pam admitted. "They don't. I guess he's drifting."

"I was always pushing you to find someone else, and I feel kind of responsible," Brenda admitted. "I still think you were an idiot to let yourself get so involved with a kid, but it kills me to see you unhappy."

"I'll get over it."

"How was your date with Buster Martin?"

"He's nice. He took the boys on a pony ride."

"You going out with him again?"

"I don't know. Maybe. Maybe not." Pam leaned against the sink, her arms folded, her head bowed. "You know, for the past couple of months, every time the phone rings, I offer a little prayer that it will be Joel. When I stop doing that, I'm going to cooperate more with your find-Pam-a-man campaign."

"Is that why you always sound so down when I call? Because I'm not Joel? But what would you say if you picked up the phone and it was Joel? Would you ask him to come back? Would you insist he marry you, or would you play it his way?"

"I don't know," Pam said, shaking her head. "Nothing has changed really. All the obstacles are still firmly in place. When I think about it, I really don't get past hearing his voice, finding out how he is."

Chapter Thirteen

"But you can't be gone next Sunday," Brenda insisted as they wandered down the mall toward Dillard's department store. She was holding Scott's hand. Pam was pushing Tommy's stroller. It was Brenda's day off, and as usual, she was spending part of it with her sister and nephews.

"Why not?" Pam asked.

"Well," Brenda began, her mind racing, "because I'm having a party. Yes, a party. And I want you and the boys to come."

"You haven't mentioned anything about a party," Pam said, her voice suspicious.

"Well, George and I thought we'd have a little announcement party for Robert and Jessica."

"And you want Scott and Tommy to come to an *announcement* party?" Pam asked.

"Well, not exactly an announcement party," Brenda said. "More like a congratulations picnic. Yes, I thought a picnic would be nice so that your boys and Robert's twins could come. Don't you think that sounds like a good idea?"

"Not particularly. The weather in April is a little iffy for picnics."

"It's the end of April. And if it's too cold, we'll use the party room at the apartment complex. An inside picnic. If it's as nice as it is today, we can go across the creek to the park. So you see, you can't go out of town. You'll have to postpone your little junket until the following weekend."

They stopped to order four Orange Juliuses and sat on a bench in the center of the mall.

"I have to be in town the following weekend. I've got a retirement party. But I guess we can leave Wednesday or Thursday and be back by Sunday. Be careful, Tommy. You're going to spill it."

"Why don't you just wait and leave Monday morning?" Brenda suggested.

"No, I'm restless and ready to go someplace after being cooped up with the boys all winter. Which do you think the boys would enjoy more—San Antonio or Padre Island?"

"Oh, Padre, definitely. They'd love the beach. And the weather should be perfect on the Gulf."

"Yeah, I think you're right. I just kind of dread the thought of keeping up with the two of them on the beach. The ocean makes me nervous, and I thought they might like the riverboat ride in San Antonio. Or maybe we could do both, stop in San Antonio on the way to Padre."

"Great idea. I tell you what, sis, if you'll wait and go after the picnic, I'll go with you."

"You would?" Pam said, her face lighting up. "That'd be great, but I thought you didn't have any vacation time coming for six months."

"Well, the store's decided to close the Zodiac Room for a few days to do some redecorating. And, yes, I know, they just redecorated, but there're a few more things they need to do to get ready for the Hong Kong

Celebration. So I can go and help you with Scott and Tommy, and we'll have a wonderful time at the beach.''

Brenda threw their cups into the trash receptacle, hoping that was the end of the conversation. It had worn her out. *Oh what a tangled web we weave, when first we practice to deceive!* she thought. One lie led to another. She just hoped she could keep them all straight. And now she had better put some thought into planning this picnic she was going to have. Actually, it sounded like fun.

"Come on, Scott," Pam said. "Let's go get Grandma a birthday present.''

"I think it's nice of you to do something for Robert and Jessica," Pam said. "I want to help. It makes me feel good to see people so happy."

"You were right about them," Brenda said. "Once Robert started courting Jessica instead of taking her for granted, the woman bloomed like a rose in May. We went with them to the symphony Friday night, and she looked like a duchess. Robert couldn't take his eyes off of her. What may have started out with Robert as a need to bring order to his life has turned into a genuine love affair.''

"Yeah. It reads like one of those old-fashioned romances. The plain unappreciated governess ends up beautiful, loved and the mistress of the manor house."

They had reached the entrance to Dillard's. "What shall we get Mom?" Pam asked.

"Not another set of iced-tea glasses or a blouse. Let's get something different.''

"How about a sexy nightie?" Pam asked. "Or some pretty lingerie?"

"For *Mom*?"

"Why not?"

"You're right. Why not?"

When Brenda got home, she called George. "Guess what? We're having a picnic.''

She explained how she invented the picnic to put off Pam's plans to take the boys on a trip. "And I had to promise to go with her, so she'd wait until Monday. I hope she'll have company on her trip, but it won't be me."

"Do you still think you've done the right thing," George asked, "telling Joel to get his tail down off that mountain, as I believe you so delicately put it? Maybe he was just calling to check on them like he said. Maybe he didn't want to hear all about your sister's despondency and be made to feel like a total cad because he had gone away like she told him to do. You know, sometimes, my dearest, it's a bit difficult for us men to know just what it is you women want."

"I don't know if it was the right thing," Brenda said, looking at the grouping of family photographs on her bedroom wall. There was one of her and Pam taken when they were still in pigtails. They hadn't always gotten along, but they'd always been important to each other. Sisters. "Time will tell, I suppose. My sister may hate me for the rest of her life."

"Don't overdramatize, dear. She might be angry as an old troll, but she won't hate you. I just don't understand why you couldn't have just asked her outright instead of all this blooming subterfuge."

"If I asked her, I'm afraid she would have said no. You know how Pam is—she'd analyze his motivation, weigh the pros and cons, take into consideration what was best for the boys, discredit her own feelings, and in the interest of 'doing the right thing,' she'd say no. But if he just shows up, if she sees him standing there, I think she'll follow her heart. She's missed him so, George, more than she'll ever admit. But I know my sister, and she's really hurting. The poor darling has been operating on sheer willpower since that boy left. And wise or stupid, I think this business with Joel has at least got to be allowed to play its course. Otherwise, Pam will spend the rest of her life wondering how it might have been.''

"Your parents aren't going to be very happy about this," George warned.

"I realize that. But Pam can't live her life for Mom and Dad. She can't even live it for those boys. At some point she has to do what is best for her and let the rest fall into place."

"'Follow her heart,'" George mused. "When did you decide to follow your heart?"

Brenda smiled at her reflection in the dresser mirror. "I think when you bit into that McDonald's hamburger knowing that you were just going to hate it and saying, 'I say, this is jolly good.'"

"Is that the best you can do?" George sounded disappointed. "That's not very romantic, and I consider myself a rather romantic fellow."

"Actually, I knew something was going to happen when our eyes met that first time in the mirror over the bar at Lucky's. I had been watching you, admiring you, then you caught me at it and smiled. That smile made me feel warm all over, and I knew you'd be special. And after we had our first real date, when you insisted on driving all the way out to the lake for our first kiss because you wanted it to be in a beautiful place, that was nice, too." Brenda leaned back against the headboard, her smile still in place. Nice memories.

"It was beautiful, wasn't it?" George said. "With the moonlight on the water, the waves lapping against the shore, the night birds calling and the cicadas serenading."

"The kiss wasn't so bad, either," Brenda recalled.

"No, I'd say that was a rather red-letter kiss. Listen, my love, what if I exit this dreary office in a few minutes and meet you for a drink at Lucky's? This conversation makes me want to spend a romantic evening with the woman I love.''

''Oh, I'm sorry, darling,'' Brenda said, hoping she sounded disappointed, ''but I need to... actually, I promised to help Pam. She's run into a real bind on a job she's doing tonight. I'll see you at home 'bout six.''

Goodness, Brenda thought as she hung up the phone. For a basically honest person, she certainly had been telling lots of fibs. But she didn't want to tell George she had a four o'clock appointment with her doctor.

She and George had gotten along much better since she stopped talking about pregnancy with every breath she took. Pam had been right about that, too, as well as about Jessica and Robert. Funny how her sister could be so insightful about other people's situations and full of doubts about her own.

If this visit to the doctor turned out to be a false alarm, Brenda didn't want to have raised George's hopes needlessly. And she tried not to allow her own hopes to soar. But she had a hard time keeping her hand steady as she touched up her makeup.

When she backed her BMW out of the garage, she felt as though she had swallowed a bucket of butterflies. Her stomach was a fluttery mess. Calm down, she told herself. What will be, will be. And no matter what the doctor said, life was good as long as she had her George. And that thought calmed her, because it was true.

AT FIVE FIFTEEN Brenda used the pay phone in the lobby of the North Park Professional Building to call her husband's office.

''Liz, this is Brenda Harrington. Is my husband by any chance still there?''

"He just left. But I see him talking to Mr. Rothbaum out in the hall."

"Would you please tell him I've had a change of plans and to meet me at Lucky's for a drink?"

Brenda felt like skipping across the parking lot, so she did. She felt like singing at the top of her lungs as she drove down the highway, so she did. She felt like giving her husband a red-letter kiss when he walked up to the bar, so she did.

"All *right*!" the bartender hollered. "Now that's what I call a kiss."

Other patrons in the bar began to applaud.

"My goodness," George said, looking a bit silly with lipstick smeared across his mouth. "What was that all about?" But about this time, he caught sight of the writing on the mirror over the bar. *"George is going to be a father"* was spelled out in large letters with bright red lipstick.

George's face blushed a matching red to the delight of the happy-hour patrons. "Is it really true?" he asked his wife.

Brenda nodded. "I just came from the doctor's. Our baby's due in December. Some kind of Christmas present, wouldn't you say?"

They kissed again. By this time, they were surrounded by a crowd of well-wishers who were happily clapping and catcalling their approval.

"Congratulations, George," a male voice yelled.

"Nice going, George," yelled another.

Then a woman started singing "Rock-a-Bye, Baby," and everyone—customers, waitresses, bartender—joined in. Brenda wondered if it was possible to be any happier.

PAM KNEW THE MINUTE SHE OPENED the front door. Her sister and brother-in-law were standing arm in arm on the front porch, looking like the cat that ate the mouse.

"And to what do I owe this unexpected surprise?" she said.

"Oh, we just thought we'd stop by and see our favorite sister-in-law," George said, his normal crisp accent slurred. "Actually, you are her sister but my sister-in-law, and we decided that we should come to see both of you."

"Well, both of me invite you in."

Brenda, car keys still in hand, helped her husband over the door sill. "Where are the little guys?" George asked, looking around.

"In bed, where most little guys are at eleven o'clock at night."

"Eleven o'clock! Imagine that, my darling, precious wife. It is eleven o'clock? Have we lost some time?"

"I don't think so. It took a few hours for you to consume all that beer."

"Ah, yes. The beer. I say, weren't those chaps lovely, buying me all those beers?"

"Yes. Lovely," Brenda said, barely controlling her laughter. "Now, why don't you tell Pam why we wanted to come and see her."

George teetered back and forth just a bit, then drew himself up to his full height. "We came to see you, dearest Pamela, to inform you that you are going to be an aunt. We are with child!"

Pam hugged her sister first, then George. "That's the nicest thing I've heard in a hundred years. You two will make fine parents, and I have a very lucky little niece or nephew on the way."

The sisters started crying, as sisters will at a time like that, then they found themselves laughing when they realized George was crying, too. He sat down heavily on the sofa and got out his carefully folded pocket handker-chief to wipe his eyes and blow his nose. "Excuse me, ladies, it's all just a bit overwhelming."

Deciding that George didn't need any more alcohol, they toasted their good fortune with hot chocolate. "You're not going to feel too well in the morning," Pam told George.

"Oh, he didn't really drink that much," Brenda said affectionately, cuddling up against her husband. "He's just drunk on life. Me, too. Do you think it's too late to call Mom and Daddy?"

PAM ADMIRED HER HAIR in the mirror one last time. Brenda had given her a permanent, and it looked ter-rific. Brenda had also insisted on loaning her a sweater in a wonderful soft shade of yellow. "And wear those Cal-vin Klein jeans I gave you for Christmas," Brenda in-structed. "They fit really nice. And don't forget eyeliner. George will be taking pictures, and you don't want post-erity to see you with naked eyes."

"Heaven forbid," Pam said. "That would be tragic."

"I just want you to look your best," Brenda said.

"I know you do, and believe me, I appreciate all your concern. In fact, I don't know what I would have done without my sister to call me, to cheer me, to spend her day off with me. You and my boys are the brightest parts of my life."

"Ah, shucks, what's a sister for?" Brenda said. Her tone was joking but her embrace sincere. "I happen to love you very much."

"I know," Pam had said. "And I love you, too. I don't know how my bratty little sister grew up into such a lovely woman, but you sure did. Now let's stop this before we get maudlin."

Pam finished dressing the boys in their matching red overalls then carried the potato salad and chocolate cake out to the station wagon. The bushes and trees in her yard were erupting with tender little buds of life, and blades of delicate green were peeking through the dead winter grass. Pam breathed a deep welcome to the spring that was in the air.

It had been cloudy and cold this morning, but the weather had decided to cooperate and supply a sunny and almost warm picnic day. Brenda had reserved a pavilion at the park and planned to build a fire in the fireplace for roasting marshmallows and wieners. It was to be George's first all-American picnic, complete with three-legged races and softball.

Softball. Pam searched through the hall closet for her trusty glove left over from high-school days.

"Let's go, guys. Party time."

"Can Barney come?" Scott asked.

"Sure. But you keep him off my cake, or your name is mud."

Pam was surprised to see Cindy and Paul at a picnic honoring Jessica and Robert. The two couples barely knew each other. However, they seemed to be chatting amicably enough. Brenda and George were building a fire. Somehow Pam had the impression that there would be other people here, but perhaps she was a bit early. She carried her potato salad to the long table under the pavilion roof and looked around to see where the boys and Barney had run off to.

Tommy was halfway up the ladder of a very tall slide, and Pam went racing over to get him down.

Robert's twins came running up. "We'll push the boys in the baby swings," one of the girls said. "Jessica said we are in charge of watching the boys."

"I'm not a baby," Scott said.

"Scott can swing in the big swings if he's careful," Pam instructed, "but don't push him very high. And you have to watch out for Barney. He doesn't understand about swings."

Pam got her chocolate cake out of the station wagon. She'd made a sheet cake to feed all the people she thought would be here.

She motioned for her sister to come talk to her, but Brenda just waved. "Cake looks good," she said.

"Come here, Brenda." Pam tapped her foot while she waited for her sister to saunter over. "Okay, what gives?" she demanded. "I thought this was going to be an announcement party?"

"Well, Jessica and Robert decided they didn't want a lot of fuss made over them just now. They're going to have a very small wedding, then they're planning a reception when they get back from their wedding trip. But we decided to have just a little gathering anyway."

"You might have told me," Pam said, not trying to conceal her irritation. "I could have gone ahead and taken my trip. And I made potato salad for two dozen and a sheet cake."

"I'm sorry, sis. I guess I should have told you. But you know how I've been this week with my head in the clouds. You'll just have to forgive me, honey. Come on over by the fire and have a beer."

"Brenda, this is queer. Where's the man you're trying to fix me up with? After all, here I am permed and wearing eyeliner. Which tree have you hidden him behind?"

"I don't know what you're talking about. Well, just look at that," she said pointing at Scott, who was running toward the parking lot as fast as his three-year-old legs would carry him. Barney was loping along beside him with Tommy a distant third. "Now what do you suppose has gotten into them?"

Then Pam understood everything.

A very familiar old blue van had pulled into the space beside her station wagon, and a slender, auburn-haired young man was getting out. The sunlight caught his hair and turned it to red gold. It was the most beautiful hair Pam had ever seen.

Slowly, she started for the parking lot. Was it just another dream? She felt like she was in one, walking in dreamlike slow motion.

Barney got to Joel first and started jumping up and down, howling like a banshee. Scott fairly leaped into Joel's arms. Tommy's little legs churned faster as he covered the last few yards. "Joel," he called, arms waving. "Joel."

With Scott on one arm, Joel knelt to pick up Tommy with the other, but Barney lunged and knocked him over. Then flat on his back in the grass, Joel was attacked by two excited boys and a crazy dog. Laughing, he put his arms across his face to protect himself from Barney's tongue. Both boys were straddling him now.

Scott looked over his shoulder at his mother. "Mommy, Joel's come back! He's come back!"

Tommy just kept saying his name, "Joel! Joel!"

Not to be counted out of the melée, when Barney wasn't licking, he was barking.

Even as she picked up speed, as she ran to join the joyous scene by the parking lot, Pam thought, *I want to remember this moment for the rest of my life.*

When she reached them, she plowed her way in among the bedlam. She was like Tommy—all she could say was "Joel, Joel," over and over, like an idiot. She pushed Barney away so she could kiss him, not caring that the dog had preceded her. Joel was laughing so hard, he was gasping for breath.

Scott and Tommy decided they wanted to kiss, too, and then all of them, including the dog, were competing for space to plant kisses on Joel's dear face. Pam thought of something else to say besides his name. "I love you. Oh dear, God, I love you."

Scott and Tommy thought that sounded fine. "I love you, Joel," Scott said between kisses.

"I wove you, Joel," Tommy said as he crawled back onto Joel's chest.

Barney just barked.

"Does this mean I can stay?" Joel gasped.

"I don't know. We'll have to take a vote. Hey guys, do you want Joel to come live in our house?"

This brought a new round of excitement, with both boys offering a continuous stream of yeses.

"Yes," Pam said, "you can stay forever and ever and ever. I've never been so miserable in my life since you left."

"What about terms?" Joel asked through another round of kisses.

"Whatever you want. I'm finished with trying to out-guess the future. I'll take whatever you and the fates bring me."

Joel struggled to a sitting position. The boys piled in his lap. He ducked as Barney licked his ear.

"Will you marry me?" Joel asked. There was grass in his hair, grass covering his sweater. Grass stuck to his lips.

"You don't have to say that," Pam said, picking grass from her tongue.

But from behind Pam came her sister's voice. "Pamela Sue Hunter Sullivan, for God's sake, the answer to that question is yes!"

As EVENING FELL, the shadows from the fire danced across the roof of the pavilion. Hot dogs had been roasted and eaten along with lots of potato salad and Brenda's baked beans. A corner of the sheet cake was missing.

Pam had only nibbled at her food. It was enough to feast her eyes on Joel. His slender body had taken on a lean hardness, and he was tanned, a bit weathered. His hair looked as though he'd cut it himself. He'd been working at a sawmill, he said, loading and unloading trucks, and he'd learned to ski.

Pam leaned over to give him a sip of beer, his arms being occupied with two nodding boys, one on each side.

"We'd better take these two tired soldiers home," Pam said. *Now it's my turn,* she thought. She told Joel that with her smile.

Good-nights were said all around. Cindy and Paul told Joel again how glad they were he was back. Robert and Jessica invited everyone to their wedding. The twins excitedly announced that they were going to be junior bridesmaids. Brenda and George said they wanted Pam and Joel to be their baby's godparents.

Joel took the boys and Barney in the van. Pam followed in the station wagon. The van had a burned-out taillight. Such a disreputable old vehicle, but she couldn't imagine Joel driving a status car like Brenda's BMW. The old van would probably serve as their second vehicle for a long time to come.

She felt as though happiness were flowing in her veins and her skin was made of joy. She wasn't riding in a car, she was floating. The home to which she was going was now complete.

Together, she and Joel pulled off the boys' sand-filled shoes and grass-covered overalls. Pam watched as he carried first one and then another groggy boy to stand in front of the toilet before they were tucked in with a final kiss.

"I'll see you guys in the morning," Joel assured them.

Then it was just the two of them. They stood in the hall outside of the boys' room. "You want a cup of coffee?" she asked, not knowing if they should sit and talk in the kitchen or if he would mind if she took him straight to bed. All evening she had let the boys cling to him and relish his physical presence. Now she ached to lie in his arms, to fill herself with his body.

"You look wonderful," Pam said.

"I can't imagine why," he said. "I've just spent the worst three months of my life. Then I couldn't stand it anymore. It seemed so ridiculous for two people who loved each other to be apart. So I called Brenda just to see what was happening with you, and she told me to come down off the mountain, that my family needed me."

"She was right."

"And you and the boys are all the family I need, Pam. Really. If you don't want any more babies, I can live with that decision. Scott and Tommy are terrific."

"Why don't we just wait and see what happens? And in spite of what my sister says, you don't have to marry me."

"Maybe not. But I do need to marry those boys. They need to be able to introduce me as their father and not their mother's live-in. And I'd sure be proud to introduce you as my wife."

Joel fished around in his pocket and pulled out a small felt bag. "I can't afford a diamond, but I wanted to give you something. This will have to do for now."

It was a silver-and-turquoise ring bearing a tiny thunderbird. "An Indian guy I worked with at the sawmill made it," Joel explained. "He said the thunderbird is the sacred bearer of unlimited happiness. Sounded good to me."

"Me, too. Oh, Joel, it's beautiful," Pam said, sliding it onto her finger. "And now, would you mind terribly if I withdrew the coffee offer?"

He opened his arms to her. And so their life together began.

You'll flip . . . your pages won't!
Read paperbacks *hands-free* with

Book Mate·I

The perfect "mate" for all your romance paperbacks

**Traveling • Vacationing • At Work • In Bed • Studying
• Cooking • Eating**

Perfect size for all standard paperbacks, this wonderful invention makes reading a pure pleasure! Ingenious design holds paperback books OPEN and FLAT so even wind can't ruffle pages – leaves your hands free to do other things. Reinforced, wipe-clean vinyl-covered holder flexes to let you turn pages without undoing the strap . . . supports paperbacks so well, they have the strength of hardcovers!

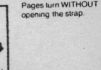

Pages turn WITHOUT opening the strap.

SEE-THROUGH STRAP

Reinforced back stays flat.

Built in bookmark

BOOK MARK

BACK COVER HOLDING STRIP

10 x 7¼ . opened.
Snaps closed for easy carrying. too

Available now. Send your name, address, and zip code, along with a check or money order for just $5.95 + .75¢ for postage & handling (for a total of $6.70) payable to Reader Service to:

Reader Service
Bookmate Offer
901 Fuhrmann Blvd.
P.O. Box 1396
Buffalo, N.Y. 14269-1396

Offer not available in Canada
* New York and Iowa residents add appropriate sales tax.

BM-G

Harlequin American Romance

COMING NEXT MONTH

#293 APPEARANCES ARE DECEIVING
by Linda Randall Wisdom

More than anything, Caryn Richards wanted two things: to keep her personal secret forever and to catch the culprit whose pranks troubled her magazine. When security expert Sam Russell arrived, she was grateful for his help—but she didn't plan on him capturing her heart. If he discovered her secret, would it destroy or strengthen the love a man felt for a woman?

#294 PEPPERMINT KISSES by Karen Toller Whittenburg

New lawyer Dana Ausbrook learned fast that the candy business was anything but sweet. Her first job was to sue for custody of a candy recipe—a wedding gift given to her mother forty years before. But the wedding had been called off, and since then the bride and groom had founded rival confectioneries, each fighting for the wonderful secret to Peppermint Kisses. And now Rick Stafford had come to plead the groom's case and stayed to court the bride's lawyer. The candy business would never be the same again.

#295 THE SHOCKING MS. PILGRIM by Robin Francis

Staid and sensible Libby Pilgrim would never have kidnapped Joshua Noon without a very good reason. And what better one than the protection of her beloved Maine coastline? But now, after a broken rudder and strong currents, Libby, Josh and their little boat were drifting out to sea, and Libby was quickly learning the hard way that crime did not pay.

#296 FIRES OF SUMMER by Catherine Spencer

Five years ago, Susannah Boyd's husband had lost his life rescuing their infant son from kidnappers. Now Susannah was trying to make a new life for herself and her boy in the safety of the rural Alaskan Panhandle. But fire-fighting pilot Travis O'Connor challenged her isolation. Would she refuse his love to protect herself—and her son—or could she find the strength to risk, and love, again?